CW01584412

DAMAGE

'Proctor knows his business inside out: exact, matter of fact and utterly to the point, this is writing with the unnecessary parts stripped out.'

TARIQ GODDARD

Author and publisher

'A highly enjoyable, big-hearted debut, full of fascinating detail. Historically vivid and humming with contemporary resonance.'

CHARLIE HILL

Author, *Encounters With Everyday Madness*

'A labyrinthine crime tale of courage and morality set in the darkest days of the last century. Proctor's prose crackles with atmosphere as it lowers you into the flaming depths of the Birmingham Blitz, while his vivid, troubled characters struggle with its central question – how do you retain your humanity in a burning world? An impressive debut from a writer to watch.'

JENNY LECOAT

New York Times bestselling author

'A pacy and exciting book full of authentic characters that I really cared about. The world-building is so strong, the place and time felt utterly convincing, and this is a story I won't forget! A pressure cooker of a novel. I love this book.'

ELIZABETH LEE
Author, *Cunning Women*

'In *Fire Damage* Nigel Proctor gives his reader a searing evocation of life during the Birmingham Blitz in prose so vivid we can taste the smoke. His detectives Harry and Annie lead a cast of characters whose lives are as ruined as the bombed out back streets they inhabit. This is crime fiction which shines a timely spotlight on human behaviour — its best and its worst — during terrible conflict. *Fire Damage* is a wonderful debut for fans of Phillip Kerr and Dominic Nolan.'

NATALIE MARLOW
Author of the critically acclaimed
William Garrett series

'A tense portrayal of wartime Birmingham, murder and moral quandary.'

KATE MASCARENHAS
Author, *Hokey Pokey*

Jessica,

FIRE DAMAGE

NIGEL PROCTOR

Hope you enjoy my take on Bron Yr Aur.

Nigel

To Caroline, Rachel and Katy, with all my love.

In memory of Reg and Nell Harvey, Ernest and Gertie Proctor, George and Georgina Shepherd and my parents, John and Sheila Proctor – so much of this story is their story.

First Floodgate Crime paperback edition April 2025
www.floodgatepress.co.uk

A version of the chapter *Tuesday 19 November 1940* previously appeared in Floodgate's *Night Time Economy* anthology as *Under Fire*.

A catalogue record for this book is available from the British Library.

Paperback ISBN: 978-1-7394395-2-1

Fire Damage is typeset in Monotype Series 110 & Series 371

Cover design by Tor © Floodgate
Text design by Peter Burgess

Printed by ImprintDigital.com

CONTENTS

The fire itself will test the quality of each man's work

1 CORINTHIANS 3:13

TUESDAY 19 NOVEMBER 1940

Reg Miles ran. Ran through a world of black and orange. A world either burning or burnt. His chest hurt each time a boot struck the pavement, hobnails flinting on the stone, sparks swallowed by the maelstrom. With every stride, his Auxiliary Fire Service axe swung out from his belt and slapped back against his thigh.

Thumping his chest with a fist, he coughed and breathed in through his mouth. Tasted smoke and brick dust. Smelt scorched paint and smouldering timber.

He spat grit.

Coughed again.

Ran on.

Let them be safe, dear God, let them be alright. I don't ask for much, Lord, but I am asking for this.

Earlier, deep in the fire and dark, no thoughts, just instinct, he dug with his axe, his gloved hands wrapped tight around its rubber grip. Sixty crews, he reckoned, they were at least sixty crews strong now – some pumping water, tamping flames, others diving deep into the rubble, hoping to find survivors, expecting the worst.

Sixty crews, all getting nowhere. And he was separated from his. Working on his own. A beginner's mistake. But this was *his* patch, *his* backyard.

And then.

'Over here,' Reg shouted to no one in particular. 'There's someone here.'

A voice shouted back: 'Who's that?'

'Does it matter?'

Reg recognised the voice and then the face: Arthur Shaw – Artie to his mates, styled after some American bandleader – a man he knew to nod at, not a close friend, not a friend at all. But any man was the right man to be here just now. And there was another man behind him, a man unknown to Reg but a useful pair of hands, no doubt. Any hands being useful at this time.

'Come on, Arthur Shaw, give us a help here.'

'OK, Reggie,' Shaw said. 'What needs doing?'

Reggie?

No one called him Reggie, no one but Agnes.

'That. Can you hear that?'

'Hear what?'

'That,' Reg said, raising a hand and pointing.

A distant sound. A circular keening – rising, falling, repeating, shouting – hoarse but vital.

'There's someone in there,' Shaw said.

Reg bent down like a rugby prop forward going in for the ruck and scrabbled at broken masonry.

The bombs had hit just before 11pm, falling onto the south side of New Building. Nobody was sure how many – nobody cared, not now, the details could wait for later – but what they were sure of was the devastation: the broken concrete, the twisted steelwork, the incandescent flames, the nostril-scorching sulphurous smoke rolling up and out of the impact crater, as if the explosion had opened a gateway to Hell.

And the people.

The crying, screaming, pleading people, shambling through the murk, like so many shades walking the earth, not knowing where they were, not knowing they were already dead.

There was an explosion nearby and then another. The third man clambered down the rubble and slid in next to Reg and Shaw. He glanced up at the sky.

Reg smiled at him. 'Don't worry,' he said, 'that ain't the Jerries this time, that's just some of our stuff going up.'

The man looked puzzled. 'Our stuff?'

'Ammunition,' Reg said. 'They don't call us the Birmingham Small Arms Company for nothing, you know?'

Working away, the three men widened the gap in the fallen masonry. Almost on cue, the moaning stopped.

'Right,' Reg said, 'it's stable for the moment, let's see what we're dealing with.'

Unclipping his AFS lamp from his belt, Reg flicked open the black-out hood and rotated the on-switch. A faint yellow gleam lit up the rubble. He shoved the torch into the hole and pushed his head in as far in as he was able.

'Hello?'

'Hello.' A weak voice, a woman's voice, a young woman's voice.

'We're here,' Reg said. 'And we'll get you out. Is it just you in there?'

'No,' the girl said. 'Mrs Charles is here too but she's out cold. At least I think she's out cold. I don't know. I can't really see. She's breathing though. A bit ragged, it is. A bit of a snorer, actually.'

'Hold on,' Reg said. 'Just hold on. What's your name, bab?'

'Maureen,' the voice said. 'Maureen Unwin.'

'Well, you hang on in there, Miss Maureen Unwin and we'll soon have you both out, you and Mrs Charles. You won't have to put up with her snoring then. I'm Mr Miles, by the way.'

'Thank you, Mr Miles.'

Reg turned to face the other men. 'It's not good,' he said, 'not good at all. As far as I can see, the two of them are right at the back, behind a concrete lintel. The lintel, it's fallen across in a diagonal and is holding up a ton of bricks. One wrong move, it's all going to come down.'

'What you want to do, Reggie?'

Reg pulled off his jacket and rolled up his shirt sleeves. 'Some-one's got to go in and dig under it. It's the only way we're going to get them out.'

'You can't go in there,' the third man said, 'it's far too dangerous.'

'He's right, Reggie,' Arthur said. 'I mean look at the size of you. If anyone's going to bring that lot down, you are.'

'Like I say, someone's got to do it,' Reg said.

Shaw smiled. 'If you're crazy enough to go in there, we're definitely going to need a bigger hole.'

As soon as the gap was large enough, Reg bent double and waddled forward, lamp held out in front of him. He peered into the gloom. It was dustier now, particulates falling from the roof like malevolent snow and that could only mean one thing: movement up top. And movement up top threatened further collapse.

Then there was the heat.

Reg couldn't see any flames but he could sense the fire was all around – watching, waiting, biding its time. He would have to move fast, he'd known that all along but now he'd have to work double-quick.

He could see the girl more clearly – she had her knees up to her chest, her eyes closed – and he could hear the other woman, her breath heavy, rasping, uneven, fading.

'Maureen?'

The girl opened her eyes. 'Mr Miles?'

'I'm here.' Reg looked back over his shoulder. 'Arthur Shaw?'

Shaw's face appeared in the gap, a distant silhouette in a far-off, different world. 'Yes?'

'You better get in here.'

'Me?'

'You.'

Reg went down onto his front and crawled forward until he was level with the lintel. Using his axe, he scraped away at the ground, pushing debris under and behind him. Inching forward, he coughed. The falling dust was thicker now and it wasn't just dust.

Smoke.

The hole was filling with smoke.

And it was hotter, too.

Much hotter.

The flames weren't far away, their time for biding over.

'You alright in there?'

Reg glanced back. 'Who's that?'

'Ned. Ned Lucas. Is that you, Reg?'

'There's two women trapped in here,' Reg said. 'And there's a fire burning somewhere around us.'

'Understand. We're running a hose now,' Lucas said. 'Water pressure's a bit down but let's see what we can do to get that fire out.'

'Ta,' Reg said, pulling aside a piece of masonry and pushing himself forward. 'Maureen Unwin, you better still be with me.'

The girl coughed. 'Course I am, Mr Miles, where'd you think I'd be?'

Reg smiled at her tone, at her cheek. 'Good girl. How's Mrs Charles doing?'

'Not good. I can't hear her no more. I can't hear her, Mr Miles.'

'You hang on, Maureen,' Reg said, 'I'm almost with you.'

Reg reached forward and pulling with his hands and pushing with his feet, wriggled into the shallow dip beneath the lintel. It was a proper squeeze but with a deep breath and one final shove of his boots, Reg came up and out the other side.

Maureen Unwin watched as a dirt-blackened and smoke-shrouded shape appeared from the hole. 'Maureen,' the figure said.

'Mr Miles?'

'That's me.'

Reg looked around. He saw a pair of legs – one foot wearing a shoe, the other not – sticking out from behind a fall of bricks. 'Mrs Charles?'

Maureen nodded and Reg moved towards the older woman. But as he crawled closer, he could see she was dead. Her eyes were open and staring, her jaw gaping, a loose denture on her lower lip. An iron rod pierced her left side and the ground beneath her was a blood-thickened shadow.

He pushed himself backwards, back towards Maureen.

'Is she dead?'

'Yes. she is.'

The girl gulped and dry sobbed.

'Now come on, Maureen,' Reg said, reaching out, patting a shoulder. 'Let's get you out of here.'

The girl looked down at the crawl space and shuddered. 'I can't go under there, I can't,' she said. 'It's tiny.'

The smoke was thicker now, the air hotter.

'I got through, didn't I? And look at me,' Reg said.

The girl nodded. 'You did.'

'And if I did...'

'I can.'

'That's right. Arthur? You there?'

Half a face underlit by torchlight appeared in the gap above the lintel: Ned Lucas. 'What can I do, Reg?'

'Ned, this is Maureen, Maureen, Mr Lucas.'

'Hello,' the girl said.

Lucas smiled. 'Alright.'

'He's going to help you through, aren't you, Mr Lucas?'

'I am, Mr Miles.'

'All you've got to do, Maureen, is lie down and crawl forward a bit. I'll be here pushing and Mr Lucas over there will grab your hands and pull. Easy. Alright?'

Maureen bit her lip and looked unconvinced. 'You say so.'

'I do,' Reg said.

'Can I close my eyes?'

'Best not,' Reg said.

The girl lay on her front and started to move forward into the gap and under the lintel. Reg crouched over her, holding her by the waist and pushing.

Without warning, part of the wall to Reg's left cracked, bricks fell and flame spat. Reg felt the heat across his back, smelt cloth smoulder.

The girl screamed.

'Ned?'

'I've got her.'

'Then get a move on, will you?'

Reg loosed his grip and the girl slithered away, her feet disappearing from sight, pulled clear by Ned Lucas.

'Reg, you better get out now.'

'There's a dead woman in here, I'm not leaving her. She deserves better.'

'Just leave her, Reg.'

Reg crawled down and around the rubble to where Mrs Charles lay. He twisted onto his side and as gently as he could, pulled her body free.

'Sorry,' he said, as if she was still capable of hearing. 'Sorry but I'm doing the best I can.'

He dragged the woman's body over to the lintel, easing her into the gap, head and shoulders first.

'Can you reach her, Ned?'

'Just about.'

'Then get her out 'cos I don't want to be in here much longer meself.'

Reg watched as the corpse's feet disappeared.

The lintel moved for a second time, more bricks fell, more flames, more smoke. And steam.

There was steam in the air now.

'Lord,' Reg said, 'don't let this be it.'

Throwing himself to the floor, he scrapped with the earth, a terrier at a rat hole, and twisted himself forward.

Something overhead moved.

Reg felt whatever it was press down on the small of his back and then there were hands wrapped around his wrists, his arms, his shoulders, pulling, pulling, pulling. He was drawn free just as the lintel collapsed and the space behind him vanished forever, backfilled by fire and debris.

Minutes later, near midnight, Reg Miles stood on the street and looked back at the BSA works. Lit by flames, the southern end of New Building was entirely flattened but somehow, by some miracle, a large part of the structure appeared intact. Sides were missing but the interiors were untouched. It was almost as if a skilled surgeon had taken a surgical saw to the place, removing the damaged tissue and bone and nothing else.

Overhead but elsewhere bombs still fell, the air shuddering with each distant explosion. Other people's problem now, not his, not for the moment. He felt someone at his back.

'Reggie?'

'Arthur.'

'You like to cut things nice and tight then.'

'I was only doing my job. Doing what felt right.'

'Maybe,' Shaw said. 'But the right thing for someone else is not always the right thing for yours truly.'

Reg nodded. 'Yeah, so it would seem. What happened to you, by the way?'

Shaw smirked. 'Made sense to give way to the professionals.'

A young works lad, no more than fifteen, came racing towards them. 'Mr Miles!'

'Saul?'

'You live in Highgate Street, don't you?'

'I do.'

'It's been hit. Hit bad. Loads of houses is down.'

'Loads? How many?'

'I don't know. Just loads. Most maybe.'

Reg Miles ran on and turned the corner into his street. Into a scene he didn't recognise. Into someone else's life. He was anywhere but home.

To his left, a frontage torn away, a side collapsed, a bent chimney stack and a bedroom wall. An exposed fireplace below a wall-mounted mirror, the only wall left of what had been an upstairs bedroom.

To his right, water trickled from splintered pipes, dripping onto brick and timbers. It looked like a child's play set, stomped on in boredom and petulance.

He wiped smoke and dust from his eyes and bowed his head, not wanting to look at where his house had once been.

'Reggie?'

A voice in the gloom followed by a figure, a shape.

'Reggie.'

Running now, the figure leapt forward and wrapped its arms around his neck.

'Aggie?'

'Oh, Reggie,' Agnes Miles said, burying her head into his neck. 'Reggie.'

Reg pushed his wife away, put a hand on her left cheek. She looked up at him, smiled through the tears and smut that covered her face.

'Emmy?'

'She's at Nell's. We were in the shelter and now she's asleep on the front room settee. Well, got her eyes closed, at least.'

'She's alright then?'

'She's fine, Reggie. We're all fine. We're all safe. Our house too. Look at it, look at our little house.'

Through the dust, the ashes, the darkness, the flames, their house on the corner, still in one piece.

Reg raised his head to the heavens, said a silent thank you to whoever had been watching over Agnes and Emmy. And over the bricks and mortar he'd become so attached to. Sentimental, he knew but he loved his house – their house – for what it meant to his family and the home it offered. He hoped whoever it was up there could see through the burning, smoke-filled sky and know just how grateful he was.

If there was anyone or anything up there, apart from the shadow of the Luftwaffe and the promise of more death and destruction.

WEDNESDAY 20 NOVEMBER 1940

1

The body, when they found it, was under a door, in the garden of an abandoned house. At first, they thought the poor child was a victim of the previous night's raid, blown clear by the explosion and then covered by tumbling woodwork. But neighbours said the property had been empty for months, ever since the old woman who'd lived there died.

And then there was the matter of the child's injuries – or lack of them.

'Who found her?' DS Harry Marsh said, not particularly caring which of the two young coppers in front of him answered.

'A gang of kids larking around this end early hours today,' PC Hayward said. 'They told some ARP bloke and he called us.'

Marsh nodded. 'Does he have a name, this ARP bloke?'

'Suppose he must but we don't know it,' the other PC said, the one Marsh didn't know, a hint of a smirk on his face, a lit cigarette behind a cupped right hand.

Marsh looked at him. 'You being funny, Constable?'

The unknown copper dropped his head. 'No, Sergeant, sorry, Sergeant.'

'What's your name?'

'Smiley, Sergeant, Victor Smiley. Vic.'

'Right, PC Victor Smiley,' Marsh said, 'at least we now know what you'll be up to for the next hour or so.'

'What's that then?'

'Go get me this ARP man's name – I suspect whoever took the call down the station did their job somewhat better than you – and better still, get his address, he and I need a word.'

Smiley nodded. 'Yes, Sergeant.'

'And your cigarette, Constable...'

'What? I've only got a couple left.'

Marsh shook his head. 'I don't want one, I want you to put that one out.'

'Now?'

'Now.'

Smiley flicked the ash from his cigarette, licked his fingers, twisted off the lit end. He put what remained of his smoke into a breast pocket.

Marsh turned and walked down the side of the terrace. Behind him, he heard the words *Hun Stuff* and *Passchendaele* and knew exactly what the one constable was telling the other.

As he rounded the far corner of the block, a flash gun went off, burning a residual image onto the policeman's corneas. The photographer looked up and nodded. 'Just getting in early, Sergeant Marsh. Killing time, so to speak.'

'Thank you, Mr Wall,' Marsh said, looking down at the girl, 'most thoughtful. Got a good wide shot, have you?'

'I have.'

'Well carry on then. We'll need a decent one of her face too.'

The photographer frowned – as if he needed telling his job, as if.

Marsh watched the man reposition his camera before turning his full attention to the girl.

No more than ten, maybe eleven.

Her eyes closed, she could have been resting.

Her hands folded over her chest, in prayer.

Her head propped on an embroidered cushion.

The dead girl had a certain serenity about her.

Like a marble figure lying on a tomb.

'Sergeant Harry Marsh,' a woman said, the voice as singular as its owner. The accent was somewhat refined, the harsher characteristics of its Ulster origin either redacted or burnished but the undertones remained in place, conveying education while maintaining a sense of authenticity. A sense of earthiness yet intelligence.

'Dr Penny,' Marsh said, without turning, 'I'm honoured.'

'You should be. We're shorthanded and when the roster calls, well, she's a harsh, harsh mistress, who won't be swayed by rank and privilege, no matter how early the hour.'

Marsh looked round and smiled. 'It's good to see you, Moira. How are you?'

The woman laughed. 'I'm top, how you doing?'

'Better than she is.'

'Aye, that'll be right enough.'

The photographer collapsed his tripod and moved away. 'I'll hang back a bit, let the good doctor have a looksy. Let me know if there's anything in particular either of you need, Sergeant,' he said.

'Will do,' Marsh said, with a nod.

The policeman and the doctor watched Eric Wall walk away. With his baggy trousers, short jacket, bowler hat and bow-legged gait, the photographer was the spit of Chaplin's Little Tramp.

Moira Penny glanced over at Marsh. 'What? No Dr Watson today?'

'Dr Watson?'

'DC Hancock, your literal partner-in-crime.'

And Marsh felt his stomach turn and churn. The very feeling he'd had many times over the last five days – a feeling of incompleteness, a sense of loss which would, he hoped, eventually subside and permit him to grieve – washed over him again. Deep down, he maintained a lingering belief that, at any moment, Ray Hancock would appear from around a corner, before laughing and pumping Harry Marsh on the shoulder, as he always had.

But Ray Hancock was gone.

Gone forever, like a person met in a dream who is all too real until the moment of waking, at which point they vanish, never to be seen again, leaving behind nothing but a profound sense of absence. That was how Harry Marsh felt when the news broke.

It was how he still felt.

'Coventry,' Marsh said. 'Ray was visiting his sister in Coventry the other night. The night the Jerries hit town.'

Moira Penny's hand flew to her lips. 'Och, I didn't know.'

'Why should you?'

'I'm sorry. He was a good fella, a good friend, especially to you.'

Marsh nodded. 'He was.'

They stood, neither able to look at the other, a frozen moment outside of time.

The DS took a deep breath, dropped his leather murder bag to the floor. 'Ladies first,' he said, gesturing at the corpse.

Moira Penny smiled, accepting his levity as it was meant: deflection from any acknowledgement of common grief. 'Let's take a look at this poor weean then,' she said.

The doctor bent her knees and leant forward.

Harry Marsh reached into an overcoat pocket and pulled out a Rybar inhaler. He put it to his mouth, squeezed the rubber bulb and breathed in.

'Are you in trouble there?' Moira Penny said.

'It's the air,' Marsh said. 'It's damp this morning, that's all.'

'Does your doctor know?'

'Know what?'

'That you're suffering again, man.'

'But I'm not.'

'But you are, I can see that. It's as plain as the inhaler in your hand.'

'No, I'm not,' he said, 'I've got a slight chill. Always makes it worse, does a slight chill.'

Moira Penny shook her head. 'Men, stubborn the whole bloody lot of yous. So, what have we here? God, she's young.'

Harry Marsh pulled a pair of rubber gloves from his case. Snapping them over his hands, he walked around the dead girl and stood next to her head. 'First impressions?'

Dr Penny glanced up. 'It's too neat. All too tidy. Look at her hands, they're folded. And her skirt, it's smoothed down. And her hair, it's like it's been brushed.'

The DS nodded. 'I agree. How do you think she died?'

'Harry, give me a chance here.'

'Well?'

'Will you shut up, have away with yourself and make me some space?'

Marsh smiled, took a pace back and watched Moira Penny examine the body. He liked the doctor. He liked her directness, her honesty, her immediate application to the job at hand. She was like a blinkered racehorse out of the gate, straight ahead without hesitation or distraction. They'd first worked together three years ago, just after she'd arrived in Birmingham from Belfast via Glasgow. A gruesome case of violence in marriage, dismemberment, remains disposed of in a lime pit that had once been a coal hole and a desperate defence based on the Law of Coverture. A defence that never stood a chance.

The case was a sordid series of events but the beginning of a friendship.

'No signs of obvious violence, apart from this wee scrawb,' Moira Penny said, lifting the neckline of the girl's dress and pointing at a mark.

'What is that?' Marsh said.

'It looks like an abrasion, I would say something's been ripped away from her neck.'

'Like what?'

'I have no idea. But removed after death, almost certainly.'

'Why after death?'

'There's no sign of blood in the scratch and that implies that there was no blood circulating at the time, that her heart had already stopped.'

'Anything else?'

The doctor pushed open the lid of the girl's left eye. 'Well, there's this.'

'What's that?'

'Those red marks inside her eye.' Moira Penny opened the girl's right lid. 'Inside both eyes. Petechial haemorrhaging, they're a key indicator of asphyxia caused by some obstruction of the airways. Enough to suggest that she was possibly strangled or smothered. But given there are no real marks on her neck apart from that slight scratch, I'd have to say smothered.'

'Alright,' Harry Marsh said. 'Anything else?'

'You'll be glad to know her pants are still in the right place.'

'I am.'

'But as you asked so nicely, there is something, something else...' Moira Penny leant close to the girl's lips and sniffed. 'Definitely something else. I need to get her down to the General, open her up, run some tests but her lips are sticky – there are a few fibres stuck on them – and there's an odour of some sort.'

'Odour?'

'Smell, Harry, odour means smell.'

The policeman pulled a face, a face full of pretend hurt. 'I know what an odour is, I'd just like to know what this particular odour is.'

Moira Penny laughed. 'I'm just joshing with you, Sergeant Marsh. Seriously, there's something sweet and chemical on her lips. It's possible she was drugged before she died.'

'Drugged implies premeditation.'

'It does and given everything I've seen so far, I'm as certain as can be that this poor girl's a victim of human agency – and I'm not talking about whatever fell from the sky last night.'

2

Reg Miles sat in the canteen, dunking one of Aggie's ginger and honey biscuits into his mug of tea, when a voice boomed out: 'If it isn't the great hero.'

Reg looked up to see Arthur Shaw barrelling towards him. 'Mind if I join you?'

Reg shook his head. 'If you want.'

'I will then,' Shaw said, putting his mug down and sliding onto the bench next to the big man. 'You alright today, Reggie?'

'I'm alright.'

'That was quite a night though, last night, quite a night, I'd say.'

'It was.'

'You going in like that. I thought that was the last I'd see of you, I did. I thought: he's not coming out again, he's not. That's what I thought. He's in there and in there he's staying. And then you came out. I've never seen anything like it.'

Reg chewed, nodded, swallowed. 'I'm sure you have.'

Arthur Shaw sipped and smiled. 'I have not. I was only saying to the lads earlier: *You should have seen that Reggie Miles last night. You won't believe what he did. I tell you, you won't.* And you know what? They didn't. I had to swear it was true. Swear it was true on my old girl's grave. They believe me now, though. Yes, they do.'

Reg drained his mug and stood. Shaw followed him with his eyes. 'You do that a lot, Reggie?'

'Do what?'

'Put your neck on the line for other people, people you don't know.'

'It's my job, I guess.'

Shaw shook his head. 'No, Reggie, you said that last night but it's not your job.' He waved his hands around the room. 'This is your job. This place. The lines and the lathes. The nuts and the bolts. The bullets and the shells. This is what you get paid for. What you did last night, you didn't have to do that but you did it all the same. Why did you, why did you do what you did?'

Reg shrugged. 'I was there.'

'And now you're here?'

'I am,' Reg said.

'So what did you make of that lot this morning?'

'What lot?'

'This morning, that lot outside. You must have seen them.'

Reg nodded. 'I did.'

How many had it been? He hadn't counted. Hundreds of men, maybe more. Some he knew, some not, stood there, barricading the main gates, demanding their wages. Demanding that despite the obvious difficulties, they should get paid on time. And he sympathised. He did. But he had a job to do – two jobs, you count the Auxs – and sometimes, no, almost always, you had to forget the personal, push your own worries right down, just do what needed doing.

Especially at times like now.

Shaw picked at a tooth with a fingernail. 'You a man of faith?'

'What?'

'Do you believe in God, in the afterlife, in all of that? Is your reward waiting for you in heaven, Reggie? I only ask 'cos you sure seem in a hurry to get there.'

'Nice talking to you, Arthur, you take care,' Reg said, turning and moving away.

Shaw laughed, reached out a hand, grabbed Reg by the elbow. 'Don't be in such a hurry, Reggie. You and me, we've got stuff in common, stuff to talk about. Loads of stuff in common, loads to talk about, I know we have. Tell you what, when we get off, let me buy you a drink. It's the least I could do, after last night. After what we shared, we both deserve a drink and I'm happy to buy. Alright?'

'I don't much drink, Arthur.'

Shaw dropped his hand and Reg walked away.

'See you later, Reggie. See you later.'

3

Smith. The ARP man's name was Smith. Stanley Smith. An ordinary name for an ordinary man. Not that anyone was ever ordinary – Marsh knew better than to make such an assumption – it was just that sometimes an individual appeared to lack anything that marked them out. Self-contained, maybe that was a better description. The sort who kept himself to himself and only got involved when pushed but somehow always knew exactly what was what, when it came to his neighbours.

Sitting in Smith's front room, the policeman looked around. A black and white photograph of a young girl about to turn into a young woman hung over the fireplace. The photograph was mounted on cream card and sat behind glass in a simple black frame. The cloche hat suggested the picture had been taken some time in the Twenties.

'Your daughter?'

'Yes,' Smith said. He looked up at the picture. 'It's a few years ago that. Married now she is and living in London. At least I think she is. Haven't heard from her for a while. She's not in touch so much, not since her ma died.'

'I'm sorry.'

'It happens.'

'Mr Smith?'

The ARP man turned his head, his eyes rheumy, his skin grey. From tiredness, from a cold, from day-to-day living, the cause of Stanley Smith's condition wasn't obvious and the DS wasn't in a hurry to ask – it was a look many if not most people wore these days. Harry Marsh knew he did and was constantly surprised by the pale old man who stared back at him from his shaving mirror every morning.

A pale, tired old man.

Either his all-enveloping weariness would pass in time or he'd get used to it but whichever way, the end result would be much the same: it wouldn't bother him any longer.

Marsh opened his police notebook. 'The girl?'

'The one under the door?'

'How was she found exactly? What were the circumstances?'

'Some kids. They'd been playing down that end. Anyway, they found her and then they came running up the street and they found me.'

'How did they find you?'

'They knocked on me door.'

'Just like that?'

'I'm a local ARP bloke, they know me and they reckoned I'd know what to do.'

The policeman nodded. 'And these kids, do they have names?'

Smith widened his eyes and nodded. 'There were three of them. One was Tommy Perks. The second one was Patrick Slater. And the third was Vincent Lee. That's it, Tommy, Patrick and Vincent, that was them. Not that Vincent was really with them like, he sort of loitered behind, like a bad smell.'

'And do they live locally?'

'Tommy and Patrick live in the next street up. Tommy at 32, Patrick at 45, I think. Vincent lives at 19 Smith Street, with his aunt. Great-aunt, actually. Bit of a one that one is, I can tell you. Had quite a life.'

Marsh ignored the invitation for gossip. 'Thank you,' he said, writing down the names and addresses. 'And why did you call the police, Mr Smith, rather than just getting her body collected? Isn't that the more usual thing to do these days?'

Smith shook his head. 'If she was a bomb victim, maybe, well, yes, that would have been the thing to do but this, this just didn't seem right. The girl lying there, under the door, like she'd just gone to sleep or something. That house, it's been empty a bit and though the street's something of a ruin, that house, it's not been hit. So I'm thinking, whatever killed that poor kid, it weren't no bomb, I'll tell you that. And she looked so peaceful, like she'd just dozed off. No, it wasn't right, that's why I called you lot. That poor little thing, couldn't leave her lying there, not all alone like that, could I?'

The stairs led down and away, further into the earth. The tiled walls became stone walls and the ceiling dipped. As the space around him darkened, Harry Marsh felt his chest tighten. He could smell dirt and blood and cordite – or thought he could. The walls were mud brown now and folding in on him, the stairwell turning into a gullet, which with one inhale would draw him down into a lightless place.

He stopped and slowed his breathing. Moira Penny turned and looked back at him.

'Harry?'

'I'm fine. Let's just get on with this, eh?'

The doctor nodded and moved off. She reached out and turned on a light. The darkness receded and Marsh took a step forward.

The stairwell opened into a large chamber, iron-framed beds and medical equipment arranged neatly along the side walls. A string of electric lights, slung from the ceiling, ran the length of the room.

'What is this place?'

'It's a hospital ward doubling as an air raid shelter. Or should that be an air raid shelter doubling as a hospital ward? You tell me, Harry, I'm not sure I know anymore.'

Marsh followed her across the room and out into another corridor. 'And where does this lead?'

'The Lewis's building. The basement.'

'Lewis's? The department store?'

'That's the one. See that big door? Big doors, to be precise.' The doctor pointed to a set of floor-to-ceiling double doors, barely visible at the far end of the unlit corridor.

'Yes.'

'That's Lewis's basement and our temporary morgue, if we need it.'

'A morgue?'

'Thinking is, during an air raid, we keep our living patients closest to the hospital, the dead ones? Well, it doesn't matter where we keep them, does it?'

Harry Marsh shivered, both at the thought and the chill in the air.

'Ah, here we are,' Moira Penny said. 'My well-appointed offices. Age before beauty, Harry.' She shouldered open a door and gestured. Marsh entered.

His chills doubled down.

There was a white stone table in the centre of the room. Its surface was grooved and canted, with a rose-shaped plughole at one end. A lead downpipe ran from the plug hole to a gutter in the floor. A hand water pump stood next to the slab, water dripping from its extendable nozzle into an old white bucket – the first bucket in a row of buckets, some full.

A glass-fronted cupboard, attached to the opposite wall, was filled with chemical bottles of various sizes. A table, laid out with a selection of hammers, saws, chisels and pliers, sat against the same wall.

In the far-right corner, there was an annex and in the annex Marsh could see two redbrick pedestals, six feet apart, a long concrete block laid across them. An open coffin rested on the block.

'Must say it all looks very up to date,' the DS said. 'No expense spared, if you ask me.'

The doctor laughed. 'Victorian,' she said. 'The General's original pathology room.'

Harry Marsh walked over to the table and looked down at the body that lay there. At the body covered up to its chin by a plain white sheet. A body looking so much smaller than he remembered and he remembered how small she'd looked when he first saw her.

How young and vulnerable.

And small.

'Poor kid,' Harry Marsh said, was all he could say.

'Yes,' Moira Penny said, 'a poor wee bairn.'

'Anything to tell me?'

'What do you think I've been doing with my time?'

Marsh smiled. 'Not planning to waste mine, I hope.'

Dr Penny smiled back. 'I never would, Harry, would never dare.'

'So..?'

'So. The eyes were the first clue. We were right about that—'

'You were right about that.'

'I was but I didn't want to sound too smug.'

'Is that even possible with your accent?'

'You're a fine one to talk about accents.'

'That's true enough.'

Moira Penny frowned, tried to look cross, failed. 'Now, if you'll only shut up and let me tell you what I know, you might learn something.'

'Roger that.'

'Good boy.' The doctor walked over to the table and picked up several small cellophane envelopes. 'These two packets contain fibres I took from her mouth and lips,' she said. 'And these other two are fibres I took from her nostrils and her lungs.'

'What sort of fibres?'

'Cotton, maybe. I need to get them under a microscope but my guess is cotton and possibly, given their colours, cotton from the cushion.'

'The cushion was used to suffocate her then?'

'I'd say almost certainly. I can't find any injuries that would indicate any other form of death. Her major organs, they're exactly what you'd expect in a girl of her age. I'm about to send the lab some blood samples but her insides don't display any obvious sign of arsenic or cyanide poisoning, either deliberate or accidental. My guess? If there is a drug in her system, it's more likely to be a sedative than anything else. So, what with the petechial haemorrhaging and the fibres and all, good money's on the cushion.'

'And her lips? You said they were sticky and there was an odour?'

Dr Penny laughed and glanced down at one of the metal pails. 'You won't believe this, Harry, but it may just have been chocolate on her lips. There is certainly something that could be chocolate in her stomach contents, along with what looks like bites of cake. The lab will let us exactly what, eventually. Don't worry, I've already made your case and told them to pull out all stops.'

Marsh nodded, 'Thank you,' he said, trying not to think about what was in the bucket at his feet. 'And time of death?'

'Given the progression of rigor mortis and core body temperature, twelve to eighteen hours ago.'

'Before midnight then?'

'Almost certainly.'

'And her age?'

'Pre-puberty. No more than eleven.'

Harry Marsh pulled the sheet away from the girl's chin. 'And this mark? The one on her neck.'

His friend shrugged. 'Whatever was removed, it definitely happened post-mortem, as I said earlier.'

'Identity tags?'

'It's very possible.'

The policeman wiped a hand across his forehead. His skin was clammy. Being this far underground was starting to feel uncomfortable. Or maybe it was the girl's presence, reminding him that eventually he'd be underground permanently.

Him and everyone he loved.

And just how many of his friends already were.

The doctor reached forward and took the girl's right hand. 'And then there's this.'

Harry Marsh watched as Moira Penny unpeeled the girl's fingers, pushing them back and away from her palm. 'What's that?'

The doctor moved the hand towards the light. 'This. Can you see it?'

Harry Marsh craned his neck and peered at the girl's palm, at where Moira Penny was pointing. He could just make out some faint blue lines. 'Is that writing?'

'It is. Very faded but writing all the same.'

'And what does it say?'

Dr Penny shook her head. 'I'm not sure. The one word looks like *panic*, the other could be *turtle* – I just don't know, it's not really legible enough.'

'*Panic* and *turtle*? What's that meant to mean?'

'Search me, Harry.'

Marsh took a step off, rubbed a hand across the back of his neck. 'Do you think she wrote it herself?'

Moira Penny shook her head. 'Well, if she did, it means she's left-handed but no, what's there looks like an adult's writing to me – see all those curls and curves. Maybe it's something she was told to remember but to be honest I really don't know and anything I say now would be pure assumption. And I know how much you hate assumptions.'

The policeman watched the doctor fold the girl's hand and lay it back on the table. 'What is it, Moira? What else is there?'

'What?'

'This assumption you obviously do have. The one I won't like.'

'It's not an assumption exactly, Harry, but there is one other thing, well, a couple of other things, actually.'

'Yes?'

'Her skin tone. What do you make of it?'

Marsh looked at the girl. 'Difficult to say in this light and given her condition. What do *you* make of it?'

'It's olive. It's subtle, yes, due to the death pallor I didn't notice it at first but her skin has a definite olive hue. And then there're her features.'

'So?'

'I'm not convinced she's British. If I had to say, I'd say she was from the Mediterranean, maybe. Southern Europe certainly.'

'Mediterranean? Are you sure?'

'No, I'm not sure, that's why it's an assumption. However...'

Moira Penny took a bag from beneath the wall table and opened it. She pulled out a light tan frock. Marsh recognised it at once – the dress the girl had been wearing when she was found.

'This,' Dr Penny said, 'this implies something different again.'

She held out the dress and pointed at a label stitched inside the neckline: *Made in Germany*.

4

The afternoon passed in a mist of mechanical routine, with nothing to mark it out from any other day. Reg Miles drew up schedules, ticked off manifests, settled full-blown arguments and half-cocked petty disagreements and generally let the hours follow the pattern they'd followed many times before. Reg wasn't bored and distant but then neither was he engaged and fully present. There were times when the man felt he was living his life at one step removed, as if everybody else was on the other side of a semi-transparent safety curtain – like the one they had at the music hall – and that he was a spectator, waiting for the curtain to rise and the action begin.

This was one of those times.

It wasn't that he was ambitious and wanted to be elsewhere, not really. At one point in his childhood, he had imagined he'd be happiest, machete in hand, hacking his way through impenetrable jungle, on the brink of discovering a long-lost city. That had been the influence of too much Edgar Rice Burroughs on an impressionable young mind. Later, even as he grew out of Tarzan and his adventures, he still harboured a desire to travel. Difficult now there were three of them but maybe after the war they'd find a way.

Leaving school and dreams of Africa behind, Reg, at thirteen, started working in the local barber's as a floor sweeper and before long was charged with lathering up faces, in preparation for wet shaves. On one Saturday his old man had turned up. Drunk, he demanded *Little Reg* give him a shave. The barber had protested that the boy wasn't ready, that he hadn't been trained up but Reg's dad insisted.

As Reg nicked his father's neck for the fifth time, the white soapy lather seeping bright red, the older man had opened his eyes and looked at his son. 'Reginald,' he said, 'you ain't cut out for this, you ain't.'

A week later the boy found himself standing at the gateway to the BSA factory, wax paper wrapped sandwiches in one hand, bottle of pop in the other.

Clocking off, Reg hung his overalls in his locker and dragged on his jacket and overcoat. He slung his gas mask over one shoulder and put on his cap. He yawned and hoped that tonight would be a quiet one. He'd now worked five days in a row at BSA and five nights as a volunteer fireman, so tonight was his night off, unless it was an extreme emergency. Yes, a quiet night would be good, given that Agnes had a night shift herself and that Elizabeth Margaret would need minding. He'd have his tea and then a read of the Mail, see if there was any news of the Villa second team – they'd all been taken prisoner at Dunkirk, dozy sods – and have a cigarette or two.

Agnes being at work, she couldn't object if he smoked a couple of ciggies, as long as it was out the back.

Perfect.

Stepping into the drizzle, a figure moved across in front of him. 'Reggie Miles.'

It was Arthur Shaw, accompanied by two other men. Reg recognised one – he was Shaw's associate from last night – the other he didn't know.

'We'll have that drink now, Reggie, shall we?'

5

The policeman and the doctor leant against the iron railings that ran across in front of the hospital. They hadn't spoken for five minutes. Moira Penny stood several yards off, downwind, smoking the one cigarette she allowed herself daily, careful that her fumes didn't go anywhere near her friend.

'German, she's German?' Marsh said, eventually.

'Possibly.'

'But how? What's a young German girl doing in Birmingham?'

'You're the policeman, you tell me.'

'Funny. Very funny, Moira.' The line of his chin giving lie to his words.

The doctor sighed. 'Her clothes are not new. In fact they're quite old and somewhat dated but they're well kept, well tended. They've been repaired a few times but repaired with care. Also, they fit her well. Which is odd, given how old they seem.'

'Hand-me-downs,' Marsh said. 'They could be hand-me-downs. Which means—'

'There's an older sister.'

'A close female relative, certainly. And those words—'

'*Panic* and *turtle*?'

'Do they mean anything in German?'

Moira Penny shook her head. 'You're asking the wrong girl here, Harry, I don't have a word of German. I haven't a clue, sorry about that.'

'You can't be good at everything,' Marsh said, smiling.

'Oh but I can,' Moira Penny said, 'just not German, as it turns out.'

Marsh laughed. 'Something's not right,' he said. 'Something's not right about that girl.'

'What could be right about the death of someone so young?'

The DS frowned, nodded and shrugged, all in one awkward movement. 'That's true but that label, *it's* not right.'

'What about the label?'

'*Made in Germany* – shouldn't that be in German if it was German?'

'That's a good point, Harry.'

'And anyway, you don't think she's German, do you?'

Moira Penny trod her cigarette out. 'No, I don't. I wouldn't want to judge anyone on the colour of their skin but her complexion, her features, her dark hair, she's not German. At least, not northern European. Italian, Greek, Turkish, somewhere in the Balkans, maybe, but not German.'

Marsh sighed, almost angry now. 'I agree. And anyway, if she was German, she'd be interned by now, along with the rest of her family. And that's another thing, why isn't anyone looking for her? Why hasn't anyone come forward and reported her missing?'

'Maybe because her family has been interned,' Moira Penny said, 'and she's all alone.'

'Maybe,' the policeman said, 'maybe but I'm not buying that. A girl that age? Living on her own? Even in these times? No. There's something here, something else we're missing – I'm missing – and I don't know what it is.'

'If you knew what it was, it wouldn't be missing now, would it?'

Marsh laughed and then smiled. 'Were you always so quick?'

'Always.' Moira Penny said. 'And talking of quick, time for a quick drink?'

The policeman shook his head. 'Thanks but I'd better be off home.'

6

Arthur Shaw's pub of choice was The Malt Shovel, on the corner of Munoz Road and the Coventry Road. It hadn't changed much, not in many years and it had been many years since Reg Miles was last in the place.

'The Shovel's a great little boozer. You been here before, Reggie?'

'Not for a long time, Arthur.'

'Barred, were you?'

'No, like I said, I don't drink much.'

Shaw looked at Reg's long, solemn face. 'I was joking, Reggie, just joking.'

They went in through a side door and entered the snug. It was small with stained, wood panels. The room smelt of cigarette smoke and something else, something prickly and woody, camphor maybe. Two old men in black felt hats, dark coats with astrakhan collars and biblical beards sat in the corner, playing cards.

One of Shaw's associates – the one Reg didn't recognise – went over to them, said a few words and the elderly men collected up their pack and soft-shoed out. The man then settled himself onto a stool by the door, resting his leg against its lower panel.

Arthur Shaw sat down. 'What you having then, Reggie?'

'A glass of mild, I suppose.'

'Baz,' Shaw said to the broader of the two men, the one who was mostly at his side, so it seemed, 'get Reggie here a pint of mild, I'll have a pint of Aston.'

Baz grunted and went to the serving hatch.

'You're a brave man, Reggie Miles, a proper brave man.'

'If you say so.'

'But I do, Reggie, I do. Cigarette?'

'No, you're alright.'

'Mind if I do?'

Reg shook his head.

'Ta.' Shaw pulled the cap off a metal cigarette lighter and scrolled the plastic wheel. A flame sparked. The lighter was bomb shaped and had what looked like a radio tower painted on its side. Next to the structure were the numbers *1939*.

Shaw caught Reg looking. 'You like this? It's from the New York World Fair, mate of mine brought it back. You want it? It's yours.' Shaw pushed the metal cap back onto the cylinder, reached across and dropped the lighter into the breast pocket of Reg's jacket, patting it flat. 'There you go, don't say I don't ever give you anything. Never say that, Reggie, never.'

Baz walked back to the table, put down two of the four pint glasses he was carrying, turned and joined his friend by the door. Heads bent together, the two men began a conversation, at a low rumble.

'Baz, he doesn't say a lot but he's a good bloke,' Arthur Shaw said, after half emptying his glass in one gulp. 'You a good bloke, Reggie?'

'I do my best,' Reg said.

Shaw looked at Reg. It was a forensic stare, one of assessment and evaluation, entirely professional and completely without passion. Reg had seen a similar look on the face of a doctor some years earlier, when being treated for suspected pneumonia.

Or it could have been the look of a big cat, peering down from its perch, high in a tree on the savanna, deciding which member of the passing impala herd was the weakest.

Either way, it was impassive, unemotional, unsettling.

'Yes,' Shaw said, 'I think you do.'

Reg picked up his drink and took a sip.

Shaw laughed. 'That's not a sip, this is a sip.' Shaw drained his glass. 'I needed that, I can tell you. You really don't drink much, do you, Reggie?'

'No, like I said, not that much.'

'Didn't think so.'

Shaw held up his empty beer glass. Baz walked across, took the pot from his boss's hand and looked at Reg. 'You want another?'

Reg shook his head. 'No, you're alright, this'll do me.'

'Suit yourself, won't be asking again,' Baz said with a shrug and walked over to the serving hatch. He leant on the counter. 'Barkeep, when you've got time.'

Arthur Shaw smiled at Reg. 'No manners that one, no manners at all. So what makes you do it?'

'Do what?'

'Do good.'

Reg shook his head. 'Good? I just do what needs doing, that's all.'

'And what reward do you get?'

'What do you mean?'

'All this doing good. All this putting your neck on the line for people you don't know, what reward do you get?'

'Same as anyone else.'

Shaw dipped his head to one side and then back up again. 'And you think that's right, do you? What with everything's that going on today, you don't think you should get some sort of reward? Some additional benefits?'

'For what?'

'For going above and beyond, Reggie, for going above and beyond.'

Reg stood. 'I better be off.'

Baz returned to the table and put a fresh pint in front of Shaw. Shaw looked up. 'Don't be off so soon, keep me company a bit. That's all I ask.'

Feeling Baz's breath on his neck, sensing he had no choice, Reg sat down again.

'That's better,' Arthur Shaw said, raising his pint. 'Cheers.'

'Cheers,' Reg said.

'You must see stuff, Reggie, see a lot of stuff.'

'Like what?'

'You being an auxiliary fireman and all, you must see a lot of stuff.'

'I don't know what you mean.'

'In the ruins. On the bomb sites. In the houses. There must be stuff that you think: *I'd like that*. Stuff, you know, just lying there, waiting to be picked up. You must have seen some proper valuable bits and pieces.'

'Maybe.'

Shaw laughed. 'There's no maybe to it, Reggie. You ever take anything?'

Reg felt as if he'd been slapped hard and everything he'd ever believed brought into question. 'No,' he said, 'I have not.'

'But you have been tempted.'

Reg shook his head. To say *Yes* would be to tell the truth but it would also reveal something of himself he would prefer remain concealed. But then to not tell the truth was inalienable to him. To his image of himself as an honest man. And he was an honest man. 'Occasionally,' he said.

Shaw laughed again. 'I knew it. I just knew it. Didn't I say, boys, didn't I say? Even the great Reggie Miles can be tempted.'

The two men at the door looked over and nodded, not sure what they were agreeing with but aware that something required their assent.

Arthur Shaw put down his glass. 'I don't blame you, Reggie, no one can blame you. The way I see it, you put your life on the line night after night for people who don't know your name and even if they did, they wouldn't care. So you do this for them, the least you should get back is a little, let's say, remuneration. And answer me this: shouldn't bravery be rewarded? And what I'm proposing, it's only the law of salvage after all.'

'It's also called looting and you can get shot for looting.'

Shaw smiled. 'If someone abandons something because they think it's been destroyed and you happen to find it intact and pocket it, is that looting, Reggie, is it?'

'No—' Reg said.

'Quite.'

'It's more like grave robbing.'

Arthur Shaw snorted and laughed, the discordant sound of chalk snagging on a blackboard. 'Funny, Reggie, you're funny. But how about this? You see a building, its walls are out, there's a roof about to come down sometime soon and you become aware that on that roof there is a considerable amount of lead. What you going to do?'

'Report it, what else?'

Shaw shook his head. 'Oh Reggie. Reggie, Reggie, Reggie, Reggie, Reggie. What you could do is let me or someone like me know and that someone can get it cleared for you. Get it made safe. I know how overstretched you firelids are, how overworked. Why give yourself any more work when someone else can sort it all out and you can make a little something on the side?'

'Something on the side?'

'It doesn't have to be just lead, either. People like a bit of furniture too and you wouldn't believe what some will pay for household appliances, even gear that's slightly, let's say, the worse for wear – you know, a bit of fire damage here and there, a dent or two. There's always somebody prepared to buy what you've got to flog. That's the kind of world we live in these days – it's a seller's market and no mistake. You want to be part of that, Reggie? 'Cos let me tell you, what we're seeing now is just the start. As things get tighter, there's going to be a big demand for all sorts of stuff over the next year or two and trust me, you want to be in at the start, 'cos there won't be any openings for latecomers. You a latecomer, Reggie? I don't think you are.'

Reg looked at Shaw. From the way the man's words rose and fell, even the pauses and repetitions, he could see this wasn't his first time: here was a man used to delivering this sales patter.

'Same goes for the factory, Reggie, same goes for the factory. Who's going to miss a load of metal that's got bent out of shape by a Jerry bomb and is no use to anyone apart from a scrapper, who's going to miss that?'

'What you saying, Arthur Shaw?'

Arthur Shaw picked up his pint pot, looked Reg in the eye. 'You wouldn't be the first to help himself, Reggie, or to help me, and you won't be the last. And anyway, you owe me this.'

'Owe you?'

'Who had your back last night, Reggie, who had your back? And think of it as cash in hand, Reggie, a bit of extra cash in hand. You think about that, you think what you could do with that little bit more. That little bit extra that you deserve because of what you do on a nightly basis. You could afford some special treats for that nice little family of yours. Be a shame if you couldn't give them a little something extra now and then. I mean, we live in dangerous times, Reggie, best to treat your nearest and dearest the best you can while they're still here, while we're all still here, 'cos if you don't, well, they could be gone just like that.' Shaw clicked his fingers. 'Live the good life today, Reggie Miles, that's what I say. Or at least live the best life you can. You think about that: the best life you can. Wouldn't that be something? And all with an extra bit of tin in your pocket.'

7

Harry Marsh walked Moira Penny to Navigation Street. He waited until she was on board the 53 tram and it was heading off towards the Bristol Road, before strolling to New Street Station.

Perched on a Third-Class bench, he closed his eyes and listened to the train clack over the expansion joints as it threaded out of the terminal and towards Moseley. Somewhere in the distance, far beyond the blackout, there was a war going on but for the moment, alone in the dark, with just the mundane and comforting rattle and sway of the carriage to keep him company, Marsh was as far removed from the conflict as was possible. It was a temporary respite, he knew that but one he welcomed.

Yawning, he set his internal alarm clock for fifteen minutes, let his head droop forward and fell asleep.

In what seemed only moments later, the train grumbled into Moseley station. Harry Marsh woke, stood, reached around the blackout, pushed down the window and unlatched the door. Leaving the darkened carriage, he stepped onto an even darker platform. The row of overhead lights which ran down to the stairs were unlit. The Waiting Room windows were blacked out, its double wooden doors closed and barred. The Station Master's office was also dark. The only indication of life, a faint tang of cigarette smoke hanging in the air. It was as if the station was being mothballed for when better times arrived.

Little did Marsh know then that within twelve months the station would be closed as part of increasing efficiencies driven by the war effort, never to reopen.

Walking out of the station, Harry Marsh crossed over Woodbridge Road and turned left, heading towards his flat. Pausing, he decided to stop off at The Trafalgar Hotel. He'd find the most smoke-free nook and have a nightcap. Jeannie wouldn't mind, in fact she'd understand.

As he crossed Trafalgar Road, he heard a disturbance coming from the yard behind the pub. Pushing through the wooden gates, he saw four men in front of him, fighting. Or rather, two handing out a beating and two receiving that beating.

The two handing it out were in police uniform.

Of the other two, one was flat on the floor, the other was on his knees.

'Alright,' Marsh said, 'what's going on here?'

One of the policemen – a sergeant – turned his head. 'Get out of here you,' he said, 'if you know what's good for you.'

'What did you say?' Marsh said.

'Didn't you hear him proper?' the other one said. 'Sod off or else.'

'Or else what?'

The two policemen turned and squared up to Marsh.

'You thick or something?' the constable said.

'I'm not thick,' Marsh said, reaching into his overcoat and pulling out his warrant card, 'but I am something.'

The constable shone his blackout lamp at the card, swallowed a few flies and then looked at his companion.

'Who are you then?' the sergeant said.

'Detective Sergeant Harold Marsh, Birmingham City Police, R Division. And what have these men done to get your heavy hand laid upon them at this time?'

The sergeant moved in close. Marsh could smell hair lotion and the vinegar bite of sweat. 'Irish is what they are,' he said.

Marsh nodded, suggesting agreement. 'Irish?'

The constable coughed, cleared his throat. 'That's right,' he said.

'And so they deserve a beating? For being Irish, they deserve this?'

'They do,' the sergeant said. 'Best to keep these bogtrotters in their place. Lets them know what's good for them.'

'And what you going to say to the guv'nor when he hears about this?'

The constable looked confused. 'The guv'nor?'

Harry Marsh shrugged. 'Chief Constable Moriarty. Him being a *bogtrotter* and all, not sure he's going to be that pleased when he finds out what's been happening here. Nor, I'd say, are all the other Irish boyos who just happen to be in the Brummagem police.'

'Yeah but they wear the uniform so they're our Irish,' the constable said, repeating something he'd heard, an unconvincing sneer on his face.

'Maybe they are but with an attitude like yours, I wouldn't want to test any loyalties,' the DS said. He looked at the two Irishmen, who were now stood back up. 'Where you from, lads? And if you say Ireland or any other facetious stuff like that, I'll let these two have another whack at the pair of you.'

'Balsall Heath,' one said, while the other looked at his feet. 'Just down the road, it is.'

Marsh smiled. 'I know where Balsall Heath is and I suggest you get back across there right now.'

The shoegazer looked up warily, anticipating a trick. 'Now?'

'Now usually means now.'

The two men nodded, hesitated and then hurried out through the gates.

Harry Marsh peered at the sergeant and then at the constable, sizing them up, wondering what would happen next. 'Any reason I shouldn't report this? I'll take anything, anything at all.'

The sergeant was breathing hard, biting back whatever he wanted to say, like a dog gathering breath before barking – or attacking.

And then the siren started.

A howling tone which rose until it was joined by another tone: a banshee cry, deeper, more resonant, more primeval. As the tones commingled and peaked, the whole sound decayed into a repeating, otherworldly cycle, a choir of ghosts who sang in half steps and wails.

The three policemen looked at each other, any and all animosity chased away by the need for self-preservation.

'There's a shelter at the station,' the constable said. 'We should go there.'

'You go,' Harry Marsh said. 'Go on, go.'

The two uniforms stared at the DS, looked at each other, looked back at Marsh.

'We alright here?' the sergeant said.

'Not really,' Marsh said, 'but right now I'm less alright with what's soon to be raining down on our heads than with the pair of you.'

The three policemen left the yard just as the pub was emptying. At the corner of Trafalgar Road and Woodbridge Road, Marsh watched the sergeant and constable pick up speed and leg it down the pavement towards the police station, disappearing into the crowd of disappointed drinkers.

The first bomb landed.

It was behind him, back towards the train station but the shock-wave almost took him off his feet.

Staggering, he glanced over his shoulder. From what he could see through the smoke, the bomb had taken off the front of the detached house next to the station. Bricks and timbers were spread across the street but the side walls and back wall were still standing. Dust fell like rain, covering everything in a cloud of mourning grey.

Jeannie.

Christ.

Jeannie.

Where's Jeannie? Is she at home? Is she safe?

Part of Harry Marsh wanted to go back, check for survivors but his overriding priority was Jeannie – he needed to find Jeannie. He consoled himself with the fact that the damaged house had been dark and appeared deserted when he passed it a few minutes earlier but one thought nagged away at him: didn't blackout make every house seem that way these days?

He turned and ran for the first time in a long time, speeding up Woodbridge Road towards the bakery – he and Jeannie lived in the flat above his dad's old business. The family home, as had been.

In an odd inversion, it had been his parents who moved out, not him. Moved out after Dad sold the shop, the older man knowing that despite what he had always hoped, his son would never follow him into baking. His mom and dad lived in a small cottage in Alvechurch, these days. The downstairs of the house doubling as a tearoom and they made what little money they could from catering for a dwindling number of day-trippers – and then made what little money they had go as far as possible.

Marsh was almost at the bakery when something moved in his peripheral vision.

Something in a doorway opposite.

Something on the other side of the road.

A figure crouching, bent double, hands folded across chest, neck bent forward, chin almost touching sternum. A motionless figure but not dead.

He crossed the road. 'You alright?' he said, as he approached.

The figure looked up: a young woman, her arms wrapped around a baby.

'Christ,' he said, reaching out a hand, 'you'd better come with me.'

'I can't,' the woman said. 'I can't move. I just can't.'

'If you don't move now, you might never move again,' Marsh said, his words well-meant but sounding harsher than intended. 'Come on, let's get you and your kid somewhere safe.'

Somewhere safe?

Ha.

Somewhere a bit safer, maybe.

Wherever that may be.

If there was such a place.

He reached down, caught her elbow, pulled the young woman to her feet.

They were in the middle of the road when another bomb hit.

Loud, close, bright, the street lit up and driven by instinct, Marsh threw himself over the girl – she was hardly more than eighteen, if that – and the baby.

He felt something hit him hard in the back and his ears dulled down, the world retreating to a distant rumble at the far end of a very long tunnel.

He smelt burning and a moment later realised his coat was on fire. Ripping it off, he threw it to the ground and stamped down on the smoking material. There were white streaks on the coat's back – phosphorus, it could only be phosphorus.

Incendiary bombs. The Jerries were using incendiary bombs.

He spun around, looking for the bakery – it was intact but the garage down the road was on fire.

Another bomb fell but a way off this time, the explosion somewhere further down the Alcester Road. And in that moment, it was like a thunderstorm rolling into the next valley, the lightning still visible over the crest of the hill – close but no longer threatening.

'Come on,' he said to the girl. 'Come on.'

The policeman took the young woman by the arm and led her to the pavement. They stopped on the kerb and she looked up into his face. Reaching out her right arm, she slapped Marsh across the cheek, as hard as she could.

He flinched. 'What?'

'We was safe in that sodding doorway, me and the bab was safe until you come along,' she said. 'Safe. You should have let us be, you should, mister.'

The girl ran off down the street, clutching the baby to her bosom. Marsh watched her go. At least there were no more explosions – not for the moment.

'What you been up to, Harry Marsh?'

He turned to see his wife standing a few yards off, smiling at him.

'Jeannie,' he said.

'That's me, Harry. How you doing?'

He stumbled towards her, threw his arms around her waist, hugged her tight.

'You should be in the cellar,' he said.

'That's where I'm heading,' Jeannie said. 'What I didn't know is that you were out here playing around with some young thing while I wasn't looking.'

Harry Marsh laughed. 'I love you, Jeannie Marsh.'

'And I love you, Harry Marsh. Now, let's get downstairs and don't forget to bring your coat with you – you're going to want to clean it up a bit before you mend it.'

THURSDAY 21 NOVEMBER 1940

1

The all-clear sounded at four-thirty in the morning. Upstairs, back in their flat, Jeannie went into the kitchen and Marsh sat down at the dining table. A square, brown table with fold-out wings, Jeannie claimed it was made of oak, he suspected it was a cheaper wood. No matter, his wife loved it and every Monday would rub wax deep into its grain, buffing the surface until it shone.

Harry Marsh sat back, removed his tie and loosened his collar. He checked his breathing: a little jagged but not too bad considering, not enough to warrant fetching out his inhaler. No, this was fine, he'd clear his head and forget about it.

Jeannie walked into the room, her blonde curls rim lit by the glow from a wall lamp.

Just as he remembered her.

He'd never been to Hertfordshire and this wasn't the way he'd have chosen to make his first trip but he'd had no say in the matter: Hertfordshire it was. Not that he remembered much about the journey.

Not that he remembered anything about the journey.

The shells exploded and the world turned yellow.

Snot yellow.

He felt tears in his eyes and fire in his lungs and then nothing, apart from delirious flashes of men shouting, crying, screaming and above, in and between all the noise, his father's voice: *You will not, it's against our every belief, against our duty to God. You will not fight in this war. I forbid it.*

The old man had once said these words, or something very similar – Harry Marsh wasn't sure exactly what, not anymore.

Nor sure of anything, not anymore, in that jaundiced, burning light.

There was a journey, a period in hospital, a transfer to the Voluntary Aid Detachment at Knebworth for convalescence and a few days spent in semi-stupor. Eventually, as the bandages were removed, he was able to open his eyes and the first thing he saw was her face.

Jeannie's face staring down at him, fringed by a white cap and backlit by soft window light but he knew she was smiling. He just knew.

'Private Marsh,' she said, her accent light but unmistakably southern, 'how are you today?'

'I don't know,' he said, 'you tell me, you're the doctor.'

She laughed. 'No, I'm not,' she said.

'Then you must be an angel.'

Later, as she pushed him around the grounds of what had been Knebworth Golf Club, she told him how her father was a local pig man, her mother a cleaner and how she herself had been in service before the war. When the club became a VAD – a Voluntary Aid Detachment – she asked her employers if she could volunteer. They agreed and here she was, in a different kind of service. At times, it felt to Harry that her service was meant just for him.

Had only ever been meant for him.

Discharged from both care and army, Harry Marsh returned to Birmingham but even weeks later he couldn't get Jeanette Rimbert out of his head. He hadn't known it when they were together but now they were apart, he realised just how he felt.

How much he missed her unearnt kindness.

How much he missed the coolness of her hands.

How much he missed her.

Returning to Knebworth, he went down on one knee and proposed. They married six months later. On leaving the church, the newlyweds were saluted by two rows of wounded soldiers, crutches raised in a crude bough above their heads – a bough which corralled and funnelled the couple back to Birmingham and a future as bright and as flawed as a piece of newly minted Brummagem ware.

Back in the Midlands, the couple moved into his old room above the bakery, Harry Marsh joined the Birmingham City Police and Jeannie Marsh née Rimbert got a job behind the counter in Shufflebothams – a posh grocery store on the corner of Woodbridge Road and Alcester Road.

In the here and now, Jeannie slid a glass into his hand. He looked up. She twisted the stopper from a bottle of Hennessy and poured a sizeable glug into his tumbler and then an equal measure into hers.

'Brandy? I thought you were making tea,' he said.

'And I thought we could use a drink,' she said, sitting and raising her glass. 'Cin cin.'

'Cin cin.'

They drank and it could have been any lazy night in winter, apart from the blackout on the windows and the odour of fire and dust clinging to their clothes.

'Well,' Jeannie said, over the rim of her glass, 'tonight's been something of an entertainment, can't deny that.'

'It has,' Marsh said. 'It really has. I only hope that little girl and her baby got wherever they needed to be.'

'Who was she?'

'No idea. I pulled her out of the doorway opposite just before the second bomb hit.' He frowned. 'I thought I was doing her a favour but you know what, maybe she was right, maybe she'd have been better off if I'd left her where she was.'

'You ask me, she looked as good as any of us do these days.'

They drank in silence.

Jeannie pushed the brandy bottle across the table. 'There's more,' she said.

'Thanks, love.'

'Did you hear about The Narrows, by the way?'

'That private club on the corner of Brighton Road and Oxford Road?'

'That's the one.'

'What about it?'

'It burnt down end of October. There were these two women in the shop today, proper would-be nobs, don't like them much – they may be regulars but that doesn't mean I have to like them, does it? Anyway, they were talking about that poor Italian family killed in the Oxford Road the same night. One said they deserved it, being Italians and what were they doing in England anyway? To be fair, she got told off by her friend, who'd known them a bit and said they were lovely people. So, the first woman then said that the fire at The Narrows started well after the bombing finished and her husband reckoned it was set alight on purpose, for insurance, or something like that. What do you think, Mr Copper?'

'I don't know, love. Sounds a bit far-fetched to me, though.'

Jeannie frowned and looked Marsh directly in the eye. 'You're thinking about that young girl again. I can tell.'

The policeman touched his cheek – the slap still felt fresh.

Jeannie refilled his glass. 'Don't you worry. You did what you thought was right, Haz, you always do.'

2

Reg Miles stood on the edge of the site and stared around in the early morning murk. Looked for factory buildings he'd known for almost twenty years, now either gone or damaged beyond repair.

The machine shops were devastated, the gunsmiths' building rubble. Word was that over one thousand machine tools had been lost and that rifle production was at an end until the new year, at least.

Motorcycle production had been cut back, too. He suspected that their seven-day-a-week production run, which had resulted in nearly one thousand new machines coming off the line weekly, would have been substantially reduced – by exactly how much, no one was saying.

Or as was more likely, no one had any idea.

And in amongst all this carnage, over fifty people had been killed and nearly twice that number injured. Reg knew a great deal of the workforce by sight, many by name, and he would say a prayer for them at some point – at the point when he stopped praying for his family, that is.

Even now, two days later, the bomb damage still smouldered, throwing up curlicues of dust and ash. There was a heavy scent of charred timber and creosote in the air, too, an odour which took Reg back to a summer before the war. A summer when he'd spent several Sundays knotting and treating the new wooden fence that ran across the bottom of their garden. He was proud of that fence, it was the first thing he'd built when they moved into their new end-terrace council house back in '37. As he sank in the posts and hammered on the crosspieces, it finally felt as if they were putting down roots, claiming this territory as theirs and no one else's.

A proper home for him, for Agnes and for Elizabeth Margaret.

Or Emmy, as they called her.

Then September 1939 came and everything was made uncertain once more.

Now Emmy went to school, satchel on one side, Mickey Mouse gas mask on a strap, nestling in the small of her back.

And his wife's skin was sallow, her hair yellowed, both effects of the constant exposure to airborne sulphur in the workplace. Aggie was his *canary girl,* as women affected in this way were called.

He hoped the effects were no deeper than cosmetic.

Reg yawned, stretched out his shoulders and tried to wake himself up.

Last night's emergency shout – the second night in a row – had been the worst yet and he was tired, tired beyond anything he could have imagined only a few weeks earlier.

After leaving Arthur Shaw in The Malt Shovel and walking home, he and Agnes had crossed in the kitchen – she was on a late and on her way out – and he'd only been sat down for minutes when the alarm sounded and Ned Lucas came banging on his front door.

'Looks like a bad 'un again, Reg.'

The two men had rushed Emmy round to Reg's sister and then raced down to the station, pulling on their jackets and jumping onto the Heavy Unit, as it moved across and out of the yard.

Bombs, fire, water.

Water, fire, bombs.

Incessant, cyclic, never-ending.

And then afterwards, when the seemingly impossible happened and it did end, the discussion, the chat, the concern that Birmingham was running out of water: that drawing from the canals was alright for the moment but if another main went – and given more nights like this, it very well could – that might be it for the city. All these wood-framed buildings, all so close to each other, in a matter of hours, a firestorm would wipe Birmingham from the face of the earth.

The conversation was terrifying.

And now, this morning, there was Arthur Shaw to worry about.

What should he do about a man that he found terrifying in a quite different way?

Shaw seemed so confident in himself and his business affairs. So confident that he could say as much as he did to Reg without fear of reprisal, or comeback of any sort. Without fear that Reg would report him.

And that puzzled Reg, made him doubt anything he thought he'd learnt about people.

What made a man so self-assured that he could tell so much to someone he hardly knew without worry? He was either a fool or very successful.

Or maybe both.

Was it possible to be a fool and be successful at the same time? Reg had met a few chancers and charlatans over the years. Tricksters, snake oil salesmen, men good with the gammon, men who pretended to know more than they did, to be capable of more than they were – and some had gone on to become very successful.

So maybe yes, it was possible to be a successful fool.

A charismatic fool – full of stuff and nonsense but plausible, all the same.

Only deep down, Reg doubted Shaw was a fool.

There was something about the man, something about the fixed stare of his deep-set eyes and his oddly neutral manner of speaking that suggested detachment – he could have been an actor reading someone else's lines. Even so, Reg's overall impression was one of menace, of threat – a sense that if Shaw didn't get his way, someone would suffer.

And it didn't matter who.

Lord, was the war – the home front – destined to be full of men like Shaw? Men who took what they could from wherever they could and damn the consequences?

And not just the home front, the whole of life, maybe.

Taking a deep breath, Reg Miles straightened his collar, tamped his gas mask to his side and walked in through the works' entrance. He'd make an appointment to see Byfield, that's what he'd do.

No great harm could come of that, after all.

3

Jeannie Marsh appeared in the bedroom doorway, peignoir sliding off one shoulder, hair across her forehead, her eyes only half lit. 'You're off early,' she said, 'given you've only just got your head down.'

'Things to do,' Harry Marsh said, holding his overcoat out in front of him, examining the back.

'That's seen better days,' Jeannie said, slipping past him, heading towards the bathroom. 'You sew like a drunken sailor.'

Marsh squinted. 'It's not too bad, is it?'

'It's awful.'

He heard a tap run, a glass fill, a gargle and a spit. 'Do you think I should get a new one?'

Jeannie looked up from the sink. 'Only if you don't want to be taken for a gentleman of the road.'

The policeman smiled.

'Not that you could be mistaken for a gentleman of any sort,' Jeannie said, with a smirk.

'Thanks.'

'My pleasure.'

Marsh followed his wife back into the bedroom, draped his coat over the end of the bed.

'If you think I'm doing anything with that,' Jeannie said, 'you have got another think coming.'

'I didn't think anything of the sort,' he said, knowing his lie convinced neither of them.

Jeannie lay on the bed, propped herself up on a pillow and looked at her husband. 'Why so early?'

'I'm going to pop in and see Charlie.'

'Charlie Tighe?'

'Do we know any others?'

'Oh we know a few right Charlies but only one Charlie Tighe. What do you want with him?'

'It's probably nothing.'

'Coming from you, *probably nothing* almost certainly means *probably something*. What's up, Haz? You about to do something you know you shouldn't?'

Marsh stopped at the junction of Woodbridge Road and Trafalgar Road and banged on the side door to The Trafalgar Hotel. After a minute, he banged again and then heard a window creak open above his head.

'Who's that?'

The DS took a step back, craned his neck, looked up at Charlie Tighe peering down at him.

'Charlie Tighe, it's Harry Marsh.'

'Harry Marsh? Do you know what time it is, Harry Marsh?'

'I do.'

Two minutes later, Tighe opened the door. He wore a plaid dressing gown over a white vest and threadbare pyjama bottoms. His feet were stuffed into a pair of old slippers, the backs trodden down and broken by years of careless use. He had a scent of old smoke and bitter spirits about him, which hadn't stopped him pulling, if the red pucker on his neck just below his left ear was anything to go by.

'Good night, Charlie?' Harry Marsh said, stepping into the pub corridor.

Charlie guffawed and shut the door. 'Not bad, Harry, not bad.'

'Anyone I know?'

The landlord rubbed a hand across his unshaved chin. 'Her name's Philippa – or Phyllida – and no, I don't think you'd know her.'

'She still here?'

'Why?'

'I need a word and I'd rather no one walked in on us.'

'Don't worry, mate, she left as soon as the all-clear sounded. Her husband's due home sometime today and she wants to make sure there's still a house for him to come back to. And if there is, she wants to make sure it's nice and tidy.'

'A good housewife, eh?'

'Seems so.'

'But not a good wife, apparently.'

'There's a war on, Harry, in case you've not noticed. And we can't all be like you and Jeannie, so don't be so sodding judgemental.'

'I'm a copper, I'm paid to be sodding judgemental.'

'Does the copper want a cuppa?'

'He does.'

Harry Marsh sat at the kitchen table and watched Charlie Tighe warm and swirl the pot before spooning in a mound of tea. His friend's idea of measurement was careless, almost cavalier, as if he didn't have to worry about rationing.

Pouring in boiling water, Charlie dropped the lid on the pot, covered it with a knitted caddy and carried it to the table. He took two mugs off the washer and put them next to the pot. A jug of milk and a bowl of sugar were already in place, as was an ashtray containing two lipsticked butts.

Charlie dragged out a chair and sat down. 'What's this about then, Harry?'

'There was a bit of a fracas in your backyard last night, just before the raid. You hear anything?'

The landlord poured tea into both mugs and pushed one across to his friend, avoiding eye contact. 'You can do your own milk and sugar.'

Marsh wrapped his hands around the mug, enjoyed a moment's warmth. 'Thanks.'

'Just before the raid, you say?'

'Just before the raid.'

'What sort of fracas?'

'Two local coppers, one a sergeant, were setting about two Irish lads.'

'In my backyard?'

'Yes.'

Charlie Tighe shook his head. 'No, didn't hear a thing. I was working the public bar, mind you and that's at the front of the pub.'

Marsh nodded. He reached over, picked up the milk, splashed a drop into his tea. 'How about seeing something? You see anything? Not necessarily at the time, let's say earlier.'

Charlie raised his cup, sipped. 'Maybe.'

'What's a *maybe*?'

'There were a couple of young Irish fellas in last night. They started in the front bar and then moved into the snug. Took a set of dominoes with them. Nice enough blokes.'

'What did they look like?'

'Like I say, a couple of Irish boyos. Nothing out of the ordinary that I could see. Just two lads.'

'You seen them before?'

Charlie Tighe spooned more sugar into his cup, stirred, concentrating hard on the spoon, watching the tea spiral and settle. 'No,' he said.

'But you noticed them?'

'Heard them more like, the accent's a bit of a giveaway. And it's not that we get a lot of Irish in this place – they tend to keep themselves at the town end of the Moseley Road. You know, down Balsall Heath and beyond.'

'I do know,' Harry Marsh said, nodding.

As the two men drank their tea in silence, the landlord started to tap his heel on the floor, his left thigh jerking out and to the left.

'Something you want to tell me?'

'What makes you think that?'

'I've known you a long time, Charlie, an awfully long time.' The policeman smiled and reached out for the pot. He shook it. 'More tea?'

'I'm fine,' Charlie said, stilling his leg.

Marsh refilled his mug. 'How long have we known each other?'

'Years, Harry, years.'

'How many years?'

'Thirty, I'd say.'

Marsh nodded. 'A bit more than that. First day at school, you were there.'

'I was.'

'And then every day until we left.'

'Until you left and went to that posh place. I just went over the yard into the next bit of the same school.'

'Something over thirty years then.'

'Call me a liar for four years.'

'You're a liar.'

They laughed.

'Charlie, as an old friend, what aren't you telling me?'

'I don't know what you mean, Harry.'

The DS stared at his friend, reached out, patted him on his left knee. 'Come on, what is it?'

Tighe stood. 'You mind if I have a smoke?'

'You know I do.'

'I'll open the window and lean out.'

Marsh nodded. 'If that's what it takes.'

Charlie reached into a dressing gown pocket and pulled out a packet of Players. He stood and walked over to the cooker, leant down to the still-lit gas ring.

'You'll have your eyebrows off, if you're not careful,' Harry Marsh said.

'How do you think I keep my nose hairs in such good trim?' Charlie said.

The two friends smiled at each other.

'Window,' the policeman said, pointing.

'Fair enough,' Tighe said, unlatching and then pushing up the lower half of the kitchen's sash window. Inhaling deeply and holding his breath, he turned and blew smoke out and over the yard.

'You don't work this patch,' Charlie said.

'You know I don't.'

'Know anything about this side of town? Anything at all?'

'Not much. Had a few minor dealings over the years but not so much that it matters.'

Charlie took another drag, held and then exhaled. He looked back at Marsh. 'Maybe there's not much to know.'

'I don't believe you.'

Tighe blew more smoke out of the window. 'That's up to you.'

'Charlie...'

The landlord took one long drag, stubbed the cigarette on the concrete sill and sent the butt end cartwheeling out into the yard. 'There's a bit of a difference of opinion out there at the moment.'

'About what?'

'About how best to do business during wartime, that sort of thing.'

'What sort of thing?'

Charlie Tighe sighed. 'You know, who to buy from and who does the best deals, given all the shortages, *that* sort of thing.'

'Sounds a bit dodgy.'

'Not if you know your way around, it's not.'

Marsh nodded – they had different definitions of *dodgy*, that was for sure. 'And those Irish lads,' he said, 'they know their way around, do they?'

'Might do or maybe they're just two Irish lads who were in the wrong place at the wrong time, who knows? It does happen, especially if you're Irish.'

Keep the bogtrotters in their place.

Charlie Tighe walked back to the cooker, scooped up the kettle and refilled it. He dropped the kettle onto the flame, took a cigarette from his packet and twisted it around in his fingers.

'Charlie...'

'Yes?'

'Let's just call it for what it is, Charlie. This thing we're talking about, it's the black market, plain and simple.'

The publican laughed. 'Call it what you like, Harry. Truth is, times are hard for a lot of people and if you've got the brass and want a little relief from how things are, there's always someone ready to do you a deal and no questions asked. You want something, anything, someone will get it for you – if the price is right.'

'That sounds like you're speaking from experience.'

The cigarette in Tighe's hand came apart, tobacco falling onto the floor. He looked at Marsh. 'Look, everyone's got to be a bit flexible these days, how else we meant to get by? Well, maybe not you, you're not everybody else. But the rest of us? Adapt and survive, it's what we humans do, Harry, we adapt *to* survive. We all change when we have to, when we need to. All of us. And it's not like anyone's getting hurt.'

'Tell that to those young Irish boys.'

Charlie Tighe frowned. 'Fair point.'

The publican picked up and emptied the teapot into the sink, refilling it with fresh leaves. Again, his measurements were lackadaisical, sloppy. He smiled at Marsh as he poured in the hot water. 'What can I say? I like my tea and nothing, not even old Adolf himself, should stand in the way of a decent brew, should it?'

Marsh pushed his mug across the table. 'I won't ask.'

'Best not.'

They sat and sipped, each man looking at the other, waiting for the first feint at the beginning of a duel. The first indication that some kind of response was required.

Harry Marsh finished his tea, put his mug down, stood. 'Any idea who the two coppers handing out the beating might have been? Least give me that.'

'What did they look like?'

'A young constable, barely shaving, I'd say. A bit of a rat face. Pinched, big front teeth. Not a man of original ideas. And an older sergeant with one of those mouths that look like it's permanently chewing on something distasteful. And he had a medicinal smell about him, this sergeant. Or maybe hair lotion. And sweat. I would say he sweats a lot, that one.'

Charlie Tighe grimaced, as if someone had broken wind in a confined space, then nodded.

Harry Marsh strolled across the yard and up the steps into Moseley Police Station. The desk sergeant was stood reading a newspaper. Marsh recognised him, remembered the older man from when he'd been on the beat and Marsh had been a boy.

'PC Henderson, or should I say, Sergeant Henderson?'

The policeman glanced at Marsh and nodded. 'It is. And you are?'

'Harry Marsh.'

'Harold Marsh? Course it is. Lord, it's been a while.'

'It has.'

'How're your mom and dad? I haven't seen them since they sold up and moved away. And that was just after me little sis got married.'

His sister.

Gayle Henderson.

A skinny, glamorous type a couple of years older than Marsh, he'd had a real thing about her and later, although not invited, he and Jeannie had stood at the back of the church during Gayle's wedding.

Trying out the old place for size, ain't we? Jeannie had said to an enquiring usher, pointing at the engagement ring on her finger.

'Moved to Alvechurch, if I remember right,' Alfred Henderson said.

'Alvechurch it is. They've got a little tea shop. Keeps them busy but they like it that way.'

'The Quaker Baker still making them amazing cream horns?'

The Quaker Baker – Harry Marsh hadn't heard his dad called that for years. 'He is. Well, he is when he can get the ingredients.'

Henderson sighed. 'Tell me about it. The missus is always going on to me about trying to find that little bit extra from somewhere, if you know what I mean.'

Marsh smiled. 'Hard times all round.'

'And it's going to get harder, I'll tell you. Much harder before it gets any better – if it ever does get better, that is. What we need is for the Yanks to step in. That'd sort this mess out a whole lot faster. But they were late in last time too, weren't they? Always late to the party, that lot. Mind you, you fought in the last one, didn't you? I remember you going off. Saw quite a bit of action back then, if I remember right.'

Back then? But it was only yesterday.

Harry Marsh shook his head. 'A bit. Only a bit.'

Henderson shrugged. 'Lucky that, I guess.'

Shells.

Fire-step.

Slaughter.

Gas.

Jeannie.

'Yes, lucky. I was one of the lucky ones.'

The older man folded up his newspaper. 'And now we've got this one. It's never ending. Bloody Germans. Bloody, sodding Germans. It's always the bloody, sodding Germans. Anyway, what can I do for you, Harold? What brings you in here today?'

The DS reached into his jacket, produced his warrant card and handed it over to Henderson. 'It's business, I'm afraid. I need to have a chat with a couple of your colleagues.'

'R Division? Steelhouse Lane, then. I knew you were on the job but that's posh, that is. What's it about then, this chat of yours?'

'No offence,' Marsh said, 'but I'd rather not say, not just yet.'

'No offence taken, I'm sure,' Henderson said. 'Who is it you're after?'

'Sergeant Greene and Constable Noble.'

'Ah,' Henderson said, laughing, 'them two.'

Ah, them two.

Marsh caught an inflection on those three simple words that expressed far more than was said. Than could be said without invoking some major disloyalty.

'Yes,' Harry Marsh said. 'They around?'

Henderson shook his head. 'Not here, I'm afraid. They were on last night and they're on again tonight, as I recall.'

The desk sergeant reached out and picked up a plywood clipboard. He flicked through the sheets. 'Yes, tonight. They're both on tonight. You best come back then.'

'If I can, I will. Any way to get in touch with them sooner?'

'Roger Greene lives out at the Maypole, I know that but he doesn't have a blower. Bob Noble's digs are somewhere in Kings Heath. Our clerk, she'd know, only she got bombed out last night so she's not in either. Understandable, given the circumstances.'

'Very understandable.'

'Is it urgent, this chat?'

'Not urgent exactly but I would like to speak to them as soon as is convenient.'

Henderson picked up and uncapped a pen, eager to show that he was being helpful. But then that's what Harry Marsh remembered about him: a big, amiable man who could either twist an ear or lend an ear, depending on circumstance. In other words, a decent beat copper. Marsh had liked him back then and didn't see any reason to change his opinion now. In fact, it occurred to Marsh, for possibly the first time, that it had been Henderson's pragmatic approach – his ability to balance the mandatory and the secondary, the essential against the inessential – that had influenced his own view of life. His own choice of career.

'I'll take a message,' Henderson said, 'if you want.'

'Thank you,' the DS said. 'but I'll come back later.'

'Will they know what it's about?'

'I'm sure they will,' Harry Marsh said, with a nod, turning on his heel.

4

The woman in the outer office looked up as Reg Miles walked in. She was refilling a fountain pen from an ink pot. The pot rested on an open blotting paper book, a light grey spray of dried ink across its pink pages.

With her centre parting, shoulder-length curls, eyebrows plucked into arches and severe lipstick, the young woman looked like something out of the movies. Reg had seen her around, both on the street and on the site but had no idea of her name.

She put her pen down and smiled with her mouth, not her eyes. 'Yes?'

'Mr Miles to see Mr Byfield.'

'I'll let him know you're here.' Her voice was over posh, a telephone voice which contrived to conceal her Brummie roots but only succeeded in highlighting affectation. She leant forward, picked up a handset from its cradle and pushed a cream button on the base station.

Reg heard a bell ring in the office behind her.

'Mr Miles is here, Mr Byfield,' she said.

And then a voice, clearer through the glass panel door than on the phone: 'Thank you, my dear, send him in, there's a gal.'

The young woman gestured at the door with her head. 'He says to go in.'

'I heard.'

Samuel Byfield sat, cup in left hand, pipe in mouth, examining an open ledger. He looked up and nodded at the chair in front of his desk. 'Have a seat, Miles.'

Reg sat down.

Putting his cup back in its saucer, Byfield emptied his Briar pipe into a silver Asprey ashtray and laid the pipe's black stem along one of the ashtray's four notches. Everything was done with care but nonchalance, as if nothing really mattered until Byfield decided it did.

As if time was not an issue.

Reg felt an element of unease shaded with ire and even injustice: whatever urgency drove the shop floor was entirely absent here although imposed from here – and having been instructed to enforce strict time and an even stricter routine for months, Reg was keen to get back to somewhere he knew, somewhere he understood, somewhere more substantial.

Somewhere he didn't resent being, simply by being present.

'I hear you're the man of the moment,' Byfield said, turning his attention from the exact placement of his pipe to Reg.

'I wouldn't say that.'

'I'm sure you wouldn't. But all the same, it doesn't make it any less true.'

'I did what anyone would have done.'

Byfield laughed. 'Really? You honestly believe that? You did what anyone would have done?'

'Yes.'

Byfield nodded. 'Then you have a better opinion of our fellow man than I.'

Reg said nothing.

Standing up, Byfield walked to his office window. 'How long have you been with us, Miles? With BSA?'

'Nineteen years, just over,' Reg said.

'That's a good length of service,' Byfield said.

'Suppose it is.'

'Yes, it is. And in all that time...' Byfield let his words drift off, suggesting he was searching for the right way to express himself, the correct form of engagement. 'In all that time, you've never been tempted, I don't know, to help yourself to something you shouldn't? To make the system, shall we say, work to your benefit?'

'I—'

Byfield raised a hand, fingers backlit and made translucent by an unexpected shaft of daylight, for the moment, skin no more than a fine pink glove around sinew and bone. 'I know the answer, Miles, I know exactly the sort of man you are.'

And Reg felt a thousand questions explode in his head, like fireworks at some municipal bonfire night do.

Or incendiary shells, on any night.

Do you? That's good because I don't. I have no idea what sort of man I am. A passable husband, maybe, a father who tries his best but beyond that? No, no idea. And I've lived with me for thirty-three years.

Byfield walked back to his desk and sat down, swivelled his chair to the front and leant forward. 'I served with men like you last time round. Not the most imaginative of sorts but solid. You'd have liked them, no doubt.'

Reg nodded, accepting the words without comment.

'Good men. Reliable men. Trustworthy,' Byfield said. 'Are you as trustworthy as you appear to be, Miles?'

Reg shook his head. 'How trustworthy do I *appear* to be?'

'Your manager trusts you and your men like you. It's all here,' Byfield said, thumbing a line of figures. 'But do you know what impresses me the most? What tells me that you are the man to trust? This, this little figure here, this is what tells me.'

Reg craned his neck. 'And what's that?'

'Shrinkage.'

'And what's *shrinkage*?'

Byfield smiled. 'In a way, it's the difference between what we can produce and what we can sell.'

'Isn't that a matter of quantity and quality?'

Byfield laughed. 'As I said, not imaginative. No, shrinkage is not a matter of quantity and quality, it's a matter of unacceptable loss. Of base criminality, mostly. It's about what gets stolen from the production lines on a weekly basis and ends up being sold for a fraction of its true value to whomsoever wishes to purchase it.'

'Theft. You're talking about theft.'

'Yes, Miles, I am talking about theft and what do you know about theft?' Byfield rifled in a desk drawer and pulled out a pipe cleaner. He removed the bowl from his pipe and threaded the cottoned wire from one end of the stem to the other, pulling it through with care, as a soldier would when cleaning a dirty barrel. Finally, he screwed the pipe back together, all without looking at Reg once – or saying a single word.

'Despite what you may think,' Byfield said, breaking the silence, 'I am a man of the world. I do understand that sometimes needs must and that in difficult circumstances most men's heads can be turned. Women's too, I dare say. But these aren't just *some* times, these are times of war.'

Byfield stopped and stared at Reg, expecting or at least hoping for comment on his poor attempt at Churchillian phrasemaking.

Reg stared back and said nothing.

Byfield opened a tin of tobacco and started to pack his pipe. 'I do realise that in better days you chaps had a sense that the small stuff didn't matter – the inefficiencies here, the light fingers there – but these are different times now. Difficult times.'

Reg felt his discomfort reformulating into anger. 'Am I being accused of something here? I asked to see you, not you me, Mr Byfield.'

Byfield laughed, sparked a match and inhaled. Exhaling a moment later, he peered at Reg through the smoke. 'Oh, my dear man, no, you're not being accused of anything, not at all. In fact, quite the opposite.'

'What then?'

Byfield blew on the glowing embers in the pipe's bowl. 'You asking to see me today is just perfect timing, Miles. Divine providence, even. You see, I need someone to be my eyes on the shop floor. To keep a tight check on everything that's happening below decks. I hear there's a growing market for all sorts of things out there, a black market or so they say – can you imagine? But everything we produce needs to go to the right people, the right places, that's the only way this war will be won. I have to be sure of that and I'm sure even a chap like you can understand this.'

Even a chap like you.

Reg breathed in, bit his lip, swallowed.

Byfield gestured at the ledger. 'You see, Miles, this tells me there's less shrinkage when you're in charge than at any other time, so in effect, you're already on the side of the angels, whether you know it or not.'

Reg took a breath. 'Thank you but I'm happy doing just what I do at present, Mr Byfield.'

'Yes, well,' Byfield said, lighting another match, applying it to his pipe, sucking until the tobacco caught. 'I'm not and neither are those above me – as they have made abundantly clear on more than one occasion. Tell me, how old are you, Miles?'

'Thirty-three.'

'Thirty-three, eh? At thirty-three, I was in France, fighting for King and Country. Have you ever considered that? Don't you think that's where you should be, out there, fighting for our great nation?'

'I do my bit,' Reg said. 'Working here and with the Auxiliaries, I do my bit.'

'But is your *bit* good enough? Ask yourself: is this the best I can do to repay my country for everything it's given me?'

Bridling, Reg swallowed again and breathed out through his mouth, slowly, smoothly, all the time counting towards ten in his head in an attempt to conceal his rising animosity for this man.

This pipsqueak.

This jumped-up martinet.

This...

Ten.

'Mr Byfield, I do my job well, I work hard – you know that, you've said that – and yes, I do think that staying here and doing what I do best is the best thing I can do for my country.'

Byfield nodded, opened a brown file at his elbow to reveal a sheaf of papers. Reg could just make out a coat of arms and the words *Schedule of Reserved Occupations* on the top sheet.

'As you say,' Byfield said, leafing through the pages. 'What's your current job title exactly, Miles?'

'Assistant Works Manager,' Reg said. 'I'm an Assistant Works Manager.'

'Ah, yes,' Byfield said, running his finger along a line. 'Thirty-three, you say?'

'Yes,' Reg said.

'Well,' Byfield said, closing the folder. 'Given your current position within this business and your age, it would appear you are clearly exempt from service. However, what with our current, somewhat dire situation, it may be that we all need to display a modicum of flexibility. Roles may change, people may be moved into new positions. Less exalted, less exempt positions, if you get my drift?'

Reg nodded. 'I get your drift.'

'So we have an understanding, do we, Miles? I do hope so.'

Reg grimaced. 'Yes, Mr Byfield, I understand you exactly.'

'Good man,' Byfield said. 'Good man. I look forward to hearing from you about all matters shrinkage. Now, what did you want to see me about?'

'Nothing,' Reg said, 'I thought it might be something but as it turns out, it's nothing.'

5

The DI's office door was partially open but Marsh knocked, all the same.

'Come,' a voice said.

The DS went in.

Detective Inspector Seaborne, formally of the Metropolitan Flying Squad, sat behind his desk. A young woman – smartly dressed in a tailored trouser suit, one leg folded up and over the other – sat in front of him.

'Have a pew, Marsh,' Seaborne said, pointing at a chair next to the young woman.

'Thank you, sir.'

'Marsh,' Seaborne said, 'this is Assistant Lady Enquiry Officer Annie Scott-Taylor. Miss Scott-Taylor, this is DS Harry Marsh.'

The woman smiled at him and offered her hand.

'Miss Scott-Taylor,' Marsh said.

Annie Scott-Taylor's grip was firm and certain. 'Actually,' she said, 'I would prefer just Assistant Lady Enquiry Officer Scott, if that's not an issue?'

'Not at all,' Marsh said, sitting down. 'Pleased to meet you, Assistant Lady Enquiry Officer Scott.'

'And I you, Detective Sergeant Marsh.' Her voice was clear, precise and effortless. Much like her handshake, it projected nothing if not confidence and competence.

'Right,' Seaborne said, 'So, this girl, what can you tell me, Marsh?'

Me not *us*, *me*.

'Nothing much. Dr Penny's working away as we speak. She's already pretty certain about cause of death based on injuries observed but she's still got the tissue examination to do and she's waiting for a full toxicology report. Once she has it all together, Moira – Dr Penny – will submit her findings. Also, so far, there are no obvious dabs or apparent cross-transference at the scene. It's about as clean as clean can be these days.'

'What about the geezer that called us in?' Seaborne said.

'Stanley Smith. ARP man. I went to see him. Nothing to add.'

Seaborne scratched at the corner of his mouth. 'Could he have had anything to do with it?'

Ordinary. Not that anyone was ever ordinary.

'Unlikely,' Harry Marsh said, 'he doesn't seem the sort.'

Seaborne frowned. 'And what is the sort?'

'Not Smith, I'd stake my pension on that. Besides, I've had a look at the records – he's as clean as a whistle, never put a foot where a foot should not be put.'

'OK,' Seaborne said. 'And how did this clean whistle find her?'

'Some kids were playing in the street. The play spilled over into the garden of an abandoned house. There was a door lying on the ground and one of them turned the door over. After that they went and knocked up Smith and he called us.'

'And these kids?'

'Smith gave me three names: Thomas Perks, Patrick Slater and Vincent Lee. I've asked a couple of the local bobbies to go and see them. Find out if they've got anything more they can tell us.'

'Have we got anything on them, these kids?'

'They're just kids.'

'No harm in checking them out too,' Seaborne said.

Marsh nodded. 'DC Stokes is already on it – when his crew can spare him and when he's got the time.'

When any of us have got the time for anything other than simply surviving.

Seaborne smiled, or rather twisted the ends of his lips upwards in a smug tick of pleasure – he'd been listened to. Tenting his fingers, he sat back into his swivel chair, a professor ready to criticise a talented but unfavoured student, simply for the pleasure of criticising. 'And in the meantime, any initial thoughts? I'll take anything.'

The DS nodded, wondered how much to say. He was aware that both Seaborne and Annie Scott were staring at him in anticipation. Seaborne seemed entitled, the policewoman engaged.

'Cause of death would appear to be suffocation, there were tiny blood clots in her eyes—'

'Petechial haemorrhaging?' Annie Scott said.

'Yes,' Harry Marsh said, turning to look at her, 'petechial haemorrhaging. Also, there were some unidentified fibres in her nose, her lungs, her mouth and on her lips – they're being analysed today – so it's looking as if she was suffocated. Possibly using the cushion found with her. We can definitely say that she wasn't interfered with. There's no sign of a sexual motive and...' he glanced across at Annie Scott, '...her hymen is intact.'

Seaborne raised an eyebrow. 'Good, it means we haven't got some nonce on our hands.'

'No, sir,' the young woman said, her tone dry and ironic, 'just a child killer.'

Seaborne hesitated and glanced at Annie Scott. Marsh thought he detected a half-smile on her face.

The DI nodded. 'Quite right. A child killer. Terrible. So, anything else, Marsh?'

'There's a slight abrasion around her neck,' Harry Marsh said. 'Nothing significant, more a scuff, really. It's possible she was wearing a necklace and it got ripped off at some point.'

Seaborne sat back, put his hands behind his head. 'During the attack?'

The DS frowned. 'No, the graze was definitely inflicted post-mortem and we're not sure she was attacked. There are no cuts, no bruising, no defensive wounds. Just the petechial haemorrhaging in the eyes and the fibres.'

Annie Scott turned to look at Harry Marsh. 'Could whatever was taken from her have been taken as a memento, possibly? I hear that does happen.'

'You're right, that does happen and that is possible but we can't say. Not yet, at least.'

The policewoman leant forward. 'Could it have been an identity tag of some sort?'

'Again, that's possible,' Harry Marsh said, nodding, 'but again we just can't know.'

'And if it was an identity tag,' she said, 'it was almost certainly removed deliberately so as to stop us identifying her.'

Marsh nodded for a second time – the woman was sharp, keen, quick on the uptake. 'If it was an identity tag,' he said, 'and it was removed deliberately then yes, I can't disagree with that.'

Seaborne picked up a cigarette lighter and clicked it several times, indicating his exclusion demanded some form of intervention, no matter how trivial. 'And what else? What aren't you saying? Come on, Marsh, no point in holding back, old son.'

'Moira – that's Dr Penny...' he said, turning to Annie Scott.

The policewoman smiled. 'Thank you but I had figured that out.'

'Right,' Marsh said, 'of course. Anyway, Moira doesn't think the girl's British. Or may not be British.'

Seaborne closed his lighter, put it down. 'No? Why not?'

'Her complexion,' the DS said. 'Her underlying complexion beneath the pallor, it has an olive tone. And she has very dark curly hair and brown eyes. Moira believes she could be from somewhere around the Mediterranean.'

'I see,' Seaborne said. 'An immigrant then.'

'Or refugee,' Annie Scott said.

'Both are possible,' Marsh said, 'but both are just guesswork. The dress, however, isn't guesswork.'

The young woman turned her head towards Marsh. 'The dress?'

'Her clothes are old, clean and well maintained. Repaired but well repaired. And the dress, it has a *Made in Germany* tag.'

'So, she's German,' Seaborne said, 'not Mediterranean.'

Annie Scott shook her head. 'Not necessarily.'

The DI looked confused. 'No?'

'No,' the policewoman said.

Seaborne looked at Annie Scott, his expression patronising, shading on derisive. 'You maintain an interest in fashion, no doubt. But then I can see that from how you're dressed.'

'I maintain an interest in politics and economics, actually,' she said. 'Blame it on my Oxford education, not my dress sense, if you will, sir.' She turned to look at Marsh. 'I'm guessing the tag was in English?'

'The tag was in English,' he said.

'It's a long story,' Annie Scott said, looking from one man to the other and then back again, 'but the *Made in Germany* clothes label was thought up by us – the British – years ago. It was a piece of protectionism designed to stop shoppers buying German goods rather than British goods. It was used all over Europe and it was pretty successful during the last war. But then it acquired a certain cachet. You know how it works, I'm sure: the one thing you're not allowed is the only thing you want.'

Harry Marsh nodded. 'The imp of the perverse. The desire to do things merely because we shouldn't.'

Seaborne looked confused. 'The what?'

Annie Scott turned to face the DI. '*The Imp of the Perverse*. It's a story by Edgar Allan Poe, sir. You should read him. He wrote some rather good crime stories too.'

'Thank you for the recommendation,' Seaborne said, smiling but not smiling. 'Now, you two seem to bang along well enough, which I thought you would. And that's why you're both here. Marsh, I want you and Assistant Lady Enquiry Officer Scott-Taylor to work this little girly case together.'

Harry Marsh looked over at Annie Scott. 'No offence, sir, but why?'

'No offence taken, I'm sure,' the young woman said, smiling.

'Firstly, your crew's just you at the moment,' Seaborne said, 'which isn't really a crew at all. Secondly, the victim's a young girl and there must be family—'

'None that's come forward,' Marsh said.

'No, none that's come forward,' Seaborne said, 'but there must be a family – a mother, a sister. You say her clothes are old but well-tended. Maybe an aunt, a cousin. If someone looks after her clothes, someone must know her but either this someone doesn't know she's missing yet – which given the current state of the world, would not be that surprising – or knows it all too well, if you see what I mean? Right? So, anyway, you find me that someone and when you do, our Lady Enquiry Officer here will be well placed to talk to them. It's the sort of thing women do best.'

Annie Scott laughed. 'Do best at what, talking?'

Seaborne blushed – not something that Marsh had ever seen before but something he'd now remember and treasure for all time.

'And while we're on the subject of clothing, this thing with the trousers,' Seaborne said, attempting to reclaim some sense of order. 'I think you'll find a skirt would be far more acceptable.'

'As soon as the other plain clothes officers start wearing a skirt, then so shall I, sir,' Annie Scott said, standing.

Harry Marsh did nothing to conceal his smile.

Later, station tour over, necessary introductions made, Marsh pushed a chair in front of his desk. 'It's not much,' he said, 'but I like to call it home. Take a seat.'

'Thank you.'

They sat.

Annie Scott stared over Harry Marsh's shoulder. 'Nice view.'

'Back of the Court House,' Marsh said, without turning to check the window. 'There are tunnels between here and there. Means we can transfer prisoners from the police cells to the court cells without the poor sods seeing as much as a glimpse of daylight.'

'Very efficient, I suppose.'

'I suppose,' the DS said. 'So, Assistant Lady Enquiry Officer Scott-Taylor, sorry, Assistant Lady Enquiry Officer Scott – that is how you want to be known, isn't it? Simply as Scott?'

'It is. And I think simply Policewoman Scott – Assistant Lady Enquiry Officer is awfully awkward.'

Marsh nodded. 'Policewoman Scott it is.'

'And how should I address you? DS Marsh? Sarge? Guv'nor? Or maybe it should be boss? I've been told that's the preferred form in the North.'

Marsh resisted correcting her geography. 'Guv's not appropriate and I'd really rather you didn't call me boss,' he said, 'Sarge, if you like, or even Harry, seeing as we're going to *bang along well enough*, apparently.'

And Annie Scott smiled, a glorious sunrise of a smile that lit up her face and transformed her features from merely refined into beautiful. As she did, it occurred to the policeman that before long there would be a queue of single coppers running from the door, through the building, down the outside steps and probably halfway up Steelhouse Lane – some married ones too, no doubt. She was a looker, no question about that and her rarity value – a woman working in CID amongst so many male colleagues – would give her a certain appeal.

Aware that he was staring, Marsh pulled himself back into the here and now. 'You can call me whatever you're most comfortable with, to be honest, but never *boss*,' he said. 'Anyway, tell me about yourself.'

'What would you like to know?'

'How you came to be here today?'

'I took a tram from my rooms in Rotten Park Road.'

Marsh laughed. 'Rooms in Edgbaston? Very posh.'

'Not especially, I'm afraid. Anything else you'd like to know?'

'How about your Oxford education?'

'Oh, sorry about that,' she said, 'the inspector annoyed me a bit. It's not very interesting, really.'

'He annoys me a lot,' Marsh said. 'How not very interesting?'

'You're very persistent.'

'Apparently it makes me good at my job. Or so I've been told.'

She smiled. 'It would.'

'And you're avoiding my question.'

Annie Scott smiled again. 'I'm not, not really. Born in London, educated in Brighton, a stint at finishing school in Kassel, then St Hilda's Oxford. Finally, a rather desperate secretarial course before I signed up and trained at Peel House.'

'Brighton? Roedean?'

'Yes, Roedean. You're very knowledgeable too.'

'Again, makes me good at my job.'

'To take an interest in girls' public schools?'

'To take an interest in everything.'

'I can see,' the policewoman said, flicking an eyebrow, 'that I'll have to be very careful what I say when I'm around you.'

Marsh smiled. 'And Kassel? In Germany?'

Annie Scott nodded. 'Yes, Germany.'

'You speak German?'

'I do. And French. And Italian.'

Clever then as well as confident and competent. Harry Marsh nodded to himself, glad that his initial assessment had been correct, pleased that his instincts were still good. Reaching into a pocket, he pulled out his notebook. He flicked through and finding the right page, held the book out in front of him.

Annie Scott frowned, peered, squinted. Opening her handbag, she took out a pair of glasses and put them on with an almost bashful caution, as if she was revealing a great secret – or weakness. The lenses were round, the frames tortoiseshell, the glasses complemented her face perfectly. She leant closer and took another look.

'*Panic*?'

'And *turtle*.'

'Meaning?'

'That's the point,' Marsh said. 'I don't know. Could they be German words?'

Annie Scott shook her head. 'It's possible. I don't think so. They're not words I know, certainly, but I suppose they may be some form of German vernacular. Why?'

'They were written on the palm of the little girl's hand.'

'And you didn't mention this to the inspector?'

'No point. I don't know what they mean. To be honest, they were so faint, we're not sure they even say *panic* or *turtle*, so at this point it's nothing that Seaborne needs to know about. He likes hard facts and hard collars and not very much in between.'

'Yes,' Annie Scott said, 'I did get that impression.'

Harry Marsh closed his PNB. He watched the constable remove her glasses, fold them up and slide them back into her bag.

'What did you read at St Hilda's?'

'Jurisprudence,' Annie Scott said. 'I was meant to go into the family business – my grandfather's a judge, my father's a King's Counsel, my brother's about to take silk too – but it wasn't for me. I've always liked puzzles. Solving puzzles. Working out which bits of a jigsaw go where, that sort of thing.'

Harry Marsh stared at her for a moment without saying a word and then: 'Your grandfather? Not Sir Anthony Scott-Taylor?'

Annie Scott nodded, bit her lip, maybe a little embarrassed that she'd given away too much, too soon – that Harry Marsh would now see her presence as a gift of privilege, rather than the outcome of hard work and application. 'Or Gramps, as I like to call him,' she said, hoping a dash of frivolity would shake Marsh from any such considerations.

And it worked.

The DS laughed.

Sir Anthony Scott-Taylor KC and High Court Judge – a hanger and flogger of the old school – was now and forever *Gramps*. Marsh hoped he never had reason to appear before the old man himself.

'And you?'

Marsh looked puzzled. 'Me?'

'What's your story?'

'No story.'

'There must a bit of one,' Annie Scott said. 'Everyone's got a story.'

'School. Army. Demob. Police. That's it,' Harry Marsh said, with a shrug. 'As I say, not much of a story.'

'Married, though,' the young woman said, pointing to the ring on Marsh's left hand.

'Yes, married, though,' Harry Marsh said, now conscious of the gold band on his finger. He twisted at it, turned it a full rotation.

'That's a nice ring and so unusual for a man to wear one.'

'Jeannie insisted.'

'Jeannie? Your wife?'

'Jeannie, my wife. She said that if she had to wear a symbol of her repression then I had to wear one too.'

'I like the sound of her.'

'She's a decent sort,' Marsh said.

Across the office, a man put down a phone, stood and walked towards them. Seeing that Marsh was with someone, he hesitated.

'Something up?' Marsh said, gesturing that the man should come closer.

DC Stokes nodded and stepped forward. 'Sorry to interrupt, Sarge, but something's come up, something you should know about.' He nodded towards Annie Scott. 'Maybe better in private?'

'It's alright, Stokes, this is Annie Scott. Policewoman Scott, she'll be joining my crew.'

'Has joined your crew, Sarge,' Annie Scott said.

'Has joined my crew,' Marsh said. 'Come on then, fire away, anything you need to tell me, you can tell her.'

'Right,' Stokes said, looking the young woman up and down, wondering why someone who wouldn't seem out of place in one of those magazines his wife read could possibly want to be a police officer. 'We've had a report about a little girl.'

'My girl?'

'No, Sarge, another little girl. This one's just five. Thing is, she only lives a few streets away from where we found the other one and some young lad's just tried to kidnap her. Abduct her in broad daylight, apparently. Anyway, she's fine. The lad, he got away but as it turns out, he was one of the ones you were asking after. And he's got form for this sort of thing.'

FRIDAY 22 NOVEMBER 1940

1

Harry Marsh and Annie Scott walked down the street, the weather as downcast as the terraced frontages on either side of them. The houses were stunted and prematurely aged like coal miners, their creases and imperfections exaggerated by ingrained black dust. Some were missing roof tiles, others had broken windowpanes covered over with old newspaper and sticky tape.

All had a sense of decay.

A door opened and a woman brushed dirt from the inside to the out. A couple of houses up, another woman, on hand and knee, blacked her front step. Her right arm moving with rhythm and grace in a well-practiced action, a familiar routine.

On the air, there was a smell of cabbage and drains and it was impossible to tell where the edible became the ineffable.

Two very young lads and an even younger girl sat on the kerb and watched the police officers pass.

Annie Scott stopped and looked around. 'Is this the right street?'

'It is,' Harry Marsh said.

'How cosy. What number are we looking for?'

Marsh fumbled out his police notebook, leafed through to the most recent entry, stared at his scrawl. 'Vincent Lee. Number 19.'

'It's over here,' the policewoman said, pointing. She walked up to the door and knocked. After a few moments, she knocked again.

'Alright, alright,' a voice said from inside, a clipped voice both feathery and used to getting its own way. 'Give me a moment.'

There was the sound of a latch and then the door wheezed open an inch. An old woman peered through the gap. 'Who are you then?'

'Police, Mrs Lee,' Annie Scott said. 'May we come in?'

'Police? I didn't call you. What do you want with me?'

Marsh stepped forward, warrant card in hand. 'Mrs Lee?'

'It's Miss Lee and like I said, what do you want?'

'It's about Vincent. Vincent Lee. We understand he lives with you.'

'Vincent? What do you want with him?'

'May we come in?'

Millicent Lee sighed and then opened the door fully. 'Come on in then but make sure you close the trap after you.'

The old woman turned away and the officers followed her into the house. The front room was dark and chilly. It felt as if there hadn't been a fire in the hearth since the last war. Even in the gloom, Marsh could see his breath twist and curl in the air. Peering around, he glimpsed a room out of time.

A late Victorian sitting room, its ambition curtailed by physical constraint. Dark wood, cotton lace tablecloths, embroidered cushions, empty plant pots and a large mantelshelf clock under a glass dome, resting on the floor, unwound and silent. It was almost as if the room's contents were in storage, waiting to be reclaimed.

Waiting for life to restart.

Millicent Lee stopped by the door to the kitchen. 'No point in warming a room I don't use,' she said.

The old woman sat down on a kitchen chair and leant her forearms on the cloth-covered table. The cloth was bright, intricate, expensive. 'I suppose you'll expect a cup of tea. Put the kettle on, dear,' she said, waving a clawed hand.

Dear.

Annie Scott knew exactly which of them was being addressed and it wasn't Harry Marsh.

The DS looked at the policewoman, a half-smile on his face, and she looked back at him with an expression of mock anger on hers. Marsh nodded and Annie Scott swept the kettle off the hob, filling it as noisily as she could from the kitchen tap.

'Careful there,' Millicent Lee said. 'It's my only kettle and it's a nice one.'

'Sorry,' Annie said, pulling a face behind the old woman's back.

Marsh put a hand across his lips to conceal his amusement.

'There's a teapot in the cupboard next to you and the china's on the shelf behind that curtain,' the old woman said, pointing at an Arts and Crafts drape, similar in design to the tablecloth. 'I'm sure you can see the tea caddy. The milk's already over here, so's the sugar – you don't need to be fetching them across.'

'Yes, ma'am,' the policewoman said, bending to pick up the teapot and executing a half curtsy at the same time.

Marsh left his hand over his mouth.

Millicent Lee reached forward, tapped a hand on the table in front of the policeman and stared into his eyes. 'Vincent, you say? What's the lad been up to that you need to see him?'

'Is he here, Miss Lee? Is Vincent at home?'

The old woman shook her head. 'No, he's not here, not right now.'

Annie Scott walked over and placed the teapot in the middle of the kitchen table. 'This is rather posh,' she said.

'Yes,' Millicent Lee said, eyeing the young woman, 'it is. It's self-pouring you know? Victorian.'

Marsh looked at the pot. White with a blue peony pattern and a silver lid with a ridged metal plunger, he wondered quite why some Victorian had decided that lifting a teapot was too much of a chore and why he – almost certainly a *he* – had gone to the effort of inventing something so elaborate to do something so simple.

Because he *was* Victorian and that's what they did, Marsh decided. There was nothing they couldn't complicate. It was as if unnecessary complexity added to their ultimate sense of achievement.

And of self.

Self.

He'd seen too many men sent to their death by so-called charismatic officers with a deep belief in *self* – of personal mission – to know that such conviction had not a single redeeming quality.

The old woman peered up at the young woman. 'You have warmed the pot, I hope?'

'I have, Miss Lee.'

'Good girl.' Millicent Lee waved at the chair next to her, inviting Annie Scott to sit. The wave was a small, almost imperceptible tic, so practised and performed that the hand should have worn a lace glove.

There was something about this woman that bothered Marsh, something that, like the contents of her front room, didn't belong in these surroundings.

An air of genuine difference.

Harry Marsh watched his colleague place three cups on three saucers. The crockery was white bone china with gold scalloped edges and a simple flower design. The cups had ear-shaped handles. It was an elegant rather than ostentatious tea service.

Annie turned to face Millicent Lee. 'Will you pour, or shall I?'

The old woman held up her hands – her fingers were swollen, deformed and folded at the knuckles, so much so that her fingertips almost touched her palms. 'You best, these paws ain't up to much no more. You're lucky I could get the latch.'

And at that moment, Marsh could almost see justification for a self-pouring teapot.

Annie Scott pushed the pot's plunger and pumped a measure of liquid into each cup.

Millicent Lee glanced at the young woman and then looked back at Marsh. 'Before you go asking again, I don't know where Vincent is.'

Marsh reached forward and poured milk into all three cups. 'But he does live here?'

'Sometimes,' she said.

'But not now?'

'Not now,' the old woman said. 'And even if he was here right now, he's a good boy, is Vincent. I can't see what good talking to you lot is ever going to do him.'

'We just need a little chat,' Annie Scott said.

Millicent Lee laughed. 'And what do you reckon he's done that needs *a little chat*? 'Cos *little chats* don't come about for no reason, I know your lot, I know you of old and I don't know any good that's ever come from anyone ever having *a little chat* with you, I don't.'

Harry Marsh finished his tea, pushed his cup and saucer across the table. 'It's very forward of me but Policewoman Scott, is there any more tea in the pot?'

Annie Scott frowned, bemused by Marsh's slightly pompous tone. 'I'm sure there is,' she said.

'If you'd be so kind. Miss Lee, more tea?'

'I'm fine,' the old woman said, 'but you go ahead, you help yourself.'

Annie depressed the handle. Tea swooshed and swirled into the white cup.

The three of them sat in silence as the DS drank. When he finished, he put his cup down and stood. He walked over to the Arts and Crafts curtain and pointed at it. 'William Morris,' he said.

Millicent Lee nodded. 'Yes,' she said.

'Do you like it?'

'I do, very much.'

'He was part of The Birmingham Set, you know?'

Millicent Lee looked confused. 'I thought he was from Essex.'

Marsh smiled. 'Well, yes, he was but The Birmingham Set was a group of Oxford students, mostly from Birmingham. Literary types who discovered John Ruskin and then started visiting old English country churches and medieval cities in France and Belgium. Wherever they travelled, they became great churchgoers.

That's where the whole Arts and Crafts movement started – in church.' He ran his fingers along the hem of the curtain. 'It is very nice.'

Annie Scott watched Harry Marsh with increasing interest. Even as he spoke, it seemed his mind was somewhere else and deep inside he was considering other possibilities, other options, other combinations

'I inherited it,' Millicent Lee said, her tone part apologetic, part peevish. 'I was left it. These too.' She lifted a cup in the air. 'This tablecloth as well. And everything in the front room.'

'Someone was very generous,' the young woman said.

'She was a nice old lady and I was her companion for twenty years.' Millicent Lee said, smiling at the policewoman for the first time. 'Old? She was younger than me when she passed.' She laughed. 'Don't suppose anyone will ever describe me as a *nice old lady*.'

Marsh walked back to the table and sat down. 'Oh, I don't know. You seem perfectly nice to me.'

Millicent Lee reached out and tapped the back of his right hand. 'And you're very kind and a bit forward but you don't know me. I can be a right terror. But only to those who do know and love me, mind. Well, know me. Not sure anyone loves me.' She smiled, her face a web of cracks in an old wax seal.

Marsh laughed. 'I'm sure that's not true.'

Millicent Lee smiled again. 'You'll have to ask my family but I know some call me *The Old Crow*. They don't know I know but I do.' She cackled. 'The Old Crow, I ask you.'

There was a pause.

Harry Marsh leant forward. 'I'm sorry to ask again but about Vincent...'

There was a sigh, followed by an odour of lavender and denture cream. 'He sees my niece from time to time. She and her husband, they're good to him. George, especially, believe it or not.'

'Your niece?'

'Edith Furrell, she lives over the street, behind the cobbler's shop. She might know something.'

'Thank you, Miss Lee,' Marsh said.

'But if you do find him, go gentle,' the old woman said. 'He's a confused boy but he's not a bad boy.'

'Confused?'

Millicent Lee shook her head. 'People say he's simple but he's not simple, he's just, well, he's just a bit different, that's all.'

'Different? How?'

'He's not always sure about things.'

'What things?'

She shrugged. 'Everything, really. Anyway, what's he got to do with anything you might be interested in?'

'There was a young girl last year,' Marsh said. 'She said that your nephew—'

'Great-nephew.'

'That your great-nephew, well, that he gave her sweets and then asked her to take off her dress.'

'No,' Millicent Lee said, bristling, 'it wasn't like that, I promise you, whatever that girl said.'

Annie Scott looked at the old lady. 'If not that, what?'

'She misunderstood him, that's all. He was just trying to be nice, I'm sure.'

The policewoman nodded and looked at Marsh. 'You're sure?'

'Yes, young lady, I'm sure. Anyway, I thought this was all dead and buried. The police at the time seemed to think it was. Didn't think there was anything to it, not after the girl's mom and dad admitted she had what they called a *lively imagination*.'

'There was another report around the same time,' the DS said, 'that involved a bedroom window and your great-nephew.'

Millicent Lee shook her head dismissively. 'That was nothing either, he was just in the wrong place at the wrong time. Anyway, what are curtains for? Somebody wants privacy, it's easy enough, just pull them shut. Or get some nets or something.'

'Well, yes,' Marsh said, 'but yesterday—'

'What about yesterday?'

Annie Scott looked down at her notebook. 'Do you know the Warners?'

'Joe and Mary Warner?'

Marsh glanced over at Annie Scott. She averted her gaze, looked down at her shoes, a pink hue on her cheeks. 'Yes,' he said. 'Joseph and Mary Warner. Vincent was seen with their youngest girl yesterday.'

'Was he indeed?'

'He was.'

'And?'

'Miss Lee,' the policewoman said, 'Vincent offered the girl sweets, if she went for a walk with him.'

'Sweets? What sort of sweets?'

'We don't know,' Marsh said, 'and to be honest, that's beside the point.'

'And did she go with him?'

The young officer shook her head. 'No, a girl's neighbour – a Miss Lucy Potter – saw what was happening and chased Vincent off.'

'Chased him off?'

'Yes.'

'Chased him off? You make him sound like some sort of animal. And I bet she did it at the top of her voice too. I know that Lucy Potter, I know what she's like: all show and tell she is. I wouldn't send her up an alley to catch a pig, so don't be accusing Vincent of anything based on something that flibbertigibbet said.'

'We're not accusing Vincent of anything, that's not our intention,' Marsh said, 'but the Warners spoke to one of our constables and we do need to speak to the boy.'

'Why? No harm was done, was it?'

'Not this time,' Annie said.

Millicent Lee blanched and then reddened, the tips of her cheekbones spotted with crimson. 'Not this time?'

Annie glanced at Harry Marsh. He raised a hand in a gesture of caution. 'No,' the DS said, his voice low and calm, 'not this time. But we do need to speak with him. Just in case.'

'In case what?'

'Miss Lee,' Marsh said, 'sometimes it's the people we think we know best who surprise us the most.'

The old woman tutted and glanced from one police officer to the other, her look one of assessment, dissection, calculation. 'This is about that other girl, isn't it? The dead one,' she said, 'the one they found round the corner. The one under the door. It's about her, isn't it?'

'Not necessarily,' Marsh said.

And Millicent Lee snarled. 'In other words, yes.' She braced her clawed hands on the tabletop and pushed herself upright. 'I think you'd better go now. I can't help you.'

'Miss Lee—' Annie Scott said.

The old woman shook her head. 'Vincent's not here, I don't know where he is but I'll tell you this: he's what some might call a bit odd maybe but he's not a bad boy. Now, like I say, I think you pair best be off.'

Millicent Lee followed the police officers into the front room. She watched Marsh open the door and Annie Scott step out onto the pavement. The DS turned and looked at her. 'Miss Lee—'

'Leave us alone, you've said enough already. Just go.'

'I'm sorry if we've upset you, Miss Lee,' Marsh said, 'that wasn't our intention but we have a job to do.'

'I'm sure you do,' the old woman said, 'just next time, do it better.'

Millicent Lee closed the front door. There was the sound of a lock clacking into place with finality, like a full stop at the end of a novel.

'Sorry,' Annie Scott said, 'my fault.'

'How's that?'

'*Not this time* and mentioning the girl's parents by name?'

'And naming a witness. You're right, it wasn't good,' Marsh said, 'but never mind, we've all said stuff without thinking. Best to get it over and done with now. I'm sure it won't happen again.'

'It won't.'

'Good.'

The policewoman raised an eyebrow. '*Up an alley to catch a pig*?'

'Bow-legged.' Marsh half-smiled. 'And in this case, I suspect, promiscuous.'

'How very unpleasant,' Annie said, with a shake of her head.

Looking over at the cobbler's, the front door was closed and the blinds were drawn. The business had obviously been shut for quite some time and there was no indication when, if ever, it would open again. A passageway, topped with a brick gothic arch, ran down the side of the shop.

Harry Marsh stepped onto the cobbles and walked across, Annie Scott followed. 'You know a lot about The Birmingham Set,' she said, as they reached the opposite pavement.

'I think they preferred the name Brotherhood,' Marsh said.

'Still, you obviously have an interest.'

'A few of them went to my old school, actually.'

The young woman stopped walking. 'King Edward's, you went to King Edward VI? The Birmingham Grammar School?'

The policeman nodded. 'I did.'

The policewoman smiled. 'It's where my grandfather, where Gramps went.'

'It is.'

'You knew and you didn't say?'

'No reason.'

They stepped onto the pavement.

'You must be clever then,' Annie Scott said. 'I hear it has quite a rigorous entrance examination.'

Marsh shook his head. 'Not clever really, more lucky, I'd say. The right exam questions came up on the right day.'

Annie Scott laughed. 'And modest. You go where I went if your parents have the money, you go where you went if you have the brains.'

'Both of us were lucky then.'

Marsh stopped under the arch and looked up at the brickwork before turning to face his companion. 'All that talk of churches,' he said, 'it gave me an idea.'

And there it was: the something, *the other possibilities* the young woman had sensed earlier.

'Assuming the dead girl is an immigrant,' Marsh said, 'how many expatriate communities are there in Birmingham? Specifically, how many southern European communities are here?'

'I wouldn't know.'

Marsh waved a hand. 'No, why should you? As far as I'm aware we have some Serbians and some Croats. Quite a number of Italians. A Turk or two. And at least a handful of Greeks. And then of course, there are the French. In other words, quite a lot of people but not so many as to be unmanageable.'

'Where are you going with this?'

'It's where they go, that's my point.'

'It is?'

'Church. Assuming they go to church, where would they go?'

Annie Scott smiled. 'I see. Yes, where do they go to worship? We should definitely find out.'

'We should. Someone, somewhere might recognise our girl.'

They walked down the side passage and up to the back of the shop. Marsh reached out and knocked on the door.

Edith Furrell was to the point. 'Vincent? No, no idea. I've got problems of my own, thank you, and thankfully he's not one of them. I do see him from time to time, when he's in trouble with Aunt Millie, or thinks he is, more likely, her bark's far worse than her bite – he comes over here then, begging refuge, he does. But I don't know where he is right now. You should speak to Aunt Millie, she lives opposite, she might know.'

Harry Marsh looked at the woman in front of them: tired, aged before her time, troubled by God knows what but still sparky, still resilient – like a striking strip on an old box of matches.

Annie Scott nodded once. 'We already have, Mrs Furrell, and she told us to speak with you.'

Edith Furrell shook her head. 'Right, thanks Aunt Millie, thank you very much indeed.'

'Mrs Furrell,' Marsh said, 'do you have any idea where we might find Vincent, right now?'

'Not really,' the woman said.

'Parents,' the policewoman said. 'What about his parents?'

'His mom passed two years gone. His dad – my eldest brother Wally – he's a bargee. It was a bit after Marge died that Wally sent Vincent to some school just off the Fazeley canal. Said it would be good for him. A local family put the lad up for a time but he didn't stick at that for long. And then Aunt Millie took him in.'

'Your brother,' Marsh said, 'would it possible to speak to him?'

'Good luck with that. Wally's somewhere between here and London right now but when he's back, you'll find him down Gas

Street, that's where he moors the *Crown Victoria* – that's his ship. Can't say when he's going to be back though.

The DS opened his PNB, took out a pencil, wrote down the name. 'Any other family?'

'No,' Edith Furrell said, 'not round here.'

'And no idea where we might find the boy today?'

'He did some work for Worsey's,' Edith said. 'But they let him go a while back.'

'Worsey's? The coal merchant on Shenstone Lane?'

'That's the one.'

'Mooooom!' A boy's voice shrill and piercing from somewhere inside the house.

Edith turned as a young lad, pale-skinned, sandy-haired, freckled, pushed past her and ran across the yard. 'Freddie, what you up to?'

The boy grinned over his shoulder and ran on.

'Mooooom!'

Edith glanced over her shoulder. 'What is it, Colin? What's happened now?'

'Mooooommy!'

'I have to go,' Edith said. 'Colin, what is it Col, what's Freddie done to you now?'

The police officers turned and walked away.

A butcher's boy pushing a bike had entered the yard and was talking to Freddie in no uncertain terms, a hand wrapped in the boy's collar. The younger boy appeared scared but resolute.

'What do you think?' Annie Scott said. 'Do you believe them?'

'Millicent Lee and Edith Furrell? Yes, I do believe them. I think they're telling us the truth,' Marsh said, 'but I don't think they're telling us the whole truth – and won't be, any time soon.'

The man who ran the yard at Worsey's had no idea about Vincent Lee's whereabouts and even less interest.

Yes, the boy had worked there for a while but that was months back. And he hadn't been on the books for long. Turns out, he was unreliable, a bit odd even. He made people uncomfortable, even the horses weren't easy round him and you can always trust a horse to sniff out a dodgy sort. The lad had only done a few rounds – no more than that – and then they'd let him go. Had to let him go. Complaints, see? Some woman said she found him inside her house, halfway up the stairs. No, haven't seen him since. Might have gone back to his dad's barge – the *Crown Victoria*, think it's called – his old man does the Grand Union to London run, with his whole family, like. God help him if it wasn't difficult enough before the war but now, what with the bombings, why would any sane bloke do that to his family?

Harry Marsh thanked the man and the two police officers left.

'Where next?' Annie Scott said, her tone light and excited, more a young girl on a Sunday treasure hunt with friends than a police officer on the trail of a suspect.

'Back to the factory is probably best,' Marsh said. 'We'll speak to uniform, remind them to keep an eye open for Vincent. And for the *Crown Victoria*, see if that brings any results.'

'Good idea.'

'Tram or walk?'

'Oh, walk every time,' the policewoman said. 'Don't know the city very well yet, give me a chance to get my bearings.'

They walked down Summer Lane, turned left onto Constitution Hill and strolled past St Chad's cathedral. Annie Scott stopped and stared at the red brick building. At the sheeting over the roof, the shuttered main entrance: both the result of an incendiary bomb, which had crashed through into the south aisle. The device had smashed open a number of central heating pipes and the ensuing flood had extinguished the flames, minimising any internal damage. For some, this was the Hand of God in action, for others it was simple good fortune.

'Designed by Pugin, wasn't it?' she said.

'I believe so.'

'It's very like Munich cathedral, you know?'

'Really?'

'Yes. Very. The style is called *hallenkirke*, or brick hall church. What's it like inside?'

'Not as nice as it used to be,' Marsh said.

They walked on.

'There's a pub just behind St Chad's, The Gunmakers Arms, we should go there some time.'

The young woman laughed. 'Are you asking me out, Detective Sergeant? Whatever would Mrs Marsh think?'

Marsh smiled. 'More a professional courtesy, actually. The Gunmakers is where most of the Steelhouse crews drink, those that do drink, that is. You should get to know it.'

'Then you must take me there, good sir.'

'I will,' the DS said, with a nod. 'And you should follow up on our church idea. When we get back to the factory, you can get on with that.'

2

The morning had been one of routine and predictable tedium: clearing up the mess left by the previous shift and doing his best to make sure his own team didn't leave similar disorder in their wake. Reg Miles was happy that nothing too challenging, nothing too unexpected – nothing unexpected at all – took place. Even so, dinnertime couldn't come soon enough.

Sitting down on a bench in the canteen, Reg put his tin dinner pail on the table, folded back its handle and twisted off the lid.

The pail had belonged to his grandfather, a miner out in the Black Country. The container was squat and round, just like the old man. And dented and blackened by years spent underground – again, just like the old man.

Or just as Reg remembered him, at least.

'You eating out a paint pot now, Reggie?'

Reg looked up as Arthur Shaw swung his legs over the bench opposite and sat down. The man's two shadows – Baz and the one without a name – sat themselves down at a nearby table.

Reg frowned. 'What?'

'That,' Shaw said, pointing at the tin pail. 'It looks just like a tin of paint.'

'S'ppose it does.'

Shaw dropped his own lunchbox onto the table – it was black, shaped like a doctor's bag, an altogether more sophisticated affair.

Of course it was.

'Brought my own today, Reggie, just like you. So, what you having?'

Reg pulled out a packet of oven-dried onion rings wrapped in greaseproof paper, a small tub of piccalilli, two pieces of bread and a snub nose of cheese. He unwrapped the onion and started to assemble a sandwich, slicing the cheese with his brown-handled pocketknife and spreading the piccalilli across the bread with the same blade. He laid in the onions and cheese and topped them off with the second slice of bread.

'Nice,' Shaw said, watching and then opening his own pail. He placed a packet of sandwiches in brown waxed paper on the table and a pint-sized military Thermos flask next to them. Unwrapping the sandwiches, he peeled back the top layer of one half to reveal tongue, mustard, pickle. He pulled out a slice of the meat and dangled it in the air. 'Ha,' he said. 'Tongues will wag.'

'Very funny, Arthur.'

'And talking about wagging tongues, you had any thoughts 'bout what I said the other night?'

Reg chewed, put his lunch down, looked up. 'A few.'

'And?'

Reg shrugged. 'Not interested.'

Shaw frowned, picked a piece of pickle from his lunch. 'No?'

Reg took another bite of sandwich and shook his head.

'Pity that but then I was only saying to the lads this morning that I'd be disappointed by you. Not surprised maybe but disappointed, all the same.'

'Disappointed?'

Shaw chewed, his right cheek blowing up like a trumpeter's pouch. 'Yeah, disappointed.'

Reg finished his sandwich, folded up the greaseproof paper, dropped it back into the tin and screwed the lid back on. He wiped his fingers on his overall. 'Don't see why,' he said, 'I didn't promise you anything.'

'And that's the truth,' Shaw said, 'the proper truth of it. You didn't promise me anything, nothing at all. And why should you?'

'Quite,' Reg said, standing.

Shaw pulled a face. ''Cos you want it all for yourself, that's why. Whatever you can find, you want for yourself. Maybe you're already on the take, maybe you didn't need me to suggest anything 'cos you'd already figured it all out.'

'What?'

'You don't fool me, Reggie Miles, not for one moment do you fool me.'

'I don't know what you mean.'

'No one's as clean or as straight as you. Not one man or one woman alive, come to that. We've all got our price, 'specially at a time like this.'

'A time like what?'

'A time like what we're living in, Reggie. A time when it's every man for himself. Look around you. There's so much you could have and I'm not just talking about what you find out there, I'm talking about in these four walls too. A little bit of imagination and there's a lot to gain, nothing to lose. That's what I say.'

'Same as you said the other night.'

Arthur Shaw guffawed. 'Ah well, some things can't be said often enough, some things bear repeating. And then repeating again. 'Course there are some people they shouldn't be repeated to. Unsuitable people who should not know anything about our business, if you get my drift. You been speaking to any unsuitable people, Reggie, have you?'

Reg shook his head, picked up his pail and started to walk away.

'How's your little girl? How's she doing?'

Reg stopped, dropped his head. 'What?'

'I know you're a proud family man, Reggie, I know that about you, so I'm only asking: how's the family? I saw you with your missus this morning. Good-looking woman her, something of a belter, even if she has picked up a bit of local colour. You're a lucky man. Tell you what, if there's a god in heaven, your little girl will get her looks, not yours.'

'What you saying now, Arthur?'

'Nothing, nothing at all. Just that you're a good family man, or so it seems to me.'

Reg turned on his heel and was back at the table in a single pace. 'You leave them out of it, Arthur Shaw, you leave them right out of it, right now.'

'Out of what, Reggie? Leave them out of what?'

Reg raised a clenched fist, brought it level with his chin, the knuckles white, the folds of the fingers red.

Shaw took another bite of his lunch, chewed and smiled, white bread mashing between yellowed teeth. He swallowed, licked his fingers and smiled again. 'Delicious that,' he said. 'I do like a bit of bread and tongue. Especially with mustard and pickle. Proper nice. You going to do something with that hand by the way, or you just going to stand like that all day?'

Reg looked at his hand, dropped it to his side, feeling foolish and exposed. 'I...'

Arthur Shaw stared at him, his eyes dead, lifeless, more the eyes of a fish with too many days spent on a wet slab than anything human. 'Yes?'

'What's to stop me reporting you? Tell me that, Arthur, what's to stop me reporting you?'

'That why you been up to see Byfield then?' The name hung in the air like the far-off rumble of a heavy truck on a distant road and Shaw laughed. 'Tell me, what did you say to him? Can't be anything about me 'cos what have I said or done that you haven't already thought about doing yourself? What?'

'I didn't say anything.'

'No?'

'No.'

'That's 'cos you're a good man, Reggie-boy, a good family man.' He paused and stood. 'And let's keep it that way, eh?'

'And what's that meant to mean?' Reg said, squaring up to the smaller man.

They stared at each other, neither blinking, each challenging the other to look away first, like two boys in the schoolyard.

'You watch yourself, Arthur Shaw, because I'm watching you. From now on, I'm watching you.' Reg broke the lock stare and walked away.

Somewhere behind him, he heard Arthur Shaw laugh again and then fall silent.

3

Annie Scott followed Harry Marsh into the main CID office. It was busy. Men talked on phones, typed up notes with single finger jabs, smoked, joked and generally got on with the day.

And it was all men.

Not a woman to be seen.

Anywhere.

As they walked across the room, heads raised and eyes followed them. Marsh was conscious of arms being nudged, of snap judgements being passed, of whispers half meant to be heard, knowing that Annie Scott would be all too aware of the ruction she was creating. Aware of what impact her presence would have – was having – and how she would be judged, not only now and by her looks but in the future, too.

And not by her actions and results either but by her sex.

By appearance rather than ability.

A year from now, if she was too successful, she'd be *that pushy woman*, or if not successful enough, *that silly girl*. In other words – for many of her colleagues – she couldn't win.

And never would.

The DS glanced over at the young policewoman.

Head high, face relaxed but confident, she had something he couldn't name until he could: she had poise and composure. A poise and composure bestowed by an expensive education. He doubted Roedean had been her choice – she was simply the beneficiary of wealthy parents, who were able to afford what they thought best for their daughter – and Marsh didn't hold it against her as he'd long understood how the fortunes and misfortunes of birth cut both ways. Having fought alongside men from all walks of life during the last war, he'd seen courage, cowardice and fear displayed in equal measure, without concern for class distinction.

Social status.

Wealth.

Or lack of it.

And after all: poise and composure?

There were worse things to have in this world.

In this job.

They stopped at the desk in front of Marsh's alcove.

Stokes looked up from his PNB, the left corner of his mouth ink-stained from where he'd been chewing his pen. 'Sarge?'

'What are you doing here?'

Stokes smiled. 'Writing up my notes.'

'Very funny,' Marsh said. 'Who gave you permission to sit there?'

Stokes smiled again and tilted his head in a facetious manner. 'After I gave up that tip, well, I thought—'

'This desk is already taken, Stokes.'

'Who by? Ray doesn't want it no more, does he?'

Harry Marsh nodded, leant forward, rested his hands on the front edge of the desk, his knuckles white, a pulsing vein on the side of his head. Annie Scott could almost smell ozone and see the thundershower about to break over a Cornish cliff face.

When the DS spoke, his voice was preternaturally calm and all the more unsettling for it. 'Sod off out of it, Stokes. This is Policewoman Scott's desk now. Go and find yourself another sodding desk in another part of the sodding office, preferably somewhere I can't see you. And if I do see you again today, it'll be too soon. You understand?'

Stokes stood, folded up his notebook and slid it into his pocket. 'I just—'

Marsh raised a hand. 'No excuses, man, none,' he said. 'Just go. Sod off. Now.'

Stokes cast his eyes across the office, looking for support, sympathy, an offer of solidarity. He was met with the sight of swiftly bowed heads and people overly busy. Without saying another word, he walked away.

The DS pushed the vacated chair towards Annie Scott. 'Believe you've got some calls to make.'

The young woman nodded and watched the DS yank at his hat with one hand and pull off his coat with the other.

She removed her own hat and coat and looked at what was now her desk. It was just as she'd seen it yesterday – unchanged, as it had remained unchanged for days.

A blotter, a notebook, a phone, a photograph of a young woman and child, a copy of the *Sports Argus* and a dirty teacup with crumbs in its saucer, pushed to one side, it all added to a palpable sense that she wasn't alone. It was as if she'd boarded the *Marie Celeste* written up by Conan Doyle or entered a small museum celebrating the life mundane: the displays banal at first sight but the overall effect of which would linger on memory's edge for days.

This space felt haunted.

The young officer shivered and told herself not to be so stupid. Draping her coat across the back of the chair and placing her hat down next to the photograph, she reached for the phone.

Harry Marsh sat facing the window, wondering whether he should seek out and apologise to Stokes. He didn't like losing his temper at the best of times – saw it as a sign of weakness, a failing, an admission of liability – and although he hadn't been fair to him, the man had crossed one of Marsh's personal red lines: he had made an assumption. An assumption that because he had been of some assistance, the DS was now under a reciprocal obligation. And that obligation was as basic as the stewardship of a vacant desk.

Well, it wasn't vacant so sod that. Never had been.

No, he wouldn't seek out Stokes: he had no reason to apologise.

And anyway, he needed to keep his new partner close.

His new partner? Was that all it took? Was Ray Hancock now a matter of history and nothing else?

Harry Marsh felt the emptiness return. The emptiness of loss shot through with a sense of the impossible: how he wanted to call over to Ray, ask him or tell him something, buy him a beer at the end of the day, take the mickey about his dedication to the Baggies, share a joke and above all, a moment of common humanity.

All now impossible.

But in itself, *that* felt impossible.

How could a man like Ray Hancock simply cease to be? Harry Marsh had lost friends before – no, not just friends, fellow soldiers with whom he had become morbidly friendly – but his mourning back then had always been anaesthetised by the industrial scale of the carnage.

Somehow, it had never felt personal.

This felt personal.

This was personal.

His phone rang.

'Marsh, get over here now.'

'That's ridiculous,' Marsh said. 'I've never heard anything so ridiculous in my life.'

'Maybe,' Seaborne said, 'but ridiculous or not, it's how it is.'

'What happens now?'

'By rights, I should speak to the Super and suspend you pending inquiries but that's not going to happen, I'm not going to let that happen, not right this moment. But you do need to tell me everything. Everything you did or said. Everything that happened. Everything. Right, Marsh?'

'Sir.'

'I'm waiting.'

Harry Marsh ran back through the events in question, examining every point after he left the hospital mortuary to catching the Moseley train, walking out of a darkened station and then breaking up the fight in the pub yard. He recalled the sirens and the bombs. The screaming and the fear. The young woman with the baby in the doorway and the burning smell as phosphorus spittled down the back of his overcoat, scorching the material beyond decent repair. And then there was Jeannie – Jeannie appearing in front of him, like a lit candle in a window, showing him the way home.

He ran through it all, as if it were a photographic album, examining the edges and corners of each composition, looking for the slightest hint of how it had come to this.

This moment.

Then he ran through the sequence again, making sure the facts were not only right but were in the correct order and that he hadn't missed out anything that could prove important.

No, there was nothing missing and nothing wrong.

And then he ran through it aloud.

Without taking his eyes off Harry Marsh, Seaborne crumpled an empty cigarette packet and dropped it into the bin under his desk. 'And you went to the station the next day?'

The DS nodded. 'Yesterday morning and yes, I did.'

'And did you speak to... what were their names?' Seaborne squinted at a sheet of paper on his desk, turned it to one side and then looked at the sheet underneath. 'Greene and Noble. Did you speak to them?'

Marsh shook his head. 'No, I didn't. Sergeant Greene and PC Noble are on nights, apparently. I did speak to Sergeant Henderson though.'

'Henderson?'

'The desk sergeant at Moseley.'

'And?'

Harry Marsh shrugged. 'He didn't have much to say.'

'What *did* he have to say?'

'That he'd tell them I was asking after them.'

'And you didn't press him?'

'No reason.' Marsh paused. 'At the time.'

'And now?'

'Well, I don't know. Henderson's alright, I knew him when I was a kid. He was a very decent beat copper back then, very fair.'

'Fair? What's that meant to mean?'

'Just like I say, fair. If something happened on his watch, maybe some boys did something they really shouldn't, Henderson used to know when action was needed but when words were better.'

'Sounds like you speak from experience.'

Marsh smiled. 'Maybe.'

Seaborne nodded. 'I won't ask, we were all nippers once.'

'It's a long time ago.'

'Longer for me than you,' Seaborne said. He looked down at his desk, ran a finger across the top sheet of single-spaced typed paper. 'OK, so Henderson didn't have much to say about Greene and Noble but it doesn't explain this.'

'No, sir, it doesn't. May I have a look?'

'I don't see why not,' Seaborne said, rotating the pinned pages through 180 degrees to face Marsh. 'It's almost certainly against regs but all's fair in love and war, as the poet once said, and we are definitely at war. Anyway, I'm just popping out for a fresh packet of gaspers. Make sure this is facing the right way round by the time I get back, there's a good lad.'

Seaborne stood and left.

Marsh picked up the papers in front of him and read:

DUTY REPORT
Date: Thursday 21 November 1940
Reporting Officers: R.Noble (Police Constable)
R.Greene (Sergeant)
Subject: Disturbance between a party of three men in grounds of Trafalgar Hotel

At 06.40PM on the evening of Wednesday 20 November, Sergeant Greene and me were on standard night patrol, when we became aware of an incident taking place at The Trafalgar Hotel on the corner of Woodbridge Road and Trafalgar Road, Moseley.

On investigating the incident, we found three men involved in a fracas of a violent nature in the back yard of The Trafalgar Hotel. We approached and asked them to desist.

On seeing us approach, one man ran off before he could be identified and both remaining men later claimed not to know who he was.

Of the two remaining men, one was lying on the floor, his face bloody, the other man was standing over him, with a broken beer bottle in his hand. It was obvious from the second man's stance that, had we not got involved, he intended to use this bottle as a weapon of some sort.

On being challenged, the man on the floor - hereafter referred to as the victim - refused to identify himself though he had an unmistakable Irish accent.

The man with the bottle - hereafter referred to as the assailant - then identified himself as Detective Sergeant Harold Marsh, Birmingham City Police, R Division. The warrant card he produced confirmed his identity.

On examining the victim, we found his injuries to be superficial and non-life threatening. We offered to call a doctor but the victim declined our offer.

When asked, neither the victim or the assailant was prepared to explain what incited the incident in any way.

Although bloodied and bruised, the victim declined the opportunity to make a report that might lead to charges of any form.

As previously stated, the assailant refused any comment.

At this point, an air raid siren sounded and we thought it best to leave the yard and seek shelter. Both the victim and the assailant did the same.

This morning - Thursday 21 November 1940 - the assailant visited our station and asked the desk sergeant if he could see us. When told we were not there, he asked for our home addresses. He did not say why although if I was asked, I would say he did not want this report or any report written up, given his actions and attitude of the previous night.

This report was typed up by Sergeant R.Greene from notes written down as soon as possible after the incident as possible by Police Constable R.Noble.

This is a true and accurate account of events as took place last evening.

Signed: R Noble R Greene
Date: 21 November 1940

Outside, the late afternoon sky was darkening in preparation for dusk. Marsh sat at his desk, watching a murmuration of starlings swarm, coalesce, dissolve and reform – a constantly evolving pirouette of dark shapes against the battleship-grey sky, never once repeating the same pattern. A mass swoop and switch, flowing as effortlessly as soot through a flue.

The policeman understood that the apparent lack of effort was deceptive – like everything in life, it required work – and up there, in the sky, sinews were tensing and releasing, hearts beating and wings stretching, making the most of what eddies and current could be found.

Work, hard work.

As they flew, the birds' calls were piercing and sharp, echoing the twang and clatter of hammers on metal emanating from the industrial landscape they flowed through and around.

The starlings circled one last time and ebbed away, disappearing from sight, heading up and over Steelhouse Lane towards Cathedral Square and then to the Central Post Office, where they'd repeat their dance for a new audience.

Or rather, create a whole new routine.

The policeman drew the blackout across the window, turned and reached into a desk drawer. He pulled out a black cosh, the surface smooth and worn, the stitching neat and tidy. He sat and twisted the weapon around in his hands, enjoying the sensation of the lead shot oozing within the leather sheath. The weapon, a memento from an early arrest, had become a behavioural aid, almost a toy, a means of distracting the body while allowing the mind to deduct, reduct, abduct – to replace unknowns with knowns and reduce uncertainty, until something resembling the truth began to appear.

Or so he hoped.

The accusation, it was preposterous, of course, ridiculous, anyone who knew him would say the same.

The series of events was accurate but the roles were entirely reversed. A mirror had been held up to reality, a particularly dishonest and distorting mirror, like the ones he'd once seen at a travelling fair – distorting and grotesque.

Yes, that was a good word for this – whatever this was – *grotesque*.

A grotesque web of lies but why?

Harry Marsh understood that the best lie was always the one closest to the truth – far less to forget, far fewer possible contradictions, far less to trip over in the telling and the subsequent retellings, as would be required, if this complaint was taken forward.

Not that the complaint would go forward, he was sure of that, as was Seaborne, who had said as much by not suspending Marsh there and then. But the fact that the report had been submitted in the first place, it did mean something.

Must mean something.

But why go to all this trouble? That was the big question: what had he done to make Noble and Greene decide on this as a course of action?

What had he done to provoke such ire that required this level of retaliation?

Harry Marsh wasn't naive enough to believe that all his fellow officers were good Samaritans, out there, doing their duty for the betterment of society – he knew all too well there were bad apples in the force. He also knew that despite the fact the Birmingham Irish community was well represented in the ranks – and at the top, come to that – there was still anti-Irish sentiment amongst some of his colleagues. The Anglo-Irish war which followed the First World War and the Anglo-Irish Trade War that raged throughout most of the 1930s were two factors. And the Republic's present neutrality and even – as perceived by some – its accommodation with Hitler's Germany simply fanned embers of latent hostility.

A hostility which often meant Irishmen were the victims of random punishment beatings, even when there was nothing to punish.

Best to keep the bogtrotters in their place.

Even so, if that was all there was to it, why the report?

Why this very detailed attack on him?

What had he done that threatened them so?

No, this was about more than a simple scuffle in a pub delivery yard and if they were looking to scare him off, they knew nothing of the man he was.

Marsh sat at his desk, mulling over the possibilities. As the day had darkened, so had his mood, taking him from coincidence and spite to conspiracy and malice but no matter how he laid out the events of the night, he could still find no reason in Greene and Noble's actions.

Either on the night or subsequent to it.

What were they hoping to achieve other than to warn him off?

He coughed and felt his chest tighten. He breathed in and heard his lungs whistle. He put the cosh onto his desktop, reached into a pocket and pulled out his inhaler.

Two puffs and then relief.

'You're almost in the dark,' Annie Scott said, looming out of the gloom of the main office.

Startled, Marsh dropped his inhaler into a desk drawer, like a child caught doing something he shouldn't. He pushed the drawer shut with his knee and turned to the window. 'I'm fine,' he said, checking the blackout was firmly in place and then reaching back to turn on his desk lamp. 'Is that better?'

'Much,' she said. 'Is that what I think it is?'

Marsh followed the line of her chin. 'And what do you think it is?'

'A cosh.'

'Yes, it is.'

'Yours?'

'It is now.'

'Now?'

Marsh laughed. 'It was a present from a friend.'

'You obviously have nice friends.'

'Well, when I say friend, he was my first collar. A young guttersnipe, William Bayliss. Bill Bayliss. Sometimes known as Blackjack Bayliss. Or at least he liked to think he was known as Blackjack Bayliss.'

Annie nodded at the cosh. 'On account of the—'

'Precisely.'

Marsh leant forward and picked up the weapon. 'Bayliss was a bookie's runner for a while but one day decided he'd make more money if he tapped up other runners for their takings.'

'Tapped?'

'Literally.'

'And you arrested him?'

'Caught him in the act, actually. He put up a good scrap but in the end, well, you know, experience will out.'

'You prevailed?'

Marsh laughed. 'Even I was young and fit once. Well, fitter.'

'And this Bayliss, how come you've still got his cosh?'

'We were sitting there on the pavement, backs against some wall, both out of breath, him cuffed, the cosh on the ground between us and he said: *You may as well have that, rozzer, seeing as I won't be able to take it with me where I'm going, despite how useful it might be. No, you can have it. Something to remember me by*.'

The policewoman reached forward, picked up the cosh, weighed it in her hands, ran her fingers along the seam. 'It's heavy. Have you ever used it?'

'Once or twice, maybe.'

'Really?'

'Have you tried fitting a fifteen-inch truncheon into a trench coat pocket? Billy-Boy there's much more convenient. Much more useful.'

'Billy-Boy? You've even named it?'

Marsh nodded and smiled.

Annie placed the cosh back onto Marsh's desk. 'Yes, I can see how Billy-Boy would be more convenient,' she said, single eyebrow raised.

Marsh looked at his watch, tapped at the glass, pulled out and twisted the winder. 'Damn,' he said, 'stopped again. I really must get it looked at. What's the time?'

Annie Scott reached out her left arm, slid back the white translucent cuff of her blouse sleeve. She wore a small watch on her left wrist. The body was lozenge shaped and mounted on a fine gold mesh strap.

Expensive and no mistake, Marsh could tell that, even from where he sat.

'A quarter to six,' she said, catching Marsh's stare and pushing the cuff back down and over her wrist. 'I've identified a number of churches we may want to investigate further, by the way.'

'Excellent,' the DS said. 'Why don't you tell me about them over a drink?'

'I'll get my things,' the young woman said, turning away.

Marsh stood, pulled on his overcoat, retrieved his inhaler and after a moment's hesitation, picked up the cosh and pocketed it.

They retraced their earlier steps in reverse, going down Whittall Street and St Mary's Row. Passing St Chad's without comment, Harry Marsh led the way into Bath Street. As they walked up to The Gunmakers Arms, a distant clock struck six.

'Perfect timing,' he said, opening the pub door for Annie Scott.

'I'd rather you went first,' she said.

'Shy?'

'A little cautious, maybe.'

'Quite right,' Marsh said.

Inside, the pub was empty. A man in tweeds, late sixties, stooped but firm on his feet, appeared behind the bar. 'Harry,' he said, 'a bit early for you, isn't it, old bean?'

'Donald, this is Annie Scott, Policewoman Annie Scott. Annie, this old charmer is Donald Saunders, the landlord of this fine establishment.'

Donald Saunders walked over and offered Annie Scott his hand. They shook and he smiled. 'Well, aren't you a smasher?' Saunders said. 'If you don't mind me saying.'

'A girl does like a compliment from time to time.'

'And I like a girl who can take a compliment. What you drinking? Seeing as it's your first time in the house, the first drink's on the house.'

'Would a Scotch be possible?'

'Entirely possible.'

'Then I'll have a small Scotch, thank you. With ginger, if you have it.'

'My pleasure,' Saunders said. 'Bass Pale Ale, Harry?'

'Certainly.'

'Coming right up. Yours isn't on the house, mind. Just saying.'

'I didn't think it would be. I'll be over in a minute.'

'Righto.'

Donald Saunders walked back behind the bar, took a glass tumbler off a shelf and made a great show of polishing it. Harry Marsh and Annie Scott sat down at a table and watched him.

'He seems nice,' she said.

'Don't let appearances fool you,' Marsh said, 'Donald's been a bit of a villain in the past and when I say a bit, I mean a lot.'

'So why do you drink here?'

'Be disloyal not to. He was on the force for years and he's prepared to put up with us.'

'He was a policeman? But I thought you said—'

'That he was a bit of a villain? Yes, I did. The two things aren't mutually exclusive, you know?'

The young woman wrinkled her nose, deciding whether some new smell was pleasant or not. 'I see ... I think.'

Over at the bar, Donald Saunders raised a hand.

Marsh stood. 'Back in a tick.'

Annie Scott shook off her overcoat, folded it carefully and placing it on the chair next to her, gazed around the pub. The ceiling was lined with ornate copper panels, the floor Minton-tiled and the highly polished bar and counter topped with an ornamental canopy. A twin pipe footrest ran around the counter's base.

On the other side of the room, the walls above and around the marble fireplace were covered in terracotta tiles, their natural hue warmed by the glow from the lit glass lamps. It was a comfortable, welcoming space.

The door on the far side opened and two men in heavy coats and mufflers entered. Annie Scott noticed that the men's faces and hands were speckled grey and blue and as they passed her table, they left an odour of turned metal, oil and burnt powder in their wake.

Gunmakers, no doubt.

She smiled that there should be actual gunmakers in The Gunmakers Arms. Why it amused her she wasn't sure but it did. She glanced at her watch.

Ten past six.

'Somewhere to be?' Marsh said, placing a glass in front of her and sitting down.

'No,' she said. 'Nowhere. Just habit.'

Harry Marsh raised his pint and tilted it towards his colleague. She chinked her tumbler against his glass.

'Cin cin,' he said and drank.

'Cin cin,' she said, sipping at the Scotch and ginger, allowing the warmth to bite into her cheeks before swallowing.

The bar began to fill with the hue and sway of people at the end of the working day. Some were in for a drink before setting off for home and their tea, others for the evening, or until Donald Saunders asked them to leave, whichever came first.

Annie recognised a few faces from the station and nods and greetings were exchanged – entirely with Marsh – but no one approached them or attempted to sit with them. A couple threw a knowing glance in their direction and then swapped inaudible words. The young woman knew immediately what was being supposed and shared and felt angry. Felt a desire to stand, walk across the room and put these ignorant men to right.

'Ignore them,' Marsh said, staring at her as if her thoughts were written in a bubble above her head.

She turned to look at Marsh and realised that he'd been watching her the whole time she'd been surveilling the room. He was smiling – amused and entertained by her obvious pique. 'What?'

'Idiots say idiotic things, it's what makes them idiots,' he said, placing his half-empty glass on the table. 'Now, what have you got to tell me?'

Annie Scott opened her purse and pulled out her PNB. 'It would seem,' she said, 'that it's rather more complicated than I thought it might be. Turns out that Birmingham's somewhat of a cosmopolitan place.'

Harry Marsh frowned. 'And you're surprised by that?'

The young woman looked startled and her poise threatened to slip for a moment. 'No, I didn't mean...I didn't—'

'Don't let the accent fool you, Annie, we're not as cat-melodeon as we would have you believe. It's a bit of a disguise really, designed to put off nosey outsiders.'

'I really didn't mean to be rude. I wouldn't.'

Marsh laughed. 'No, I know you wouldn't, not seeing as who *Gramps* is and that he's one of us. I'm just teasing, that's all.'

The policewoman nodded. 'I knew that.' She raised her glass to her lips to cover her embarrassment. 'I did.'

'No,' he said, 'you didn't. It's been said we take a bit of getting used to, us Brummies. Especially our dry side. Trust me, it took Jeannie a good few years. Now, what were you saying?'

Annie put her glass back down on the table. 'I've spoken to Alien Registration and though it's a bit vague, there are,' she said, consulting her notebook, 'a number of Greek Cypriots in Birmingham, a small number. Greek Orthodox mainly but with no one place of worship. They tend to go to church in London or Manchester, when they feel the need. Less so now, given the current circumstances. There are some Turkish Cypriots too, mostly Sunni Muslims but no mosque. There also appears to be a growing number of Serbians, recent refugee—'

'Serbians? And what flavour's their god?'

The young woman smiled. 'Serbian Orthodox. Again, no church. There's talk of one being built but nothing as yet. Also, there are a few Croatians, they tend to be Catholic and attend St Catherine of Siena on Bristol Street. There is some question over their political loyalties but the ones that are here in Birmingham appear to favour our side – at least for the moment.'

Marsh nodded, sank his pint, caught Donald Saunders's eye and held up his hand in the universal sign that called for two more of the same. 'Very good,' he said, although Annie wasn't sure whether he was talking to her or the landlord.

'But the two largest populations,' the policewoman said, 'and by far the most promising are the French and the Italians. Some of the French are consular refugees and as far as anyone's aware, supporters of the Allies. There are quite a few families but they're scattered across the city. They don't attend any particular church and they're not an especially tight-knit group, it would seem, so locating and questioning them may take some time.'

'OK, I can see that.'

'And then there's The Italian Quarter.'

'Fazeley Street and New Canal Street,' Harry Marsh said.

'You know the area?'

'I know Digbeth a bit.'

'Most of the Italians down there have been here over twenty years, so there's very little internment but I have to say, there are an awful lot of registered organ grinders in Birmingham – and ice cream salesmen.'

'What can I say? We're a very musical city with a very sweet tooth.'

Annie Scott laughed. 'Now, not unsurprisingly, the Italian community's a big churchgoing community, so big in fact that St Michael's on Carrs Lane is known as The Italian Church.'

'That I didn't know.'

'Well, you do now,' she said, smiling and closing her notebook. 'What do we do next?'

The door to the outside opened and Dr Moira Penny swept in through the floor-to-ceiling blackout drape. The woman appeared flustered and confused, like someone who'd just missed a tram and couldn't understand how or why.

Harry Marsh raised a hand. 'Moira.'

The doctor smiled. 'Harry,' she said, glancing at Annie Scott with an enquiring look.

'Dr Moira Penny,' Marsh said, 'Policewoman Annie Scott. Policewoman Annie Scott, Dr Moira Penny.'

Annie Scott nodded. 'Dr Penny, good to make your acquaintance.'

'Moira, please,' the doctor said, looking down at Annie Scott's folded coat.

Annie reached across and pulled the coat onto her lap. 'Sorry,' she said, 'please.'

As Moira Penny sat, Marsh stood. 'We're having another drink. What would you like, Moira?'

'The usual,' she said. 'That'd be grand.'

'Coming right up.' Marsh walked away towards the bar, waving to catch Donald Saunders's attention as he did.

'I'm sorry,' Moira Penny said, 'am I interrupting something here?'

'No,' the younger woman said, 'we're just running over a few ideas, actually, following up on a few thoughts.'

'About the dead girl by any chance?'

'Absolutely about the girl.'

'Good, because I have some news on her too.'

'The toxicology results are back?'

'In part.'

'And?'

'Let's wait for Harry, shall we? I wouldn't want to be going through everything twice now, would I?'

'Of course not,' Annie Scott said, not sure whether she was being told off.

The DS reappeared, tray in hand, and sat down. 'Scotch and ginger, Scotch and water, pint of Bass,' he said, as he passed the drinks around, 'And to what do we owe this pleasure, Moira?'

'Not that I'm one to mix business with pleasure, as you know,' the doctor said, opening her bag and pulling out a fold of papers, 'but I thought this might just interest you.'

Marsh took the papers and flattened them. The top cover bore the letterhead *West Midland Regional Forensic Science Laboratory*. 'Hot off the press, I assume?'

'Very. And pretty rough at this point, I must warn you. Some of the stuff in here, it's as close to speculation as any scientist likes to get and the full tests are going to take weeks. But as you know, Harry, I suspected she'd been drugged not poisoned, so I asked the lab to check for a sleeping draught of some description before looking for anything else.'

'Thank you, Moira.'

Marsh scanned the first page, placed it face down on the table and started to read the next.

Moira Penny leant towards him and smiled. 'Do you need a hand there? Maybe with some of the longer words?'

The DS looked up. 'Diethylbarbituric acid in the blood?'

'That's what they think. Veronal or something very similar.'

Annie Scott sat forward. 'Wasn't there a famous Veronal poisoning case just before the last war?'

'There was,' Moira Penny said. '1913, in Brighton. Hugh Eric Trevanion. Magistrate recorded an open verdict as there was no evidence of foul play but also said that there might be grounds for suspecting murder.'

Marsh smiled. 'He did have an interesting lifestyle, I seem to remember.'

'Interesting?'

'A homosexual and a drug user,' the doctor said, watching the other woman's face carefully, waiting for some indication of prurience or otherwise.

'Oh,' the policewoman said, 'I see.'

'Anyway,' Moira said, 'I've asked for the Trevanion lab records to be sent up. That might help cut a few corners, that might.'

Marsh read on. 'And how was whatever it was delivered to our girl?'

'In a drink. Seems the girl had a glass of chocolate milk or maybe hot chocolate – which explains the chocolate on her lips and in her stomach – a wee while before she died.'

'OK. And this?' He pointed at a line on the third page.

Annie Scott squinted at the paper in the DS's hand. 'What does that say?'

'*Stomach contents include an undigested quantity of cereal cake, probably yellow maize. Possibly polenta*,' Marsh said. 'Unusual that.'

'Not if you're Italian,' Annie said.

Marsh looked at her and nodded – a connection made.

The room fell silent. The silence of anticipation. The drinkers stock still, pints frozen mid-sip, like wild animals on tiptoe, ears pricked, knowing something was coming but not knowing quite what or from quite where.

Just on its way and arriving soon.

There was a shake in the air, a shimmer, a door slammed out in the street. And then the siren sounded, rising and falling, rising and falling, rising and falling.

As it did, Donald Saunders was out from behind the bar and moving across the room. 'Ladies and gentlemen,' he looked at Harry Marsh, Annie Scott and Moira Penny, 'you are all welcome to stay but I would suggest you don't. Those of you that can get home, do. Those that can't, please find the best shelter you can. Harry, old bean, you and the girls hang back a bit.'

The room clearance was calm and orderly, conducted with a matter-of-fact acceptance and a collective shrug of drinkers' shoulders – the same shrug any one of them would use whether they'd just won a prize or lost a bet.

Two minutes later the bar was empty.

Saunders walked over and took Marsh by the elbow. 'You won't be getting home quick. Come on, this way, all three of you.'

The landlord opened the bar hatch and led the party through a door and down a flight of stairs. Reaching the cellar, Saunders swung the door shut behind them just as the earth shook.

Two hours later, the raid abated and at the Bristol Street tram terminus, a driver examined the three people standing in front of him – all were dusty and frazzled but apparently uninjured, apart from a cut on the man's right cheek. They smelt of hops and smoke, as if they'd just come from a fire in a brewery.

'Rotten Park Road?' the driver said. 'You'll be lucky. The power's out on Icknield Port Road. Going to be out until tomorrow morning if you ask me. Bristol Road's closed too, from Selly Oak onwards – there's at least one fractured water main. The trains might be running but I can't be certain, you'll need to check at New Street, you will.'

'Excellent,' Annie Scott said. 'Shanks' nag for me.'

'You can't walk that far on your own,' Harry Marsh said.

'I'll be fine,' she said, faking an optimistic smile, knowing that the last thing she wanted was a trek through the dark this soon after an air raid.

'You'll do no such thing, officer,' Moira Penny said. 'My flat's only a good stretch of the legs away and I've got a spare room – you must stay with me tonight.'

'That's very kind but—'

'But what?'

The policewoman felt the weight of the day on her shoulders as the adrenalin of the raid and then the forced march across town wore off. 'But nothing. You're very kind. Thank you.'

'What about you, Harry?'

'Moseley's not so far, Moira.'

The doctor nodded and moved off, Annie Scott held back.

'Sergeant Marsh, Sarge, Harry, you've been very kind today, I just want to say thank you.'

'My pleasure. Now you go with Moira and I'll see you at the factory in the morning, if that's alright? I know it's a Saturday but I think we need to push on, I think we may just be onto something.' He smiled. 'And Harry will do just fine.'

'Tomorrow's very alright with me. Good night, *Harry*.'

4

The stairs were wide and bright. They seemed to reach ever upwards in an infinite and inviting curlicue, as if their final destination was heaven itself. The walls that wrapped around them – forming an almost perfect cylinder – were white and punctuated with floor-to-ceiling windows. Each window a symmetrical arrangement of glass oblongs, divided one from the next by vertical and horizontal chrome strips. The glass was frosted and opaque.

Rather like the space itself.

A series of ornamental wall lights subdivided the span between the windows. Each light's casing was silver and curved like wings frozen in flight, the front glass whitely translucent, even when unlit.

Annie Scott felt that she'd stepped into a vision of the future as foreseen by an architect maybe less than a decade earlier. This future was bright and optimistic, with its clean lines and modern living – a future now made utterly redundant by the world outside.

So much change in just ten years. She didn't want to guess what life would be like in 1950 – especially not if the war was lost.

She shivered.

'This way,' Moira Penny said, from up ahead. 'Sorry the lift's not working.'

On the next landing, Moira pushed open the front door to her apartment and stood back, indicating that Annie go first. As the young policewoman stepped over the threshold, there was a click and the corridor in front of her lit up.

'Don't you worry,' Moira said from behind her, 'the blackout's in place. Now mind yourself, there's two steps just in front of you – they caught me out for a while, they did – and then it's straight ahead to the sitting room. You go there, I'll get a brew on. Or maybe you'd prefer something a wee bit stronger?'

'Do you have anything more than just a *wee* bit stronger?'

Moira laughed. 'Scotch do you?'

Annie nodded. 'Most certainly.'

'I've no ginger ale, mind. Will a drop of a water suit?'

'A splash would be nice.'

'I put a fresh ewer on the thrawl only this morning, it'll be good and cold by now. I'll just go and get it, you make yourself at home.'

Annie walked down the corridor, running a hand along the perfectly machined teak shelf to her left. She was not surprised to see an identical shelf to her right. White iron radiators were mounted on the walls beneath each shelf, both were humming but emitting very little heat.

The policewoman caught sight of her reflection in a wall mirror. She raised a finger and rubbed at the smut on her cheek and then reached back, loosening her bun. She shook her head, ran her hands through her hair and walked forward into the sitting room. Turning on a table lamp by the doorway, she looked around.

The room was huge, made all the larger by the sparse furnishing. An armchair, a sofa, an occasional table with another lamp, a slim sideboard pushed against a wall and in the corner, a Decca Salon gramophone next to a magazine rack. The rack was stuffed with what looked like books but on closer inspection, the books were leatherette-bound collections of 10-inch records.

There was a disc on the gramophone. Annie turned the machine's winder and then lowered the needle onto the revolving shellac.

Fingal's Cave.

'Now that's a good choice,' Moira said as she entered the room, carrying a jug and heading for the sideboard. 'The Rudolph Ganz recording. Not exactly late-night listening but excellent taste, all the same.'

'Oh, I hope you don't mind. It was already on the gramophone.'

'As I said, excellent taste. How much water will you want?'

'Just a drop.'

Annie watched as Moira took a small glass pipette out of a drawer, squeezed its rubber tit and drew in a measure of water. She squirted the water into the Scotch. 'That's what I mean by a drop, I hope that's what you mean,' she said.

Annie laughed. 'How very precise.'

Moira put the dropper down and walked across the room, a glass in each hand. 'Once a doctor, always a doctor, don't you know? For you.'

'Thank you,' Annie said, taking the tumbler and sitting into the sofa. She sipped the Scotch. As it slipped down her throat, the spirit left a musty aftertaste and a sense of late afternoons on autumnal moors.

Moira settled into the armchair, leant her head back and listened. 'There's something about this that always reminds me of Wagner, which is ironic really.'

'It is?'

'Given the fact that Mendelssohn was born Jewish and that Dicky boy was not such a fan of God's Chosen People.'

'I suppose.'

'Wagner even attacked poor old Felix, you know? He went into print and said how talented the man was and it was just a pity he was a Jew, as it stopped him producing anything deep and profound. How about that then? Isn't that a fine thing to say?'

Annie shook her head. 'I didn't know.'

Moira smiled and raised her glass. 'Sláinte.'

They drank.

'He loved Birmingham,' the doctor said, 'Mendelssohn, that is, not Wagner, I'm not sure that old antisemite ever came here.'

Annie looked surprised. 'Mendelssohn? Loved Birmingham?'

Moira nodded. 'He did. Especially the Town Hall, claimed it was one of his favourite venues anywhere. You know *Elijah*?'

'Not personally.'

Moira laughed her chainsaw cackle. 'The oratorio, you wee fool.'

'Ah,' Annie said, playing along. 'That *Elijah*.'

Moira smiled. 'Get away with you. Yes, that *Elijah*. It had its first performance here in Birmingham almost one hundred years ago. 1846 to be precise.'

'I didn't know that either.'

Moira sipped, sat back, closed her eyes, sank further into the chair. 'And how are you finding Steelhouse Lane, Annie?'

'My last position – and my first, actually – was in Bath so coming to Birmingham, well, it's different, certainly.' She laughed. 'And larger.'

'It would be. And do you feel out of place?'

Annie nodded once. 'On occasions.'

'But you cover it well?'

'I try to fit in.'

Moira laughed, emptied her glass in one swallow, stood and held out her hand. 'Now, for the sake of fitting in, will you have another, just to keep me company?'

'I think I will.'

'Good girl.'

Annie picked up her glass and passed it to Moira just as the needle ran out of groove. 'And I'll put another record on. Rather a novelty for me this these days, having music available whenever I want it.'

Walking across the room, Annie bent down next to the gramophone. She flicked through the other records – time for something more modern, maybe.

And then.

Perfect.

The piano introduction to *Prelude to a Kiss* spiked the air, its mood melancholic but anticipatory, the build-up to an important announcement. And then the saxophone line took the tune somewhere else – somewhere resigned, reflective and so reminiscent of late nights dancing close, in pre-war Bath.

Annie smiled at the memories and turned to watch Moira as she added precise drops of water to Scotch. 'You've just moved in, I take it,' the policewoman said.

The doctor glanced over her shoulder. 'What makes you say that now, Annie?'

'There's so little furniture and it feels, I don't know, unlived in?'

Moira placed a glass into Annie's hand and stared her in the face. 'How much furniture do you think one person needs?'

'That's a very good question.'

The doctor dropped down into her armchair, took one sip of Scotch and then another. 'Is it now?'

'It's just that, I don't know, it's a lovely flat and it seems sparse, I suppose,' the policewoman said, sitting on the sofa's edge, aware that a wrong turn had been taken.

Moira swallowed her drink, nodded. 'Everything I own, I've earnt. If that's not enough for some people then I'm sorry but that's the way it is. And seeing as that's the way it is and I'm happy with the way it is, I'm not really sorry at all.'

Annie leant forward. 'Moira, I didn't mean to offend you.'

Moira stared at the young policewoman. 'Did you not?'

'No.'

The doctor smiled, her lips glinting over the edge of her tumbler. 'How do you like it now, down here with us mere mortals?'

'Mere mortals?'

'Those of us that have to buy our own furniture so as to make our lives less *sparse*.'

Moira looked away and drained her glass.

Annie stared into her tumbler, twisted it around in her hands, watched the light refract through the etched sides and amber Scotch. 'I really didn't mean to cause offence.'

Moira raised her tumbler and frowned. 'I'm sure you didn't. Och, all gone. Do you want another?'

'I'm fine.'

The doctor walked back to the sideboard. 'It must be nice,' she said.

'What must be nice?'

'Being you.'

'And what am I?'

Moira uncorked the bottle and poured. No water was added. 'Posh, I would say. And self-assured. Never doubting yourself, or your opinion. And quite willing to express that opinion, no matter the situation. Would that be fair?'

'Possibly,' Annie said.

The doctor perched on a sofa arm. 'Annie, I don't know you from Eve but I'd say that *possibly* is almost certainly *probably*. But then that's only my opinion, that is.'

'Moira...'

'Yes?'

'I'm truly sorry if I've offended you, it was entirely unintentional. You've been nothing but kind and I've been unthinking. I'm sorry.'

'You've said that already.'

They drank in silence.

The policewoman bent forward, put her glass down at her feet, stood. 'I should be going.'

Moira laughed. 'Och, don't be ridiculous. You can't be going anywhere, not tonight. It's not safe.'

Annie smiled. 'There is a war on, you know?'

And Moira laughed again. 'There is at that. And tomorrow is another day, should we be so lucky as to see the dawn. And just so you know, I'm Belfast-born and Glasgow-educated – it would take a lot more than a wee girl like you to offend me.'

Moira opened the door and turned on the light. The room was just large enough to accommodate a bed, a bedside table and a chair. There was a clothes hook on the back of the door, a white hand basin fitted to the wall underneath the window and a free-standing mirror on the sill. 'It's not much,' Moira said, 'but I like to call it home, or at least, my spare room.'

'It's perfect, thank you,' Annie said, turning to look at Moira.

'Well, it's comfortable if not as well appointed as madam may be used to,' Moira said.

Annie pulled a face, reddened.

'Two years,' Moira said.

'I'm sorry?'

'Two years, I've lived here two years. And if it feels sparse, at least it means there's less jetsam to be discarded by whoever gets the job of clearing up after I'm dead and gone.'

Annie nodded once, looked down at her feet and closed the door.

Moira turned, walked back to the sitting room, lifted the Scotch bottle, held it to the lamp.

Maybe enough for one decent shot.

'Ach, where's the harm?'

She upended the bottle into her tumbler, rewound the gramophone, turned off the lights, pushed back the blackout and opened the window.

Prelude to a Kiss played behind her and Moira relaxed as the precision of Duke Ellington's composition – the diatonic fifths, the mirrored, rising semitones and the evaded cadences – wrapped itself around her: the song's mathematical structure so perfect, so pleasing.

Skin prickled by the cold air, the doctor sipped her Scotch, staring upwards and outwards and knowing in that moment how there was so much to understand yet so little time. Leaning further forward, she allowed the darkness to embrace her like a lover and enjoyed the calm which came with losing herself in the vast emptiness between stars.

A calm which ended when the second bombing run started just minutes before midnight and the two women scarpered downstairs to the basement.

Other residents were already there.

Without warning, a man started to sing *One Man Went To Mow.*

Everyone joined in.

SATURDAY 23 NOVEMBER 1940

1

The priest stuck two fingers into his clerical collar and pulled it around his throat. He flicked out the single metal stud and let the starched linen spring open against his black shirt, now indistinguishable from any other black shirt.

Harry Marsh looked at the surroundings, not sure what he was expecting but not expecting this: a simple desk with a reading light, one chair behind the desk and two chairs in front of it, a single bookshelf containing a number of religious works, a plain wooden cross mounted high on a white wall and a naive painting of the Madonna. To his surprise, there was nothing baroque, ornate or high church about this space, just a certain rigour. It was a room fit for function and nothing else – much like the priest himself.

Father Frederick Matthew Coughlin, a tall, lean man, with owlish glasses perched on a raptor's beak. His face was both aesthetic and skeletal, as if mortification of the flesh had turned him into a living memento mori – a constant reminder that death was no more than a missed heartbeat away. The priest's skin was closely shaven and so tightly stretched over his skull that Marsh was convinced a lit communion candle held close to the man's left cheek would be clearly visible through his right.

However, to make up for his appearance – in the knowledge that mankind cannot bear too much reality, too often – Coughlin's god had granted his representative a calm beneficence and a guileless manner, at least superficially. That and his Irish tone – a soft Cork accent, so different to the vowels and consonants spoken by Dr Moira Penny – were perfectly suited to the servant of a creed fixated on inveigling guilt before granting forgiveness.

There was an odour of wax and rosewood in the air and the policeman wasn't sure whether it came from the man himself or the desk at which he sat. But whichever, it suggested an element of carefully devised theatre – an effect designed to emphasise the sanctity of their location, despite its apparent simplicity.

'Now let me see,' the priest said, reaching the lean fingers of his right hand over the desk towards Annie Scott, without taking his eyes off Harry Marsh.

Annie Scott passed him the photograph. 'She's dead,' the policewoman said. 'Just so you know, Father.'

Coughlin laughed. 'Oh, don't you fuss, I'm used to the dead. I wouldn't be much of a priest now, would I, if I couldn't look death in the face?'

The young woman flushed, either embarrassed or annoyed.

'Ah, such a pity,' the priest said. 'Do you know what happened to her?'

'That's what we're trying to find out,' Annie said.

'Of course, of course,' Coughlin said, looking at the photograph again before offering it back to the young woman. 'The never-ending search for the story that fills the gap twixt not yet and no more. Well, I'm sorry to say, I can't help. I don't recognise her. I don't think she was ever one of mine.'

Marsh nodded. 'And you're sure?'

'That I am,' the priest said. 'She has a fine, distinctive face.'

'Well, thank you, Father,' Annie Scott said, standing.

'If it's any help,' Coughlin said, 'I would say she *is* Italian.'

The DS raised an eyebrow. 'And why's that?'

'There's just something about her. I don't like to judge people on appearances, not in my business – you'd be surprised at how many monsters walk around in beautiful skins and vice versa, of course – but this girl, her features, her hair, there's definitely something of Italy there. Something of the Italian Renaissance. Something of Raffaello Sanzio, one might say.'

'Raphael,' Annie said, as she took the photograph out of his hand. 'Really?'

'My dear girl—' the priest said.

'Policewoman Scott,' she said, her tone crackling the air.

'My dear *Policewoman* Scott, this church is not known as The Italian Church for nothing. I tend to the spiritual needs of Birmingham's Italian diaspora on a daily basis and I would say that this child is of Italian extraction. She has the look.'

Annie Scott bristled. 'But you don't know for certain?'

'No,' Coughlin said, smiling. 'I don't know, I don't. But there are a multitude of things that I would admit to knowing and not knowing – in fact my unknowns far outweigh my knowns – and this is where my faith is of such comfort: when you believe in Him who knows everything, what needs to be known on a personal level will be revealed by Him when He judges the moment to be right. And something in here...' he tapped his head with a single finger and then pointed skyward, 'and maybe up there, something is telling me that this child is Italian.'

'A small, still voice maybe?'

'Policewoman Scott,' Marsh said, 'please.'

She glanced across at Harry Marsh, clearly irritated.

'Father,' Harry Marsh said, leaning forward, 'assuming you are right and she is Italian, is there anyone, anyone at all, in the Italian community who might be able to help us further? Help us identify her.'

Coughlin ran a hand over his head, smoothed down a non-existent tuft of hair. 'Now that's a good question. It's a misconception that all Italians are God fearing and church going. Many are but some are *comunista*,' he said, the word *comunista* heavy with both accusation and heresy, 'and see both church and state as a common enemy. But just because I don't recognise a face, doesn't mean I can't see that face, I can't know that face. She may not be part of my congregation but she is Italian and someone out there will know her name.'

The priest dropped his chin into a palm and looked away, as if to commune with a divine presence. In the silence that followed, Marsh could feel Annie Scott's restlessness – her desire to be anywhere but here – it radiated from the young woman as clearly as the evening star on a cloudless night.

The policeman just didn't know why.

Didn't know what she had against Father Coughlin. Pompous and self-important maybe but it's the rare Man of God who isn't.

The priest looked up. 'You might like to talk to Mrs Gasparri. She's a washerwoman down in Digbeth and what she doesn't know, is not worth knowing. You understand what washerwomen are like, I'm sure. They see and hear more than any simple priest ever could.'

Marsh took out his PNB and looked at this far from simple priest. 'Would you have an address for her, Father?'

The day had brightened, turned white, cold, dry. There was a back note of smoke in the air but there always was these days, it was as much a part of the landscape as Birmingham's gothic arches and spires. Harry Marsh shaded his eyes with a hand and looked at Annie Scott.

'You didn't like him much.'

'And why would you think that?'

Marsh chose to ignore her sarcasm. 'Any reason?'

'I don't like organised religion,' she said.

'I can't say I noticed,' Marsh said, with a straight face.

Annie Scott laughed. 'It was that obvious?'

They walked on, turned right into Fazeley Street and headed down into Digbeth.

'The Catholic church,' the policewoman said, 'it supported Mussolini and now it's supporting Hitler. That can't be right, can it?'

'No, it can't. But to say the church supports both Hitler and Mussolini is perhaps a little unfair.'

'Well, it doesn't oppose them then. And that's much the same as supporting, in my opinion. If you don't do anything to protect your people, you may as well be the one oppressing your people.'

'Possibly true that,' Marsh said.

'And it's men like him – glib men who wear their holiness like a badge of honour and claim a direct line to God – plausible, pernicious men who don't really care for anything other than the prestige and power that being a so-called humble man of God brings, it's men like that who have let it happen.'

'This feels personal,' the DS said.

Annie Scott stopped in her tracks. 'It is, if you must know.'

'You're Catholic?'

'I was.'

'I didn't think it was a faith you could ever leave.'

'It left me.'

She walked on and Marsh followed, a pace behind. He saw her raise an arm and dab at her right eye. As soon as he caught up, she let her arm drop back to her side.

'Who?'

'It doesn't matter.'

'It matters to you,' Harry Marsh said.

She sighed. 'You'll laugh.'

'Try me.'

'My nanny.'

He laughed. 'Your nanny?'

Annie Scott smiled. 'You're laughing, I said you would.'

The DS reached forward, touched an elbow with his hand. 'No, I'm not. I already knew you were a posh lot, Annie, so you're not telling me anything I didn't know, not really.' He paused. 'She obviously meant quite a bit to you, this nanny.'

'She did.'

They walked on.

'Tell me about her,' he said.

'Nonna, I always called her Nanny Nonna. She was Italian and she raised me, in all honesty, what with Mummy and Daddy being so busy and so absent for so much of the time and Peter, my brother, away at boarding school for most of the year. She was my best friend.'

And Marsh could see the little girl that Annie Scott had been, rattling around a large town house, almost certainly in North London, having everything she wanted apart from the one thing she needed: her family.

Now, for the first time, Marsh sensed an air of loneliness about the young woman. Not a desperate loneliness, just a resigned loneliness underpinning or maybe driving her necessary independence. 'And what happened?'

'She died. Breast cancer. It got into her bones and that was it. Gone. In the end, she left me on my own too.'

'And?'

'The local priest, he said how we should be glad that Nonna had been delivered from this life of perpetual sin into the everlasting glory of God. How her pain at the end was a form of purgatory on Earth and had hastened her path to Heaven.' She dabbed at her eye again. 'Only he didn't need to mop her brow *at the end*, he wasn't the one holding her hand *at the end*.'

'You were?'

'I was.'

They moved on in silence, eventually turning right and crossing Digbeth High Street. Annie Scott pointed up at a large redbrick shop with a lunette window on the first floor. Topping the building, just beneath the roof, the name *G Makepeace* – in capital letters on a green brick banner – ran from one side to the other.

'That's a good-looking place,' the constable said.

'It is,' Marsh said. 'Unfortunately, we're going next door.'

Dwarfed by its taller, smarter neighbour, the shop to its left, with its 18th century frontage and first-floor pedimented window, looked as if it would collapse in on itself, come the next windy day.

Or bombing raid.

Harry Marsh pushed at the door. A bell tinkled as they went in.

A young woman stood behind the counter, reading a picture magazine. She looked across. 'Can I help you?'

Marsh held up his warrant card. 'Mrs Gasparri?'

The girl laughed. 'Do I look like a missus? No, you want Momma. Is she in trouble or something?'

'No, not at all,' Annie Scott said, 'we'd just like a word.'

'Go on through then,' the girl said, pointing at an old brown door. Business done, she bent down and transported herself back to a world of glamour and glitz.

'*Grazie*,' Annie Scott said, as she and Marsh walked past the girl, into the back of the shop.

'*Prego*,' the girl said, without looking up, her Brummie accent making the word sound like a two-word instruction: *Pray Go*.

Out in the yard, Mrs Gasparri was sat on an upturned metal bucket, her full-length grey skirt dangling in the suds covering the brick deck, primrose blue scarf around her head, cigarette in hand. The air smelt of smoke and soap. She looked up at the police officers as they approached, her face shuttered, expressionless.

Behind her, in what had obviously been intended as a temporary structure when built a hundred years earlier, similarly dressed women worked at a row of zinc stalls. Beating, scrubbing, wringing, they moved washing from front sinks to back sinks, their skin burnt bright pink from the constant steam. At the rear of the outhouse, a hydro extractor finished its tumbling and a pair of very young girls pulled out sheet after sheet, draping each one over the rail of a drying horse, before sliding the metal drying closet shut.

'*Polizia,*' the woman said, blowing out smoke. It wasn't a question, just a statement of fact.

'*Si,*' Annie Scott said. '*Come sta, Signora Gasparri?*'

'*Molto bene, grazie.*' Mrs Gasparri threw her cigarette to the ground, where it was sucked into and under the foam. 'And we can talk English, I speak good English.'

'In which case,' the policewoman said, 'we will speak English.'

To Marsh's dismay, Mrs Gasparri dug out another cigarette from an apron pocket and lit up. 'So, what is this about? I am here legal. I have been here thirty years, all the time legal. I despise Mussolini, yes?'

'Don't we all?' Marsh said, smiling.

'Yes,' the woman said, with a solemn nod, 'we all do.'

Annie Scott opened her purse and reached inside. 'Mrs Gasparri?'

'Yes?'

'Father Coughlin has suggested we speak to you,' the young woman said. 'He thinks you may be able to help us.'

'Help you? How? Why me?' the older woman said, her face tightening further. 'Why does the father name me?'

Annie Scott pulled out the photograph of the dead girl. 'I would like to show you a photograph.'

Mrs Gasparri reached forward.

'You should know she's dead,' the policewoman said. 'We're trying to find out who she is. Father Coughlin says you know a lot of people and may know her.'

'Let me see,' the woman said. 'Dead, you say?'

Annie Scott turned the photograph over in her hand and offered it to Mrs Gasparri.

The woman held the print to the light and stared. Then she crossed herself, left to right, neck to belly. 'Yes, I have seen her. I do not know who she is, I do not know where she lives but I have seen this face before.'

2

Cigarettes bought, dinnertime over, Reg Miles walked to his block's staff entrance and reached into a pocket for his card, ready to clock back in. He yawned and coughed, tasted smuts and dust in his mouth, especially annoying as he'd gargled long and hard first thing this morning, hoping to expunge the taste of last night. But in the kitchen, as he'd spat into the sink, he'd hallucinated water spiralling down a concrete wall like ripples on a winter pond and he was back in a blocked stairwell.

Ten hours earlier.

Outside – out in the flare and spotlight-lit dark – bombs were dropping, exploding, rending, destroying.

Despite all their best efforts to clear the stairs, there was still a man on a roof, his exit cut off by fallen masonry and high flames lapping up the walls, almost touching his feet. Long ladders were not long enough to reach him and his only hope of rescue was a turntable.

The nearest turntable was still five minutes out.

Twenty minutes later, in what seemed like no time at all and all the time ever spent waiting, the man was lowered down on a rescue line – injured, burnt, alive.

There were cheers.

'Knock off, make up, get off home,' a distant voice said, around dawn.

Then and now, Reg felt his eyelids flutter shut.

Blinking himself back into the present, he shook himself awake and slotted his card into the punch clock. He reached to pull the handle and paused. There was an engine running close by. It was irregular and choking, about to cut out. And then it backfired with a loud pop and fell silent. In the quiet, a man swore.

Without marking his card, Reg stepped back into the alley.

He saw a Guy Motors' Wolf 2 tonner parked at the far end, its driver's side engine cover open. A man was bent forward and leaning into the engine cavity. From where Reg stood, it looked as if he was about to be swallowed whole. A second man stood behind him, holding a starter handle in his right hand and bouncing it on and off his left palm.

'Need help there?' Reg said, as he approached.

The man with the starter handle looked over. 'Nargh, you're alright.' His accent was Black Country, maybe Dudley, maybe Wednesbury.

The other man pulled back and glared up at Reg. 'What do you want?' he said, in a Brummie accent low and soft with an inherited Irish inflection.

'Thought you might want some help.'

'We're fine. You can be on your way, we're just fine.'

The words *Steel Scrap* were painted on a banner that ran across the roof of the cab and the same words were painted on the vehicle's wooden sides. There was no company name. For what it was – and what it wasn't – the signage had a curiously hand-finished look, crude brushstrokes still visible in the paint's surface.

Clearly an amateur job, which didn't mean anything these days but still struck Reg as odd. 'Where're you lads from then?' he said.

The man with the starter handle stared at Reg, lifting and then dropping the tool with a soft slap against his flesh. 'You what?'

'Who do you work for?'

The man tinkering with the engine stood up and pulled the lid down on the compartment. It clattered into place. He reached forward, fastened it tight. 'And what's it to you, friend?'

'I'm an assistant works manager in this block and I'm surprised you're here, that's all.'

The handle came to rest. 'Surprised?'

'Why's that?' the other man said.

'I didn't know we had any collections scheduled today.'

'*Scheduled today?*' The repeated words had a sneer to them, the implication being Reg was an idiot for expecting anyone to have a schedule of any nature, given prevailing conditions, given that it was a Saturday.

Given there was a war on.

'He didn't know,' the man with the starter handle said, taking a step forward. 'Well, isn't that an oversight?'

Reg nodded. 'I'm sure that's exactly what it is. You got your paperwork handy?'

'Our what?'

'Your chitty.'

The Brummie-Irishman glanced over at his colleague. 'Have you got the *chitty*, have you?' His tone was facetious, mocking.

'Sure,' the man said. He walked around the Wolf's bonnet, pulled open the passenger door and reached in. 'It's here somewhere.'

Reg followed him feigning interest in the paperwork but then pushed past. Placing his hands on the top of the vehicle's side panel and his left foot on the metal mudguard over the rear nearside tyres, Reg vaulted up and into the Wolf's rear compartment. He landed on a row of boxes, covered by a tarpaulin.

The Brummie-Irishman appeared on the other side of the vehicle, right arm bent at the elbow, starting handle resting across his shoulder.

'Get out of there now,' he said. 'Now and I mean now.'

Reg bent down and pulled back the tarp.

Wooden boxes, each one bearing the same stencil mark: *Lee Enfield No.1 Mk.III*.

'I won't tell you again,' the Brummie-Irishman said and Reg felt a pair of hands reaching out from behind him, trying to grip onto his legs.

'Best get down,' the other man said, fixing his hold and then tightening it.

Without turning around, Reg kicked the hands away and knelt. He pulled at the lid on the nearest crate. It swung open easily, on well-oiled black hinges.

Reg reached in and picked up a rifle. He drew back the rear bolt, closed it down and felt the action cock the striker.

It was smooth, swift, definite.

A perfect example of a perfectly machined weapon.

He turned to face the men, rifle in hand.

3

Leaving the laundry, DS Marsh and Policewoman Scott walked across Digbeth to Bordesley Street. Row after row of run-down houses, a few with shops operating out of front rooms. One make-shift store offered vegetables, another ice cream. There was the smell of bread in the air and something sharper, something bitter.

Not unpleasant, just unusual.

'Onions,' Annie Scott said, noticing Marsh's nose twitch, 'and garlic.'

'Never eaten garlic,' Marsh said. 'So that's what it smells like.'

Annie nodded. 'It is.'

Marsh flipped open his notebook and looked at his latest entry: *Adelina Bolzano. Baker. Bordesley Street.* 'Can you see any shop names?' he said.

'No. Oh wait, what's that? Yes, there.'

Marsh followed the line of her finger. Blue writing on a yellow board: *Bolzano – panificio.*

'Here we are then,' he said, stepping over the pavement and up to the door. 'Ready?'

'Yes.'

The smell in the shop pushed Harry Marsh back through the years. Back to a time when both his parents sat, feet up, drinking tea, after a day of mixing, kneading, baking, serving. His father's face was always flush from the ovens, his mother's fingers and palms wrinkled from the number of times she'd washed her hands during service.

Looking around, Marsh stared at the different breads on display, breads he didn't recognise – breads containing herbs, onions, tomatoes. One shelf had a handwritten sign pinned to its leading edge: *panis*.

A small counter stood in front of the shelf, a row of trays beneath its glass top. Most were empty but one tray – with a piece of paper bearing the word *turtre* tucked under its front lip – contained what looked like small, square, yellow envelopes. Each envelope bulged in the centre and was crimped around the edges.

A dark-haired woman of uncertain age sat on a stool in the corner of the shop. As soon as they'd entered, her face had closed down, wiping away all trace of emotion. It was the same reaction Marsh had seen in Mrs Gasparri: a lack of expression which revealed nothing but an ancestral distrust of authority.

'*Salve*,' the woman said, her tone as flat as her stare.

'*Signora Bolzano, come sta?*' Annie Scott said.

'*Bene, grazie*, how may I help?'

Harry Marsh took out his warrant card and walked over.

Adelina Bolazano waved his hand away. 'I don't need to see what I already know. What do you want?'

Annie Scott showed her the photograph of the girl. 'Do you know this girl?'

'She's dead,' Marsh said. 'And we believe you may know who she is.'

The woman glanced at the photograph, shrugged and then sighed. 'Montealto,' she said. 'The grocer. You should speak to him.'

The next shop was an Aladdin's cave of unknown treasures, or rather, would have been when fully stocked. Right now, at this moment, there was a sense of emptiness, an almost palpable decline, it seemed the shop's glory days were well behind it and its half-full shelves were better described as half-empty. There was produce everywhere but produce surrounded by space, by gaps – it was clear something was missing, something that would never return.

A single salami hung from the ceiling in a string bag. Scraps of cheese in waxed papers lay on a shelf. Vegetables swam in jars, all pickled and preserved. A bottle of oil nestled close to a bottle of dark vinegar. A few tins of fish and tins of tomatoes were stacked next to each other. There was a tray containing two individual cakes on the countertop and there was a smell of coffee in the air. It was definitely not the Camp Coffee that Jeannie had once tried to make Harry Marsh drink – and after her husband's complaints, an experiment she never repeated – but the thick aroma of roasted beans, waiting to be ground and percolated, just like the beans his wife now brought home from Shufflebothams.

'Hello?' Harry Marsh said.

'*Salve, dottore*,' a man said, appearing from the backroom, wiping his hands on a red and white tea towel. 'Can I 'elp you?'

Marsh held up his warrant card and a flicker of concern ran like a sine wave up, down and across the other man's forehead. 'We need to ask you a few questions.'

'What's this about? Do I need to get my registration papers?'

'No, Mr Montealto,' Marsh said, 'that won't be necessary. If you were going to be interned, you'd have been interned by now, I'd have thought.'

Blankfaced, Montealto looked at the DS as if his dry tone carried a far darker threat. 'Twenty-one years,' Montealto said, the Brummie inflection in his voice suddenly more pronounced, reassuring both himself and the policeman that he belonged here. 'Twenty-one years in England. Fifteen 'ere, in this shop. Fifteen. Ask people. Ask anyone. Ask everyone. Fifteen years I've been 'ere, OK?'

Harry Marsh looked around. He may not have recognised many of the foodstuffs on sale but that didn't make them any less appetising. 'And I'm sure everyone's grateful for your services, Mr Montealto.'

'I 'ope so,' Montealto said. 'Custom's not what it was, what with people moving away and everything, but I do alright.'

Marsh turned to Annie Scott. 'Policewoman Scott?'

'Sergeant.'

Opening her bag, Annie took out the photograph, careful to keep the image facing away from Montealto. 'We have a photograph and we'd like you to have a look at it,' she said, 'if you'd be so kind.'

Montealto nodded. 'I'll take a look.'

Annie Scott turned the print over in her hands and offered it to the man. Her action was careful, considered, cautious, as if she were offering a titbit to a feral cat. 'I must warn you—'

Montealto took the photograph. 'No,' he said, looking away, looking at the ground, 'I 'ave no idea. No idea at all. This picture rings no bells.' He handed the print back to the young woman.

'Mr Montealto—'

'What?'

'We were told she lived here.'

'Who told you that?'

'That doesn't matter,' Annie Scott said.

The sine wave stippled the man's forehead for a second time.

'I don't know 'er. She is no one to me. Whoever told you she lives 'ere, they're yampy, proper yampy.'

Harry Marsh took a step forward and pointed at the counter. 'Those cakes, we'll take them.'

Montealto looked confused and then nodded. 'Good choice. Signora Bolzano over the road, she makes them and I sell a few for 'er.' He put two cakes into a paper bag and passed them to the sergeant.

Marsh smiled. 'How much do I owe you?'

'Nada,' the grocer said.

'No,' the policeman said, digging a hand into a trouser pocket. 'I must pay you.'

'Tuppence,' Montealto said, rubbing his fingers up and under his chin before putting out his hand.

Marsh dropped the coins onto the open palm.

There was a noise upstairs – it sounded like a large package had been dropped onto a wooden floor – and then footsteps, faltering, uncertain, the rhythm of an after-hours drunk. Montealto glanced upwards. ' 'scuse me, I must see to this. Look, I really don't know that girl. I've never seen 'er.'

The man turned and walked towards the back of the shop. Pausing at the door, he reached up, touched the doorframe next to his shoulder and disappeared into the darkness beyond.

As the door closed behind him, a voice called out like a whisper through cobwebs: 'Giorgio. Giorgio. *Di indula? Di indula? Helf mir. Helf mir.*'

4

The two men were hesitant, knowing that the gun was unloaded but still not knowing whether to move forward or back off.

Enjoying their indecision, Reg Miles swung the rifle from one to the other – the men flinched.

Reg smiled. 'Scrap, eh?'

'Yeah,' the Black Country man said, holding up some paperwork. 'Scrap.'

'It looks pretty good to me,' Reg said, peering down at the gun. 'Feels it too.'

'What would you know?' the other man said.

'Not much,' Reg said, 'outside the fact I've worked here a good few years and I do know good workmanship when I see it.'

'Reggie. Reggie Miles. What you doing up there playing at being a soldier-boy?'

Reg turned and looked over the top of the cab.

Arthur Shaw and his two acquaintances.

'Arthur,' Reg said.

'It's not like you, Reggie.'

'What's not?'

Shaw grinned. 'Stopping someone from going about their business, stopping them from earning a decent living.'

'I don't know what their business is.' Reg slung the rifle over his shoulder, jumped down from the lorry, shoved past the man with the starting handle and walked over to Arthur Shaw. 'What's your part in this then?'

'Part in what, Reggie?'

Reg held the rifle in front of him. 'This gun, it doesn't seem like scrap to me. Seems perfectly good, if I'm honest.'

'Know much about rifles do you, Reggie?'

'Not that much but I've done a bit of rabbiting in my time and I reckon this would shoot pretty true.'

Arthur Shaw took the rifle, held it up in the air, squinted and peered down the barrel. 'Do you know what I mean when I say the freebore's misshapen, the leade's all bubbled and the whole thing's got a bad throat? Do you? 'Cos what it means, Reggie, is that this rifle's no good for nothing, nothing but melting down. Let me tell you, give this gun to a Tommy and we may as well be putting a black cap on our heads and sending him to the gallows.'

'Really?'

'Really.'

Reg stretched out his shoulders and loosened his neck. The man with the starting handle tensed. Arthur Shaw shot him a look. The man stood back.

The Black Country man took a pace forward, a sheet of paper held tight in his right hand. Shaw glanced at him, at what he was holding. 'You got the permit there, I take it?'

'I have, Mr Shaw, I have.'

Arthur Shaw swapped the paper for the rifle. 'Put this back where it came from, eh?'

The man nodded and walked down the side of the lorry, gun in hand.

Arthur Shaw glanced at the typed sheet, turned it over, smiled and then held it out for Reg. 'See, Reggie, no problem here. None at all. None that I can see anyway. What do you think?'

Reg took the paper.

It was a BSA salvage permit, allowing scrap goods to be removed from the premises.

It was dated 22 November 1940.

It was clearly signed in green ink: *S.Byfield*.

5

The police officers walked out and into Digbeth. They headed up the High Street and were standing in the shadow of St Martin's before they spoke.

'Another fine church,' Annie Scott said, shielding her eyes and looking up.

'This one's mine,' Harry Marsh said.

'Sorry?'

'My old school's. It's where we worshipped.'

'Interesting.'

'Not very and it's not that old,' he said. 'Late 19th century, although the original was 13th century. But then that's typical of Birmingham, that is.'

'What is?'

'Ever forward,' he said. 'Even if something's old and decent, it doesn't mean we can't tear it down and replace it with something new and not as good. It's our one major flaw.'

'Just the one?'

Marsh laughed. 'That we admit to.'

The policewoman turned to look at Harry Marsh. 'You're really quite cynical, I think.'

He smiled and shrugged. 'Not true, I'm more a pragmatic optimist, actually. Shall we sit a minute?'

They sat on a stone bench beneath a tree, close to the south wall of the church.

'Cake?' Harry Marsh said, holding out the paper bag from Montealto's shop.

As they ate, the sweet creaminess of the porridge-like cake giving way to an aftertaste of lemon, a man walked across in front of them. He wore an old green trench-coat, belted at the waist with a length of rope and a beaten-up, shapeless fedora. Pages of newspaper protruded above the rim of his boots, wrapping themselves around his trouser cuffs and a hessian sack dangled from his left hand. The sack swung as he moved, the low point of each swing striking the pavement with a clank. The man looked over and nodded, Harry Marsh nodded back.

'It's a disgrace,' Annie Scott said.

'What is?'

'That,' she said, inclining her head towards the tramp. 'Surely he can do better for himself than this?'

For a moment, Marsh felt a need to correct this young woman, to explain to her that not everything in life comes as readily to everyone else as it does to some but only for a moment. He caught himself, remembering how old she was and quite how he'd been twenty years ago.

Twenty-two years ago.

How he had believed that a life lived was a matter of self-determination and then his discovery that all life – no matter how high or low born – was prey to the wild caprices of chance and good fortune. In the trenches, death made no exception for class, breeding, talent or wealth – it was the great leveller. And who it visited at any particular time could not be affected by connection or by influence, it simply arrived. There was no possible argument, no running away, no negotiation – there was just luck and that luck was an almost tangible line between life and death.

And how luck had delivered him both to Jeannie all those years past and a fight in a pub's backyard just two nights gone. A fight which for incomprehensible reasons had set events in motion that were beyond his control. Reasons he now needed both to uncover and to understand, if he was ever to regain any sense of agency in his own life.

Harry Marsh watched the tramp turn the corner and disappear from sight. 'You don't know anything about him,' he said.

Taken aback by Marsh's harsh tone, the policewoman glanced across. 'I'm sorry?'

'Maybe he prefers it this way. No home, no ties, no one to judge him or pass comment on his habits. Free to live his life as he wants to, free to live without commitment or condemnation.'

'Are you saying I judged him?'

'I am.'

Annie Scott blew air out of her mouth and Harry Marsh was reminded of a startled goldfish in a glass bowl. It was as if she was unused to criticism – maybe she was.

'Pity,' she said, 'it was pity I was expressing.'

'With just a little condemnation.'

The policewoman inhaled, paused, exhaled. 'Yes, maybe,' she said. 'Maybe you're right.'

'I am right.'

'Are you always so smug?'

'Only when I'm right.' He paused. 'And I'm always right.'

Annie Scott laughed. 'You're a funny man, Sergeant Marsh. Cynical – and I'm sticking with that – but funny.'

Harry Marsh pushed a final morsel of cake into his mouth. 'Polenta, isn't it?'

'Polenta?'

'The cake?'

The constable stopped, nibbled, nodded. 'Yes, I would say so.'

Marsh brushed crumbs off his collar. 'Thought as much. My dad, he was a baker and he experimented with it years ago. His customers never really got a taste for it so he stopped trying but this is good. I like the lemon too, gives it a proper edge.'

Annie Scott stared down at her feet and then up at Harry Marsh. 'The dead girl, there was polenta cake in her stomach.'

Marsh nodded. 'There was.'

'Made by Adelina Bolzano and sold by Montealto?'

The DS nodded again. 'Possibly. Did you notice Signora Bolzano's bread shelf, by any chance?'

'I did.'

'It was labelled with the word *panis*. And those things on the tray beneath the glass, the stuffed squares...'

'Ravioli. They're layers of filled pasta.'

'Not *turtre*? They were labelled *turtre.*'

Annie Scott shook her head. 'Definitely ravioli. I'm not sure what *turtre* means, it's not a word I know.'

'Fair enough.'

The policewoman stared at Marsh. 'I feel somewhat left behind.'

Harry Marsh smiled. 'Don't worry, it'll come to you.'

Annie Scott folded what was left of her cake into the paper bag and pushed it into her handbag, which she clipped shut and then looked over at Marsh. '*Panic* and *turtle*?'

'Exactly. Send a child out shopping, you might write stuff you don't want forgotten on her hand. What we thought were *panic* and *turtle* were actually *panis* and *turtre.*'

'Bread and ravioli, a shopping list.'

'Precisely.'

Annie Scott shook her head. 'But those words aren't Italian. I don't know what they are but they're not Italian.'

Harry Marsh got to his feet. 'Tell me, are there many Jews in Italy?'

'Jews in Italy? I don't know. I know Venice has a synagogue and a whole Jewish area, I've seen it, Rome too, I believe. Why this sudden interest in Italy's Jewish population?'

'When Montealto went into the shop's backroom, he reached up and touched the door frame. And all good Jews have a prayer scroll attached to the door frames of every living room in their house.'

'A *mezuzah*. Which they touch when they pass.'

'Yes.'

'I didn't notice,' the policewoman said, her tone terse, cross with herself, annoyed that she had missed something so obvious.

Again.

'I did, so don't worry,' Marsh said. 'Did you hear the voice that called out to him as he walked away? What did you make of that?'

'It was faint. Barely audible, actually.'

Marsh smiled. 'What did you hear?'

'I heard *Giorgio* and then, I don't really know. *Di indula* maybe? And *helf mir*?'

'Is any of that Italian?'

'*Di indula*? I don't think so. Almost certainly a Romance language similar to Italian but not, I think, Italian.'

Harry Marsh laughed.

'What's so funny?' she said.

'*Almost certainly a Romance language similar to Italian but not, I think, Italian*, that's what.'

The young woman paled, looked away, looked back. 'I don't like being teased,' she said, her words uninflected, just simple and direct.

Harry Marsh raised his hands, both in defence and surrender. 'I'm sorry. I didn't mean to cause offence, I really didn't.'

'Then what?'

The DS grinned. 'It's just that I can't imagine Ray ever having said something like that. He just wouldn't. He was never that...' he searched for the word, 'precise. Precise is probably the best way to put it.'

'What would he have said?'

'*It's all Latin and Greek to me, Harry*, or something along those lines.'

Annie Scott's expression changed. 'Ladin,' she said, rubbing a gloved hand across her forehead. 'Ladin, it could be Ladin.'

'What?'

'*Di indula* – it could be Ladin.'

'And what's Ladin?'

'It's a dialect spoken in north-east Italy, very close to the Austrian border. Some Italians up there speak German too. And *helf mir* is German for *help me*, that I do know. What *di indula* means, I'm not sure. We were looking for one common language when actually what we heard was one man speaking two different languages.'

Harry Marsh moved away, turned and looked back at Annie Scott. 'I think we need to have another chat with Signor Montealto and his house guest.'

'Montealto not Bolzano?'

'Definitely Montealto. First off, he didn't really look at the girl's photograph before saying he didn't know her – it could have been a picture of Madeleine Carroll for all the notice he took – and second, I don't see any need for a shopping list if you live above the shop in question, do you?'

The policewoman nodded. 'I think you're right – again.'

6

Reg Miles looked at the signature, confused, disappointed, pained, as if he'd bitten into something sweet only to find it was off.

Arthur Shaw smiled, stepped forward, reached for the permit. 'Seems you're not the only one who's got friends upstairs, eh, Reggie?'

Reg let the paper slip from his fingers. Shaw passed it back to the Black Country man. 'Keep this safe, would you?'

The man nodded.

'And get off with you, there's people waiting.'

'Right you are, Mr Shaw, we'll be off right away.'

Reg and Shaw watched as the tarp was dragged back into place and fastened down. The Black Country man got into the cab and the Brummie-Irishman applied himself to the starter handle. Whatever he'd done under the bonnet minutes earlier worked and the engine caught on the third turn. Even so, as it moved forward, the engine had an arrhythmic clatter.

Shaw put a hand on Reg's shoulder and pulled him to one side, back against the wall. The Wolf moved past them, belching out smoke like a bronchitic dragon.

'Enterprise, eh, Reggie? What a thing it is. Not even a war can stop men when it comes to business. Some might even say it's good for business.'

The truck disappeared around the corner and coughed its way into the distance.

Shaw moved around and stood in front of Reg, peering up at the big man. His two sidekicks maintained a distance and watched on but even at some yards off, Reg felt the threat of their presence – a presence like a fire biding its time in a cavity wall, ready and waiting to explode outwards, without warning.

'You really are a strange one, Reggie,' Shaw said, backing away and moving further down the alley. 'I can't fathom you out, not at all. Not one little bit.'

'Nothing to fathom.'

Shaw's two men were closer now, manoeuvring Reg forward, moving him on just like a pair of collies he'd once seen at a Bingley Hall dog show, steering sheep into a pen.

Or maybe wolves isolating an ageing deer and moving in for the kill.

'No hidden depths then, Reggie. No secrets? No itches that need scratching from time to time? I don't believe that. There's got to be something. Something somewhere. There's always something. There always is.'

Arthur Shaw disappeared around a corner and Reg could do nothing but follow, the two henchmen saw to that. And now they were all standing in a small, narrow alley, high brick walls on three sides and only one way out.

More importantly – more worryingly – they were cut off from any chance of being spotted by passersby.

For the first time in a long time, Reg Miles felt scared of something other than anything that fell from the sky or burnt across the earth. He wiped sweat from his brow and loosened his collar. 'Don't reckon there is,' he said. 'Not with me, leastways.'

Shaw pouted. 'Fair enough. So, what you're saying is what I see with you, that's what I get? Is that it?'

Reg nodded once. 'Guess so.'

'And what about other people? What do other people get?'

'I don't know what you mean.'

'Other people. That lovely wife of yours and that kid, what's her name? Elizabeth Margaret, that's her name, isn't it? That little buttercup of yours, Elizabeth Margaret?'

Reg frowned – where was this going? 'That's her name,' he said.

Shaw smiled. 'See? I've been asking around. Finding out things, satisfying my natural curiosity.'

'Well, I hope you're satisfied.'

Arthur Shaw grimaced. 'Not really, more disappointed, in truth.'

'Disappointed? With what?'

'With you.'

'Me? Why?'

Shaw dug out a packet of cigarettes from a pocket, pointed them at Reg. Reg shook his head. Shaw stuck one to his own lips. 'You got a light?'

Reg stared down at the man. He could sense the fire in the wall was getting impatient.

Shaw smiled. 'I know you have. I gave you that nice lighter only the other night. The night you and me had that chat. You remember that, don't you? I'll be offended if you don't.'

Without saying a word, Reg pushed two fingers into his breast pocket, pulled out the lighter and handed it over. The other man lit up and reaching out, shoved the lighter back into the big man's jacket.

'See,' Shaw said, 'a few questions here and there, I know everything I need to know about you. About you and your family. Everything.'

'And?'

Shaw drew on his cigarette, blew smoke up and into Reg's face. 'You know what people love more than talk? They love gossip. And why do they love gossip? They love to see people cut down to size, that's why, 'specially if the people getting cut down are high and mighty. Or think they are. Those that think they're better than the rest of us, people love to see them fall. That's why those Sunday rags do so well, that is. Nasty, mean gossip. People love it.'

'I don't.'

'No, you wouldn't.' Shaw said, laughing and dropping his cigarette to the floor, treading it out. 'But then you're a bit high and mighty yourself, aren't you, Reggie Miles? A little bit high and mighty you are.'

'Not really.'

'But you think you're better than the rest of us, don't you? Why else would you take yourself off to Byfield? Why else would you want a word with him if you didn't think you were better than, well, let's say, me, for example?'

Reg turned and started to walk away and then stopped – Shaw's two friends were stood shoulder to shoulder, blocking his exit.

Arthur Shaw moved up close behind him.

'You know what they say, Reggie: a bad wound heals but a bad word doesn't.'

Reg half-turned and peered over his shoulder. 'And what's that meant to mean?'

'Exactly what it says, Reggie, exactly what it says.'

'I don't know what you're on about but I don't have to stop here and listen.'

Shaw laughed. 'I know plenty of people who will listen though. Listen to everything I've got to say about you and how you carry on.'

'How I carry on?'

'What was it? *Grave robbing*, wasn't that how you described it? Yes, it was, that was exactly what you called it.' Shaw sniggered. 'Well, when people learn how you've been profiting from other people's suffering...' He shook his head. 'Let's just say, I wouldn't want to be you when word gets out as to exactly who you are really. No, I wouldn't.'

Reg swivelled around, found his right arm raised in the air, his fist clenched.

And then the one named Baz moved in and caught his arm, while the second man kicked at the back of Reg's knees, collapsing him forward, forcing him to the ground.

Baz twisted Reg's arm up and behind his back and pushed his face into the dirt. Reg felt gravel tear at his skin and in his peripheral vision, saw a leg swing back – he braced himself for impact.

Arthur Shaw raised a hand and the boot never came.

Kneeling down in front of Reg, Shaw smiled the smile of a beneficent traveller, one fortunate enough to bestow favours on the less blessed. 'And if that doesn't work, see, that thing about wounds and words, it's not just about real wounds and words, not really. Words can wound, yes, they can, 'cos bad things said about you, they can really hurt and you wouldn't want that now, Reggie, you really wouldn't.' He tapped his chest, just over his heart. 'But wounds can be in here too. Maybe the worst wounds. You hear about that poor girl, Reggie?'

Reg coughed, spat phlegm the best he could. It pooled on the ground in front of his nose. 'Which one?'

'The one they found under the door, just up from you, wasn't it? Just up and around where you live. You see, I know that too, I really do know where you live.'

Reg craned his neck, stared up at Shaw. 'I heard about her.'

'Nasty story. Sad. Poor child, dying like that.'

'Yeah, it is sad.'

Shaw nodded and put a hand on Reg's right shoulder. Despite a burning pain which ran from his neck and into his right arm, Reg turned and glared at the hand.

'I heard no one knows who she is,' Shaw said.

'I heard that too.'

'So sad that, don't you think?'

'I do.'

'But so much sadder if you know who she is, if she's part of your family. If she's your daughter.' Shaw pulled out his cigarettes, reached forward, retrieved the lighter from Reg's pocket and stood. 'You think about that, Reggie, you think how sad that would be if it was your daughter under that door. Now that's a proper wound, however you look at it. Well, not a proper physical wound but painful all the same. One it's going to take some time to get over, if ever. You think about that before you go taking yourself upstairs again, Reginald Miles, you think about that.'

Reg grunted and tried to stand.

Baz tightened his grip.

Shaw lit up and put the lighter back into his own pocket. 'I'll be taking this back, eh, Reggie? I'm sure you won't mind.'

Reg struggled against Baz's grip, managed to push himself up and onto to his knees.

The second man moved in and punched Reg in the face. As his neck cracked and he tumbled forward, Reg Miles saw white flowers blossom in purple star fields and then fade to dull mauve.

Followed by a timeless black nothing.

Unconscious, unyielding, unending.

7

Harry Marsh scanned the frontage. The window was shuttered, the door locked, the store closed. On the first floor, a net curtain flapped up and around an open window but there was no indication of life. Nothing to suggest that there would be a response, any response, should he knock.

Turning, he rejoined Annie Scott. She stood in the middle of the street, watching the curtain twist in the wind, furling and unfurling. She looked at Marsh without dropping her head. 'Anything?'

'Not a thing,' he said. 'As quiet as the tomb. What's that?'

'What's what?'

'That,' Harry Marsh said, pointing at the shutters over the shop window.

'Oh yes,' Annie Scott said, narrowing her eyes. 'Something's been painted on the shutter and then scrubbed out.'

'I agree.'

'What does it say?'

'Looks like five letters. The first's a *J*, the middle one's a *D* and the last is definitely *N*.'

'*Juden*,' Annie Scott said, 'it says *Juden*, that's German for—'

'I know what *Juden* means,' Marsh said, with a scowl, remembering those fellow officers, a few years back, who'd been to the Bingley Hall one night and returned marching to Mosley's tune of conspiracy, blood, soil and antisemitism. Weak men, persuadable men, men who'd believe any word said to them as long as it came packaged in an Upper-Class accent.

Annie nodded. 'What next?'

Harry Marsh pointed at the passageway that ran down the side of the shop. 'Shall we?'

Annie Scott followed Marsh across the road. The passage smelt of urine and she dabbed the back of a glove to her nose.

The police officers emerged into a large communal courtyard. The brick walls were whitewashed. The wash was peeling off in patches, either through exposure to direct sunlight or where it had been applied over damp brickwork – the damp, the result of blocked guttering and badly maintained downpipes. There was a wooden privy in one corner and in the other, next to a set of wooden gates, an upright pump tap and a large stone water trough. The trough was empty apart from tendrils of green slime at one end, directly beneath the tap.

They walked to the grocery store's rear entrance. Three steps led up to the door, a half-glazed affair with six small glass windows, each painted black.

There was a cellar entrance next to the steps, its wooden doors closed and padlocked, the padlock freshly oiled.

Harry Marsh mounted the steps and raising a hand, knocked on the back door.

There was no answer.

He knocked again, paused and listened, then turned the door handle.

Locked.

'What are we going to do now?' Annie Scott said.

'I'd say this glass looks a little bit damaged, wouldn't you?' Marsh said, pulling out Billy-Boy. Wrapping his right hand around the cosh, he tapped one leather end smartly on the lower-left glass window above the door handle. There was a crack and a tinkle. Marsh bent forward, pushing his free hand through the shattered pane.

'A little unorthodox,' the policewoman said.

Marsh shrugged and pocketed his cosh. 'Bomb cracked the window, most likely.'

'How fortunate for us.'

There was a click. 'Got it,' Marsh said, with a smile. He pushed the door open and went in.

Annie Scott followed.

The back room was part-storeroom, part-sitting room, part-kitchen. A couple of sacks were propped up against the wall closest to the shop. One was a sack of dried beans, one a half-sack of rice.

In the other part of the room, there was an old armchair and a small side table in front of an open range. A pipe, its bowl round and squat like a cooking pot, lay on the table next to a book. The book was in Italian and by someone called Pellegrino Artusi.

There was a smell of coffee and old tobacco in the air. For once, Marsh didn't find the smoke objectionable. Somehow, in this room, it was comforting, almost reassuring, suggesting that despite all the chaos in the world, some lives carried on as they always had and that at some point in the future all lives would be this way again.

Could be this way again, the caprice of man willing.

Directly above their heads, booted feet walked across wooden floorboards.

Annie Scott turned to look at Marsh, head tilted, eyes raised, question obvious. The DS nodded and the policewoman walked across the room to the door at the foot of the stairs. She reached out and eased the door open, carefully, methodically, half-expecting its old hinges to betray her at any time, without warning.

Marsh joined her and they peered up the steps into the dark gloom of the next floor.

In the quiet, they could hear music.

A gramophone.

A voice humming over a fiddle and piano backing.

Marsh stepped forward, put his foot on the bottom step.

The wood twisted and squealed.

He looked at Annie Scott and pulled a face.

Upstairs, the needle clattered and wailed across several grooves, like a pig squealing its last.

Harry Marsh loped up the stairs, two treads at a time, no longer caring who heard him. Annie Scott followed.

The first landing was deserted. The only sign of life, the same aroma of coffee and tobacco as downstairs.

To their left, there was a small room, no more than a junk room, containing two broken chairs, an old table and a roll of tatty carpet.

In front of them, the room that looked out over the main street, window open, curtain now still. Through the doorway, they could see a bed, a broken-down armchair and a small table, pushed back against the wall. A Bakelite wireless shaped like a bullet, with a large circular dial surrounded by a disc of orange and two matching orange knobs – one for tuning, one for volume – sat on the table. Next to it, a small, empty coffee cup.

Further down the landing, there was another set of stairs, leading up to the top of the house.

Harry Marsh raised a finger to his lips and headed towards the stairs. He realised the gesture was unnecessary as soon as he made it – their presence wasn't exactly unknown – and he felt foolish, like a young child leading a playmate on some pretend top-secret mission, only to realise that they were being watched from the house by amused adults.

As the officers emerged into the attic, Montealto stood in front of them, his arms crossed in resistance, although his face acknowledged defeat.

There was a gramophone on the floor to his left – the disc still spinning, the needle arm yanked upwards and outwards – and a small dresser and stool to his right. Three shirts were hanging from an improvised clothes line, which ran from the dresser to one of the attic's cross-beams and two candles guttered on the dresser's surface. An old rag doll sat on the floor, propped upright against a stool leg. A pair of heavy brocade curtains hung behind Montealto, cutting the room in half. Their edges overlapped and puckered like pursed lips.

The grocer glanced over at the dresser and made a move towards it.

Marsh shook his head. 'No,' he said, 'stay where you are, please.'

Montealto stepped back and pressed himself against the curtains.

Without saying a word, Harry Marsh walked to the dresser.

Montealto watched him all the way, willing the policeman to stop but realising that they were all powerless to do anything other than what they now did.

Così è sempre stato, e così sarà per sempre.

Thus has it always been, thus shall it always be.

That's how it was with people like this, Montealto knew that – unstoppable, unrelenting, inevitable.

Harry Marsh lifted a picture frame from behind the burning candles and removed the thin muslin cloth that covered it. A small silver chain slid from within the folds of the material and fell to the dresser's top, where it landed with a clink.

Marsh examined the photograph.

A young mother and her two children, one maybe eight, the other no more than two, all three alive with a piercing vivacity, which both filled and overflowed the frame.

The policeman caught his breath – even at the age of two, the younger girl's face was unmistakable. And the frock worn by the older girl, he knew it would bear a tag that read *Made in Germany*.

Marsh turned the frame around in his hands and showed it to Annie Scott.

The policewoman leant in, looked, frowned and nodded.

Replacing the photograph on the dresser, the DS picked up the item that had fallen from the cloth. It was a Star of David suspended on a chain thin and delicate enough to sit around a young girl's neck. Again, he showed the piece to Annie Scott and then looked back at the grocer. 'Observant but not orthodox, Mr Montealto.'

Montealto appeared confused. 'Sorry?'

'You burn Shabbat candles but you keep store on Shabbat itself,' Marsh said.

Montealto shrugged. 'Not all the world shares my faith and who am I to deny my neighbour 'is bread?'

'*Share your food with the hungry,*' the DS said, '*and bring the homeless into your house*?'

Montealto tapped his index finger on his right cheek just below his eye. 'Isaiah, yes? And why not, eh? It's as good advice as any.'

Marsh sighed, knowing one onerous task had been completed only to be replaced by another, far larger challenge. 'And exactly who would these *homeless* be?'

The curtains behind the Italian grocer opened and a second, smaller man stood there. He wore a dirty white undershirt, which stretched down and over red-striped pyjama bottoms and had a blanket around his shoulders. Even in the pale light, he looked haggard and ill. Stepping forward, he put a hand onto Montealto's shoulder, both as support for himself and as a sign of mutual consolation.

'Me,' he said, looking at the police officers, 'you talk mit me.'

SUNDAY 24 NOVEMBER 1940

Harry Marsh sat at his desk, mug in hands.

Unable to sleep, he'd risen before dawn, dressed and walked into town, leaving Jeannie undisturbed in their bed. The outside world was quiet, dark and cold. The night had brought a deep freeze, almost as if to compensate for the heat of the recent attacks. Each footstep was met with the crack of either frost or broken glass, both equally common in Birmingham's bomb-struck landscape. As Marsh walked, he blew on his hands, watched his breath condense in the air and felt quite alone in the world. He wasn't – he had Jeannie – but recent events had done little to reduce his growing sense of dislocation and an impression that the old madness was here again.

That chaos was the natural way of things.

Again.

Since joining the police, his whole professional life had been about bringing order where there was none or at least restoring some temporary semblance of order, when and wherever possible – but this latest case?

It was almost beyond human understanding, his understanding, at least.

Almost?

No, it was beyond anything he understood as human behaviour.

Especially now he knew the full story.

Harry Marsh didn't believe in evil as an external force. He believed in people and how some could perform the most heinous crime in moments of crisis and confusion, before spending the rest of their lives full of regret. There were always exceptions but they were wrong up top, rather than devil led.

Only this, this poor girl, this was something else.

Something else entirely.

This was the consequence of that old madness writ large. The madness which sparks and spreads, becomes an epidemic, a collective breakdown. A reminder that chaos *is* the natural way of things and peace, law and order just a temporary respite.

A veneer, a mask.

And a disappointment.

Having witnessed the failures of government which led to The Great War, so many had hoped for so much better in the Twenties – a different way of living, of doing things, of organising the world. But the world at large had different ideas and humanity lumbered blind and unthinking into this new disaster.

Maybe Marsh had been naive in hoping for a new kind of world back then – maybe it was the remnants of his Quaker upbringing raising false hope in him, or maybe it was the dream of a returning soldier that, after what he had witnessed, such catastrophe could never be allowed to repeat – but if he had been naive, so had many others.

So many others.

No, he wasn't alone, he knew that but his knowing was of no consolation. Not now, not right now, now faced with this.

This.

This what?

All of this, that's what.

The death of a young girl was bad enough – even in the best of years, such a case would harrow his waking hours – but the thought that certain individuals, for reasons unknown, were attempting at best to discredit him, at worse destroy him, circled his consciousness, like some predatory creature looking for a weakness, an opening, an opportunity.

Looking to catch him off guard when he least expected it.

Looking to pounce and devour him.

To render him useless.

He shook himself. Sod it: he wouldn't let that happen – he wouldn't let anyone do that to him.

Not anyone.

No one.

Marsh walked up the steps, shouldered open the doors and nodded at the duty officer behind the Steelhouse Lane station desk. 'Morning, Sarge.'

'Barely morning yet, Harry,' the sergeant said. 'In on a Sunday? What you up to?'

'You know what they say, Sarge, time and tide and all that.'

'I don't say that but I'm sure some do. I am about to pop the kettle on though, you want a cuppa?'

'Thanks, that'd be kind.'

'Only milk, I'm afraid, no sugar, not a grain to be had.'

'Just milk is fine.'

'Splendid. Won't be long. I'll fetch it through.'

'Thanks.'

'My pleasure, Harry.'

The detectives' room was cold, dark and lifeless. His alcove was even colder. He moved an electric fire as close to his desk as the flex would allow and turned it on. The top bar glowed and hissed as it burnt off the night's condensation, the air smelling both damp and scorched. He held out his hands and felt his palms begin to prickle.

Taking off his topcoat, he ran his fingers over the burns on its back and his cack-handed attempt at a repair and then draped it over his shoulders.

The sergeant appeared and passed Marsh a white mug. Recognising the look on the DS's face, he turned away, without saying a word – he could see there was thinking to be done.

'Thank you,' Harry Marsh said, as the sergeant walked across the office. 'Much appreciated.'

The policeman raised a hand. 'Any time, Harry. Oh, by the way, that barge you was asking after – the *Crown Victoria* – it moored up in Gas Street late last night.'

'Thanks, that's useful to know.'

Marsh turned to face the window. He stared out at the redbrick court buildings beyond. Not that they were red at this time of day, just black and threatening, the silhouette of their tall spires pricking an even more ominous sky.

He sniffed the mug, enjoyed its warm milky aroma. Then he took a sip of tea. He was grateful for the pleasure it brought, for the ordinariness of the moment, for the unchanging banality of it all. Such basic physical pleasures would never change and for that, thank God. He drank the tea and placed the empty mug on the wooden sill.

What to do? He took his cosh from his pocket and rotated it in his hands.

The previous afternoon, in the attic, the two men sat in silence, one on a chair, one on a bed and looked up at the two police officers. Marsh turned the framed photograph around and showed it to the men. 'Who is she?'

The unnamed man looked at Giorgio Montealto and muttered something under his breath. The shopkeeper shushed him.

'She's my niece,' Giorgio Montealto said.

Annie Scott took a pace forward. 'And does she have a name?'

'Liora,' the other man said, his voice low, weak, rough-hewed like a wind blowing itself out in a rocky ravine. 'Name ist Liora.'

Harry Marsh nodded. 'And you are?'

The man tapped his chest and coughed. 'Montealto. Carlo Montealto,' he said, in the same hoarse whisper as before. 'Her papa.'

Marsh took his PNB from his pocket. 'Sorry to be so brutal but I assume you know she's dead?'

Carlo Montealto turned to look at his brother. His expression was one of anticipation and sorrow. He reached over and tugged at Giorgio's left sleeve – a gentle, polite tug, a request not a demand. He spoke a few words under his breath which Marsh couldn't catch, in a language Marsh didn't recognise.

Giorgio stuck his head on one side, glanced at his brother from under a low brow, nodded and frowned. 'My brother 'ere, 'e doesn't speak great English. 'E speaks Italian, German, Ladin and Hebrew very well, but 'is English isn't good and 'e wants to apologise for that, alright?'

Despite the circumstances, Marsh found himself smiling: that a man should apologise for speaking four languages and not five.

Annie Scott stepped up next to the DS. 'I could—'

Marsh raised a hand. 'No, not now. I know what you're going to say but not now. I would rather you simply listened and took notes.'

Annie Scott tipped her chin in agreement. 'Very well.'

'If,' Marsh said, 'if I was to ask your brother a few questions, would you be kind enough to translate, Mr Monetalto?'

The shopkeeper nodded. 'Yes, I can do that for you.'

And he did.

A family living in the Italian Tyrol.

A Jewish family living in the Italian Tyrol.

So close to the border that the mother Judith and elder daughter Sophia travelled into Austria on a weekly basis for work and stayed in a small boarding house to save on daily travel costs. The father – Carlo – a tailor, worked at home and looked after their younger daughter, Liora.

The family were liked, loved even, by their neighbours as good, kind people who treated everyone fairly and equally.

Carlo Montealto was respected enough to serve on the local council.

And Judith and Sophia always returned to their home and family every Friday, in time for Shabbat.

Until 9 November 1938.

Kristallnacht.

Prompted by the assassination in Paris of the German diplomat Ernst vom Rath by Herschel Grynszpan, a 17 year-old German-born Polish Jew, Hitler ordered an all-out assault on the Jewish race, its places of worship and its businesses in Germany, Austria and the Sudetenland.

That night, led by the SA and the Hitler Youth, pogroms raged throughout Austria and the majority of Viennese synagogues were destroyed, burnt to the ground.

The local fire services stood by, watched, did nothing.

Across the country, Jewish businesses were attacked and at best despoiled, at worst destroyed. Countless Jews were arrested and deported, some to Dachau, others to Buchenwald.

Judith and Sophia Montealto were swallowed up in the eruption of violence, never to be seen or heard from again. Whether they died that night or sometime, someplace else, Carlo never found out but he knew in his heart that they were dead.

Of that much, he was certain.

And then on 17 November, Mussolini brought in the *leggi razziali* – racial laws restricting the rights of Jews – and Carlo was removed from the council, while Liora was excluded from school.

Within twenty-four hours, the Federal Commissioner in his Fascist uniform drove through the village in his black car. The Fiduciary sat next to him, dressed in black, with gold braid on both shoulders.

The tailor and his daughter stood in their shop doorway and watched them pass, knowing that life here, as they knew it, was over.

Three sleepless nights later, there was a knock on the door.

Fearing the worst, Carlo peered through the curtains, expecting a mob with torches. Instead, it was his neighbour, a fellow councilman.

He was crouched over to avoid detection and had a package stuffed into his jacket. Carlo opened the door and invited his friend in. The man declined but held out the parcel – it was wrapped in brown paper and tied up with string. 'Please,' he said, 'leave.'

Carlo Montealto took the package and the man scuttled off, disappearing into the shadows, vanishing from sight.

Sat at the kitchen table, the tailor untied the string and let the paper fold itself open, revealing a bundle of lira and a letter:

This money, which was our money, is now your money. Take it and go. We do not want to see you go but go you must. Times are difficult now for you Jews but soon they may be much worse. You must go to this man in Zurich – there was a phone number written at the bottom of the note – *he will give you all you need to travel to your brother in England. Flee there now, not only for your sake but for that of your daughter and take not only our money but our love, too.*

There was no signature.

Carlo Montealto counted out the lira, carefully placing each note so that Mussolini was face down and Il Duce could see nothing but the dark of the table's wooden surface.

All in all, the tailor counted out 5000 lira.

His friends were generous, indeed.

The journey to Zurich involved a bus to Brixen and then trains to Verona, Milan, Chiasso and Zurich. It was a long and arduous route but at least they never once dipped into Austria. After three days in transit, they stood on the edge of Lake Zurich, watching a dark grey cloud roll down and off a far mountain, before racing across the water, bringing rain.

The tailor held his daughter's hand tightly in his own and hoped it wasn't a sign of trouble to come.

A day and a phone call later, they met a man called Peters in a café. With its brown, highly polished panelling lit by orange-shaded ceiling lamps and waistcoated table service, the café was upmarket and expensive. It occurred to Carlo Montealto that even the perfume of steam and sugar in the air was beyond the means of ordinary working folk back home – not that there appeared to be any such thing as ordinary working folk here in Zurich. No, the people he'd met so far were rude, pushy and seemed determined to have anything other than a pleasant time. Maybe it was the café prices that made them so prickly.

He ordered a glass of hot chocolate that he shared with Liora.

When he arrived, Peters listened to their request and said that he could help but of course, it would not be *inexpensive*.

Carlo smiled to himself: how could it not be, given their surroundings?

He asked how much and Peters replied that this *depended*.

Depended on what?

On whether they wanted *false-real* or *real-false papers*.

And the difference?

Peters smiled, his thick jowls shifting like ripples in aspic. 'False-real are real passports that have been chemically washed to remove all pictures and personal information. Your photograph and details are then inserted in the spaces now available. These documents are impeccable and truly undetectable.'

'And real-false?'

'These are fakes, made from scratch. Very good to all but the eagle-eyed. Unfortunately, in these times, eyesight is both worse, in that some people do not see what they wish not to, and better, in that others see what one might wish they should not.'

'And there's a difference in price?'

Peters reached across and chucked Liora's left cheek. 'What price invisibility?'

'How much?'

'For the best? 2000 francs. Each. For the not quite so good, 1500 francs.'

'In lira?'

'If we must. 865 lira or 650 lira. Again, that is for each.'

Montealto nodded, felt the package of money in his overcoat pocket, knew it would soon be so much thinner, so much lighter. He wondered how much money he would need to get both him and his daughter to England and how much would be left after their travel papers had been purchased. 'Is this your best price? I only ask because, well, I must ask.'

Peters laughed. 'I am afraid to say that yes, it is.'

Carlo looked at Liora. She was chewing a sugar cube and running a finger around the edges of the paper it had been wrapped in. She sensed that she was being watched and looked up at him, licking her finger as she did. Her eyes were large, serious, curious. And then she smiled and his mind was made up.

'Yes,' he said.

Peters nodded, his multiple chins slapping up and down. 'Yes to which?'

'Yes to invisibility.'

'Very good. Do you have photographs I may use?'

'No,' Montealto said.

'This I can arrange.'

'For a fee?'

'Of course.'

Carlo Montealto nodded and reached into an overcoat pocket.

'No, not here,' Peters said, turning his head so as to cast his eyes around the café. 'It does not pay to be so forthright. You should phone me again in two days' time. I will then know if I can help you.'

'If?'

'Did I not say? In this life there must always be ifs. This is the one uncertainty that is certain. I'm sure you understand.'

The tailor wasn't sure he did.

Over the next week, flash bulbs popped, passports were rinsed and convincing travel documents produced.

Carlo Montealto was still a tailor but now he was Carlo Masiero, a Catholic from Padova in the Veneto, travelling to England to see his brother, who'd moved there in 1918.

'So nearly true, it may as well be,' Peters said, as Carlo handed over a carefully counted wedge of money, only for the big man to count the notes again, one by one, methodically licking his thumb and forefinger as he separated each from the other. 'Bon voyage et bon chance, mes petits.'

The next leg of their journey took father and daughter from Zurich to Paris by train and then, after a connection at the Gare du Nord, from Paris to Lille. From Lille, they took a train to Calais and then a boat to Dover. Dover to London had been a coach trip and then finally, another coach had brought them to Birmingham, early in February 1939.

Giorgio Montealto welcomed his brother and niece – a girl he'd never met – with open arms and father and daughter moved into the attic. For the first few months, the newly arrived pair mingled openly in Birmingham's Italian quarter but scarcely left the tightly compact streets of Digbeth. Carlo Montealto was more than aware that he and Liora had travelled on false papers and after 17 years of living in Mussolini's Italy, the last thing he wanted was to be arrested.

An arrest which would be followed by inevitable repatriation to his homeland.

Bit by bit, Giorgio found his brother pieces of suitable work: the venting of a suit now too tight after too many home-cooked meals, the turning of a wedding dress into a first communion frock, the relining of a well-loved overcoat – and Liora passed her time by either helping her father or running errands for her uncle.

Throughout all of this, the tailor was still unsettled and spent his sleepless nights tossing and turning and trying to remember how his wife and elder daughter looked, talked, smelt. Called in by Giorgio, a local doctor prescribed a sleeping draught – Veronal – which the tailor accepted with mock gratitude but never used, worried that a drugged sleep would rob him of any chance to conjure up the slightest memory of Judith or Sophia.

And then things began to change. At first the change was slow but the subsequent momentum inevitable.

On 3 September 1939, the UK declared war on Germany, following its invasion of Poland.

On 10 May 1940, Italy declared war on the Allies.

Immediately, the *Daily Mail* led a campaign to have all aliens in Britain interned – over 4000 Italians with fewer than 20 years' residence in the UK were then arrested and put into camps.

Simultaneously, across the country, angry mobs attacked Italian restaurants and ice cream parlours, while other businesses began to sack all Italian employees.

Some local authorities turned Italian tenants out of council houses.

And the front of Giorgio's store was defaced with a yellow Star of David and the word *Juden*.

That Carlo should have dragged his daughter halfway across Europe so that she could experience this, seemed to the tailor the height of God's disdain for His chosen people's mortal existence.

His dislike of His own creation.

And then in early July 1940, *U-47* sank the SS *Arandora Star*, with a single torpedo. Originally designed to carry just 500 people, the former Blue Star liner was on its way to Canada, carrying 734 interned Italian men, 479 interned German men (including a number of Jewish refugees), 86 German prisoners of war, 200 military guards and a crew of 174 officers and men.

805 people died, amongst them 486 Italians, many of them naturalised British citizens, who had been expecting to see out the war at an internment camp on the Isle of Man.

When details of the sinking and the subsequent loss of life trickled back through the Italian community by hushed and fearful word, Carlo Montealto retreated into the attic, never again to be seen in public. Despite her father's qualms, Liora still ran errands for her uncle.

In November, the bombings started and each and every night Carlo prayed that the next bomb would deliver him and his daughter from this *emek habacha*, this *vale of tears*. One night, when his brother was out playing cards and convinced that God would not even offer him, Carlo, this one small mercy, he chose to take matters into his own hands. Creeping downstairs, he took two polenta cakes from the counter. The cakes were a day old and chewy but still edible.

Next, he made two glasses of hot chocolate. He laced both with his sleeping draught and took his tray of offerings upstairs to the first-floor room, where his daughter lay on the bed, listening to the wireless.

Liora ate her cake, drank her chocolate and fell asleep.

Once she was away, Carlo shut the door, spread a towel across its bottom edge, turned on the fire's gas tap and put a cushion over his daughter's face. He knelt next to her and rested his head and shoulders across the cushion, his tears soaking into its thin cotton cover.

He drank his chocolate and closing his eyes, waited for death.

The next thing he remembered was waking up to see his brother leaning over him, his face out of focus, half-formed, as if distorted through greased glass. That and a cold breeze blowing in and across the room from a newly opened window.

'Liora?' The weakness of his own voice shocked Carlo Montealto.

His brother shook his head and turned away, a hand half-raised in sorrow and dismissal.

Later, at the height of that evening's bombing raid, Giorgio took Liora's body through blacked-out back streets and hid it under a door in the garden of an abandoned house. It wasn't a particular house and not one he'd chosen with any purpose, other than it was far enough from home and the first one he came across which best suited his needs.

Best suited *their* needs.

Hopefully, his niece would be taken as a victim of the bombings and that would be that.

About to lay the door down, he reached forward and tore the Star of David from around her neck – the fewer people who knew she was Jewish, the more chance her body would be treated with respect.

An hour earlier, holding back his tears, he hadn't known what else to do and had convinced Carlo that it was better the authorities tend to her now.

Still delirious, half alive, half dead, Carlo had agreed.

And now, back in the attic, standing in front of the two police officers, tears staining the cheeks of both brothers, the grocer shook his head in disbelief. 'It's all true,' Giorgio Montealto said, 'I'm so sorry but it's all true.' He raised his hands to his face and wiped his cheeks.

High above Birmingham, the clouds opened.

MONDAY 25 NOVEMBER 1940

1

Annie Scott appeared at his desk. 'Good morning.'

Marsh glanced up – she looked anxious.

'Sit down,' he said, 'please, sit down.'

The policewoman pulled out the chair, sat. She seemed tired, her face puffy, her eyes swollen, as if she hadn't slept for weeks.

Or she was on the point of tears, constantly.

He knew the feeling.

'How are you, Annie?'

'Shocked, maybe.' She hesitated. 'I don't know, actually. I really don't know. I don't have the words.'

'Me neither, if it's of any comfort. I mean, I don't know how I am, not that I don't know how you are. Which I don't, of course. And I certainly don't have the words. Not good ones, anyway.'

She smiled, appreciating his levity, or at least his attempt at it. 'May I ask, have you started your report?'

He shook his head. 'No,' he said, 'I haven't.'

'But you should, you must.'

'We haven't even made an arrest yet.'

'No, we haven't,' she said, her disapproval faint but obvious.

'Way I see it,' Marsh said, 'he's not capable of going anywhere, not the way he is and I reckon we'd need a stretcher to get him moved. So why not leave him in situ for the moment?' He stared at her, waiting, maybe hoping, for a challenge to his authority – she dropped her head in disapproval but none came.

The desk phone rang. Both Harry Marsh and Annie Scott glared at it, as if was an unexpected and unwelcome interloper at a funeral tea.

'I'd better get that,' the DS said. 'Marsh...What? No, I see...Well, it's quite ridiculous...Absolutely absurd...No, of course, I completely understand, I'll come over now...' He looked at Annie Scott. 'Yes, Assistant Lady Enquiry Officer Scott-Taylor is with me.'

Marsh replaced the receiver and stared down at his desk.

'What is it?'

'Seaborne wants to see us.'

'Why? Has he heard something about Saturday?'

Marsh frowned. 'No, it's to do with Noble.'

'Who?'

'A young copper from Moseley who made a complaint about me last week. He's been beaten up, he's in hospital and he's telling anyone who'll listen that I put him there.'

The hospital building rose high in the morning air. Broad and pale and angular, its frontage suggested a modernist, recently planted tombstone, or maybe a freshly scrubbed mausoleum. Many local residents weren't convinced it was the best look for a hospital but most conceded it was at least an honest one.

Harry Marsh and Annie Scott walked up the steps to the front doors, in silence. The young woman wasn't sure if words were required and if they were, what line of conversation would be most appropriate. She couldn't imagine the thoughts that were running through Marsh's head, how his emotions must be churning – what with Saturday's revelations and then the further accusations this morning.

After Seaborne's brief outline of the new charge made against Marsh and a request – no, an instruction – that she accompany him, the pair had hardly exchanged a word since standing in front of the DI an hour and a half earlier.

'Give me one good reason,' Seaborne had said, 'one good reason not to suspend you here and now.'

'Because it's not true,' Marsh had said.

Seaborne had laughed. 'Christ, I know that, Marsh. I know what sort of copper you are and I know this isn't you. But something's going on here and I need to know exactly what.'

'Believe me, sir, so do I.'

'Give me something, Marsh. Anything. Tell me everything you know and don't beat about the bush. I can't afford to lose your crew, you know how tight things are round these parts. What with Ray Hancock being stupid enough to get himself killed. Now getting shot of you? That can't happen. Problem is, this goes any further, you're out and there's nothing I can do about it. The Super will insist. He hears about this, any of this and he will insist, mark my words, Marsh, mark my words.'

'Give me the day, sir,' Marsh had said. 'Just today. If I can't sort this out by tonight, you'll no doubt do what you need to do. What the Super needs you to do.'

'Damn right I will.' Seaborne had sat back down, nodded once, glanced up. 'One day. And take Scott-Taylor here with you. Whatever you do today, make sure you've got a witness. We wouldn't want anything else to come along and run us both off the road now, would we?'

Inside, the hospital reception area was broad and light. There was a first-floor balcony on three sides, each side fronted by a six-rung railing, the top rung of which was made of brass.

'It looks like the observation deck on the Queen Mary,' Annie Scott said.

'I wouldn't know,' Marsh said. 'Only been on two boats: first time in steerage, second time in bandages.'

At reception, they were directed to a ward at the far end of the hospital.

As suggested, they took the lift and then walked side by side down a long, bright corridor, its whiteness almost painful to the eye. The doorways off the corridor were also white and blended near hermetically into the walls. There was an odour of medication and cleaning fluid in the air, the aroma of modernity, efficiency, efficacy.

'Should we be here?'

'Probably not.'

'And you mean to talk with the officer?'

'I do.'

'Inspector Seaborne wouldn't approve, surely?'

'I doubt he would but he didn't say no.'

'You didn't say you were intending to interview Noble.'

'Not in so many words, no.'

'Not in any words.'

Halfway along, they came to a row of phone booths. Harry Marsh stopped and opened the cantilevered door to the first booth. 'I need to make a couple of calls,' he said, disappearing inside and pulling the door across behind him.

Annie Scott leant against the wall and waited.

Marsh started speaking, his words a distant thrum and blur.

The policewoman looked up as a man in a wheelchair was pushed past.

Catching her eye, he grinned in an absentminded way: maybe he was imagining her presence and she wasn't real. His gummy smile was toothless and the lower lids of his eyes were red, distended and folded forward and down. He reminded her of a long-gone family dog, who in its later years had suffered from diamond-eye and hip dysplasia. Her parents had let the dog groan and moan on well beyond any measure of a good life, only for it to die, one morning, nose down in its breakfast bowl.

'Worse ways to go, I suppose,' her father had said, hiding a guilt that was to follow him to his grave.

The policewoman hoped this old man's twilight years were more enjoyable than those of her family dog. Or if not exactly enjoyable, at least pain-free.

Marsh ended his first call by clacking his hand down on the cradle several times and then redialled.

Turning her head, Annie Scott listened closely but could hear no more of this new conversation than the previous one.

Who was he calling?

And why here?

Why now?

He must have his reasons but if he did, he wasn't saying. At least not to her and she wanted to know.

Needed to know.

Felt she deserved to know.

After all, here they were, about to visit Robert Noble. Personally, she was not convinced that they should be here at all and hoped that her association with Harry Marsh – and any ongoing investigation into his actions, including his failure to arrest a self-confessed guilty man and his willing accomplice – would not damage her professionally.

Dismissing her thoughts as both unworthy and selfish, she remembered her initial assessment of Marsh as decent and honest. Despite what he had said about not judging people on appearance, Annie Scott was confident in her ability to weigh up people with a fine degree of accuracy, after only a brief time in their company. It was one of the things she believed made her a good police officer.

And Marsh was a good police officer, of that she had no doubt.

A good man, too.

The phone's handset was replaced with a final thump and the booth door opened. 'Come on,' Harry Marsh said, 'let's go and see our man.'

2

All Reg Miles could think about was a soak in the tub and then falling into bed. Sleep would come soon after, he was sure of that – even if when he first closed his eyes, all he saw was fire and all he heard was the constant rhythm of a pump, pushing water up and into the air.

That and the smell of smoke.

Always the smell of smoke.

No raids since early Friday but no escape from the thoughts that ran through his head, through his dreams either.

And now between all of this, weaving its way in and around everything, like a rat escaping from a dog through a wicker fence, there was the image of Byfield and the need to tell him what had happened on Saturday.

The need to ask if what had happened – what Reg had witnessed, what he'd been shown – was real, legal, sanctioned.

If it was all to the good, even if his beating said otherwise.

But if Byfield was part of the scam then confronting the man was the worst thing he could do.

Wasn't it?

Or was it?

Reg didn't know anymore. Wasn't sure he would ever have known, no matter his present circumstances. He hated the fact that his normal equivalence was now so thrown out of balance.

Last Saturday, after Shaw and his men had gone, after he'd come round, after the shift was over, Reg had made his way upstairs, up into the deserted offices and corridors, their emptiness the real distinction between workers and managers – the former impelled and conditioned to work on a Saturday for the good of all, the latter nowhere to be seen.

What was that old Commonwealth poster?

Together, that was it.

Together.

Fat chance.

Nevertheless, despite all his reservations, Reg had never had any other choice than to sit down at Byfield's secretary's desk and scrawl out a note: *About what we discussed, I need to see you Monday, R. Miles.*

Anodyne enough to conceal intent, intriguing enough to demand attention.

Shoving the folded paper under Byfield's locked inner door, he'd left the site, all the time certain that he was being watched.

Sunday, he'd sat in his chair – bruises and scratches explained away as nothing more than an accident at work – nursing a headache and stayed there all day, not moving an inch between Agnes and Elizabeth Margaret leaving for chapel and later returning home.

Not an inch.

'Mr Miles,' a voice said, 'you're wanted. Wanted at the gates.'

Reg turned and looked at the boy Saul, standing next to him. 'What?'

'It's your missus, says she needs to see you urgent like.'

Agnes? What was she doing here? She was on nights again this week, she should be at home, catching up on her sleep.

But at the gates, it wasn't just Agnes, Nell was there as well – the two women standing close, arms linked, mutual support. Agnes stared at Reg as he walked across, her expression feral, desperate, a cornered animal about to turn on its attacker.

'What is it?' he said, already knowing the answer and feeling his stomach tighten.

'It's Emmy.'

'What about her?'

'The school,' Agnes said, her voice choked, 'they haven't seen her since Nell dropped her off.'

Reg reached out but Agnes shook his hands away.

'What's happened? Where is she then?'

'That's what we'd like to know, exactly what we'd like to know,' Nell said. 'Elizabeth Margaret left her reading book at mine this morning and when I fetched it to school, she was nowhere to be found.'

Reg looked at his wife, said the first thing that came into his head: 'And how are you?'

Agnes scowled: stupid question, no answer required.

None offered.

3

The doors to the ward were tall and semi-glazed, the glass panels set into dark polished wood and transected by horizontal chrome rails. Beyond, the ward was light and bright, with its blackout blinds folded back and its main illumination coming from a large floor-to-ceiling window. The space was clean, clinical, cool, somewhere to rest and recuperate and so unlike the hastily converted rooms in which Harry Marsh had found himself in 1918.

A nurse stood at a square table in the middle of the ward, carelessly arranging flowers, filling time, waiting for her next real job. She looked up, turned and walked towards them, her low heels clacking rhythmically on the herringbone parquet floor. 'Yes?' she said. 'May I help?'

Her uniform was, like the ward, contemporary in its line and cut, her hat and veil tidy and practical. This young woman looked far less like the Edwardian lady volunteer that Jeannie had appeared to be when Harry Marsh first saw her – was first able to see her – and much more like the medical professional she obviously was.

Up close, she smelt of soap and antiseptic. Marsh found this curiously reassuring and it helped calm his nerves – nerves that always jangled when entering a hospital ward, even as a visitor.

He nodded. 'I hope so. Robert Noble – I believe he's on this ward.'

'And you are?'

'Marsh. Harry Marsh. Detective Sergeant Harry Marsh. This is Policewoman Scott.'

'I see. Is he expecting you?'

'Do we need an appointment?'

'Well,' the nurse said, 'it's not strictly visiting hours.'

Annie Scott smiled at the nurse. 'He's a colleague. A close colleague,' she said, implying a certain intimacy. 'And the sergeant and I, we've been on duty all weekend. You know how it is? Duty calls and all that. Professional before personal. Especially now.'

The nurse smiled back, a confidence shared. 'Do I ever.'

'Well,' Marsh said. 'Do we get to see him or not?'

Annie Scott nudged him with her elbow. 'Forgive DS Marsh, he's desperately worried about poor Bob.'

The nurse nodded. 'Of course, I understand. Constable Noble's fine. He's doing well, actually, considering. He took a nasty beating and his arm had to be pinned in surgery but we expect a full recovery.'

'I'd really like to see him,' Annie said.

The nurse frowned and sighed. 'Well, yes, OK. Let's say it's official business, shall we?'

Harry Marsh grunted. 'It is official business.'

The nurse looked at Marsh, her interest piqued. She wasn't sure she should let this man anywhere near her patient. She felt a light touch on her forearm, saw the policewoman's hand resting there.

'I do know this is somewhat of an imposition,' Annie said, 'but we don't have much time and I do so much want to see dear Bob.'

The nurse frowned, a scintilla of debate on her neatly tidied brow and picked at the watch hanging on her apron, next to the large red cross. 'You can have fifteen minutes,' she said, 'but no more. This way.'

As the nurse walked off, Harry Marsh caught Annie by the elbow and held her back. 'You should have warned me,' he said, in a whisper.

'Warned you about what?'

'That you were such a good liar.'

Annie Scott laughed. '*Beshrew me if I would do such a wrong for the whole world.*'

'That's Shakespeare, isn't it?'

'My Desdemona was the toast of the Fifth form.'

Marsh gestured towards the nurse, who was pulling a curtain away from around a bed, at the far end of the ward. 'Then lead on, Macduff.'

'Actually, it should be *Lay on, Macduff.*'

'*Lay into* would be more appropriate,' Harry Marsh said, walking away and down the room.

Noble looked up and opened his eyes. 'Christ,' he said, as Marsh's face came into focus. 'Christ on a crutch.' His voice slurred by a wired jaw, it sounded as if he was calling out from the next room, or performing a poor ventriloquist's act.

'Morning,' Harry Marsh said, dragging over a low metal chair with his foot and sitting down.

'You shouldn't be here,' Noble said. Annie Scott appeared over Marsh's shoulder. 'And who are you? Forget it, it don't matter anyway – neither of you, neither of you should be here. Why are you here?'

Harry Marsh smiled. 'This is Policewoman Scott. And we're just two police officers concerned about a colleague, that's all.'

Noble looked rough: pyjama jacket open displaying a concave chest, purple and yellow bruises down the whole of his right side, the evenness of their spread corrugated by his ribs.

Left arm plastered and suspended in the air by a pulley.

Both wrists encircled with dark-blue bruising.

Unshaven, his right eye was mostly closed – a blood-stained sclera all that was visible around a dilated pupil.

From his manner, it was obvious that he was on painkillers, probably morphine. Harry Marsh remembered his own experiences of morphine, how pleasant it had been and how the hankering for its other-worldly charm had been so hard to dismiss, even months after its administration was far from necessary.

DS Marsh tried to look sympathetic. 'Just a few questions, Bob,' he said. 'You don't mind if I call you Bob, do you, Bob?'

Noble raised a hand as if swatting at a non-existent fly. He was looking for the bell cord that would summon the nurse.

Marsh stretched up and moved the cord out of the man's reach, tying a loose knot in it to raise it even higher.

Noble jammed his head into the pillow, hiding his good eye. 'I don't have to talk to you. I don't. I won't. I don't and I won't. Got that?'

'No,' Harry Marsh said, 'you don't but I'd prefer it if you did. Otherwise, well, Policewoman Scott and I, we'll have wasted some of our tram tokens and that's not good, not given how things are right now. Is it, Constable?'

Annie Scott shook her head. 'No, not good at all.'

'I hear,' Marsh said, taking off his hat and laying it on the bed, 'I hear you've been telling people that I've been bad.'

Noble snorted into his pillow. 'You have. Just look at me. Proper bad, you've been, proper bad.'

Harry Marsh smiled. 'But we both know that I had nothing to do with this. It wasn't me that put you in here, was it, Bob?'

'Yeah, it was.'

The sergeant glanced over his shoulder. 'Policewoman Scott, be so good as to pull the curtains to, would you?'

Annie Scott looked at Harry Marsh with an expression of surprise and confusion: if she did what he asked, what was he planning to do next? Seemingly to answer her unasked question, the sergeant's left eye fluttered a wink that only she could see.

'Whatever you need, DS Marsh,' she said, her tone compliant if over obliging. 'I'll just stand here and keep *cave*.'

'Thank you,' Marsh said, remembering his schoolboy Latin and how *cave* – *beware* in English – would be uttered by the appointed boy, stood at the classroom door, to watch out for any and all approaching teachers.

Annie Scott drew the curtains together and stood against them, her back to the seam.

Marsh leant forward and tapped down hard on Noble's plastered arm. The constable winced. 'They've done an alright job,' Marsh said.

Noble glared at Harry Marsh. 'You've done an alright job, you mean?'

Marsh tapped the plaster again. Another wince. 'Now we both know that's not true, don't we, Bob?'

Noble shook his head. 'You did this to me, you did. You. You did.'

'No, I didn't, Bob, I really didn't.'

Noble grinned, inasmuch as he could grin. 'Your word against mine, Marsh, your word against mine.'

Marsh nodded. 'Now that's the first true thing you've said since I sat down, let's hope it won't be the last.'

Noble attempted to shrug but winced as pain radiated out from his shoulder, reaching into both neck and elbow, simultaneously. 'I've said all I'm going to say, so you better be going, you had.'

'No, not quite all, you haven't,' Marsh said. 'There's a bit more to tell yet.'

'You can't make me tell you anything.'

'No, I can't but I can make you listen.'

'You what?'

'I'll talk, you listen and then we'll see where we get to by the end.'

The man stared at him blank faced. 'Nothing to say.'

Harry Marsh rested a hand on the plastered arm, pushed down, felt the pulley give and then retract. Noble whimpered. 'Funny, isn't it?' Harry Marsh said, 'we've met just the twice but I feel I've got your measure.'

He leant down on Noble's arm again.

Noble closed his eyes and groaned.

'Odd really,' Marsh said, 'the first time we meet, you're beating someone up. A couple of blokes, actually. A couple of Irish blokes. And second time we meet, you've been on the receiving end of a solid trashing. Can't be a coincidence now, surely?'

'Think what you like.'

'I will, don't you worry.'

Harry Marsh reached over Noble's body and lifted up his right pyjama sleeve.

Noble squinted. 'What you doing?'

'This right wrist of yours, it looks sore. What'd you do to it?'

'You'd know, seeing as it must have happened when you beat me up.'

The sergeant laughed. 'You know what that looks like to me? That looks like a restraint injury.' He pushed a finger into the yellow and black flesh. Noble squirmed. 'Yes, it does. You ask me, someone's been holding you by the wrists and pinning your arms back.'

Noble grunted. 'I wouldn't know anything about that.'

Marsh nodded in admiration. 'It's a good firm grip too. You look closely, you can almost see the shape of the fingers. So firm, we might even get a dab off that.'

Noble glanced at his wrist and pulled his arm back and under the top sheet. 'You don't know what you're talking about.'

'Beautiful black eye, by the way, I'm assuming that was a punch to the face. Or a headbutt. Probably a headbutt. And your arm?' Harry Marsh tapped the plaster. 'How did this happen?'

'You kicked me. When I was on the ground, you kicked me, you did.'

Marsh shook his head. 'Did I? Bit harsh of me, that.'

'Yeah, it was.'

The sergeant picked up his hat and sat on the bed. Noble's plastered arm jiggled and settled. The man looked like he was about to throw up.

'Watch it,' Noble said, 'watch what you're doing.'

'See this?' Marsh said, holding out his right hand.

Noble nodded. 'I see it.'

'What do you see?'

'A hand.'

'And what don't you see?'

Noble pulled a face, 'What do you mean?'

'Exactly that: what don't you see?'

'It's a hand.'

Harry Marsh held out his other hand, turned it over from palm to knuckle. 'Now what do you see?'

'Apart from another hand, nothing.'

Marsh made a fist and waved it in front of Noble's eyes. 'And now?'

'Get away from me, leave me alone.'

Marsh opened his hand, tapped Noble on the cheek. 'Thing is,' Marsh said, 'if I'd beaten you up as badly as someone has beaten you up, I'd have cuts on my hands. Bruises, incisions, maybe a broken bone or two in my knuckles but what do you see? Nothing, you said so yourself.'

Noble closed his eyes. 'Maybe you wore gloves. Yeah, I remember now, you wore gloves.'

'Perhaps I did. Shall we ask the doctors?'

'Ask the doctors what?'

'Even if I wore gloves, I'd probably have a fair bit of bruising and if I hit you that hard wearing gloves, you'd expect to find some trace material in your wounds.'

'Some what?'

Harry Marsh laughed. 'And you call yourself a policeman? Trace material. Bits of whatever the gloves were made from – leather, cotton stitching, wool lining, bits like that.'

'That's not true.'

Marsh shook his head. 'Sorry but it is. You ever heard of Dr Moira Penny, by the way?'

'No.'

'She's Birmingham's best police surgeon and a leading forensic pathologist. She's also a good friend of mine. I've just given her a call and she's on her way here right now to give you the once over. I'm sure the doctors in this place are very good but they're not familiar with police procedure, why should they be? And I do want to make sure they – we – haven't missed anything. True, Moira's used to looking for evidence on dead bodies so a nice warm one should make a pleasant change.'

Noble stared at Harry Marsh, his face a mask of skin, patina of bruising. But somewhere, somewhere in the maze of purples, yellows and reds, Marsh detected a reaction – something between the impulse to retreat and a wash of resignation.

'Now, the way I see it,' the DS said, 'and Dr Penny will probably be able to corroborate my theory, the way I see it is that you were attacked by at least two men. One held your hands behind your back, the other let you have it with both fists and at least one application of his forehead. And then, when you were down on the ground, chances are, they both gave you a good slippering. I say slippering but by the look of your ribs, they were wearing heavy duty boots. That would account for the break in your arm too – am I right?'

Instinctively, Noble reached out a hand and rubbed it across his plastered arm, 'I'm not saying nothing, I'm not. Nothing.'

Harry Marsh smiled. 'Now, these men – whoever they were – would I know them?'

Noble dropped his chin to his chest and shook his head, either in admission or denial.

Marsh frowned and scratched at his chin. 'Assuming that's what happened, just accepting for a moment that I'm right, the question is, why would you want to blame me? What's that about? I think that's a fair question, don't you?'

Noble said nothing.

'You see, I think you're scared of me for some reason,' Harry Marsh said. 'I think you think I know something about you that you don't want me to know. That's what I think. Am I wrong?'

Noble snorted. 'Scared of you? I don't think so.'

The sergeant nodded, licked his lips, dipped his head and leant in until their noses were barely an inch apart.

Noble's eyes opened wide.

'Well, you sodding should be,' Harry Marsh said.

Startled, Noble pushed his head back into the pillow. 'You can't do anything to me. What more can you do that's not already been done?'

'I haven't done anything yet,' Marsh said. 'But tell me this, Bob Noble, you happen to know how many people are turning up dead these days? And being the state of things, what's one more unexplained corpse tripped over in the dark?'

'You can't threaten me.'

Noble reached up for the bedside cord. Marsh slapped his hand down and away.

Noble called out. 'Nurse! Nurse!'

Annie Scott opened the curtains and peered out. 'Incoming.'

'Do me a favour, make sure Bob and I have a while longer for this nice chat of ours, would you?'

'Of course,' the policewoman said, stepping out through the gap in the curtains.

Marsh watched as his colleague's feet came to a halt, shoes pointing down the ward. He saw the nurse's feet arrive. There was a pause, a whispered exchange and then the nurse turned and walked away.

Harry Marsh rested his hand on Noble's plastered arm, as if soothing a child who was seeking attention for a fictional complaint. 'OK, Constable Noble, you know I didn't do this to you and I know I didn't do this to you but someone did do this to you. Thing is, if that someone had hurt me like you've been hurt, I'd want to get back at them. I really would. But you're not doing that. No, you're not. What you're doing is pointing a finger at me and there's got to be a good reason for that.'

Expressionless, Noble stared at the sergeant, blinked and then turned his head away. 'I'm tired and I'd like you to go.'

Harry Marsh shook his head. 'I'll leave soon enough. But first, a very basic question, one I've been asking myself since first thing this morning: who benefits from me getting the blame for putting you in this state?'

Noble looked at Marsh and willed the sergeant to be anywhere but here.

Could see he wasn't going anywhere, anytime soon.

Felt the pressure on his left arm.

Licked his lips and pushed himself up against his pillow.

'Nurse,' he said, in a loud whisper. 'Nurse!'

Marsh pushed harder.

4

They stood at the school gates, staring at the Victorian red brick buildings. Children were running across the playground. Two boys chased each other in a circle, arms outstretched, imitating fighter planes. They chattered and grunted as each attempted to shoot the other from the sky. One threw his hands up into the air, where they fluttered like a parachute, before he fell to the ground and rolled over, laughing. The other whooped and ran around his friend, arms tilted in a victory roll.

Another group of boys stood in a tight circle, passing something from hand to hand. Reg Miles couldn't see what it was but he guessed it would be a bit of shrapnel, a piece of bomb casing. Something strange and alien and evidence that the enemy was real and meant them material harm – unlike the bogeyman, who was just an adult fib, designed to keep kids smaller than them in their place.

This mysterious metal, they knew this to be real.

Reg wondered what was it about war that small boys found so exciting, so liberating, when everyone else found it so terrifying.

He and Agnes walked past two girls spinning a skipping rope. A third girl was leaping up and over the rope. Not yet in rhythm, her sandals skimmed the cord, causing it to bang into her knees. One of the other girls tutted and said: 'My turn.'

Reg held the door for Agnes and they walked into a small reception area. A woman looked up at them as they approached her desk. 'Mrs Miles,' she said.

'And this is Mr Miles,' Agnes said.

'I thought it might be,' the receptionist attempted a smile – it was an unconvincing effort.

'It's about Emmy,' Reg said.

'Elizabeth Margaret,' his wife said, as if the woman wouldn't know who Emmy was.

The woman behind the desk nodded – who else could it be about?

Reg leant forward. 'You found her yet?'

The woman shook her head. 'No. Not that I know of.'

'And have you called the police?'

'The police, Reggie, you think it's that bad?'

Reg looked at Agnes. 'And you don't?'

His wife's face buckled. She never cried. Agnes never cried, it just wasn't something she did.

Until now.

'Love,' Reg said, reaching into a pocket and pulling out a handkerchief, 'I'm sorry.'

'Yes, the police are on their way,' the receptionist said.

'Mrs Miles?' A second woman appeared in a doorway at the back of the reception. She was older, with hair pulled back in a French bun. 'And Mr Miles, I presume?'

Reg nodded. 'And you are?'

'I'm Miss Fisher, the headmistress. You had better come through.'

Reg and Agnes followed the woman into her office. She sat down at her desk and took off her glasses. They swung on a leather cord and settled back against her cardigan.

Agnes blew her nose, offered the handkerchief to Reg. He shook his head and glared at Miss Fisher. 'How did this happen?'

'We've checked today's register,' Miss Fisher said, 'and Elizabeth Margaret is marked as absent.'

'That can't be right,' Reg said, 'my sister dropped her off at the gates first thing.'

The headmistress shook her head. 'This is embarrassing. It was only when Mrs Charley – your sister – only when Mrs Charley turned up with Elizabeth's reading book that we realised something was amiss.'

'Amiss?' Reg shook his head. 'Amiss? That's just not good enough.'

Agnes reached out and took her husband's left hand. 'I think she knows that, Reggie.'

'Lord,' Reg said. 'Lord above. What sort of school is it that can't keep tabs on your children? What sort of school are you running here, Miss Fisher?'

'I understand how you must feel, Mr Miles, I really do – but we are doing our best in the worst of all possible times.'

'Not for Emmy, you're not. Not for our Emmy.' He turned in his chair, pulling his hand away from Agnes. 'We should be out there now, looking for her. I should be out there looking for her.'

'Someone must know something,' Agnes said. 'What about Vivien?'

The headmistress nodded. 'Vivien Hoskins, you mean?'

'Yes,' Agnes said, 'they're good friends. They play together all the time. If anyone knows anything, Vivien will.'

'We should definitely talk to her. In fact, no time like the present,' Miss Fisher said, with a nod.

Reg unfolded to his feet. A big man, now even bigger. Fury and sorrow appeared to fill him, to inflate him, until it was possible to imagine that before long he would occupy all available space. Agnes had never seen her husband like this, he was normally so laconic, almost tacit. But now he stood broad and bright, inflamed with righteous anger – an anger that burnt so fiercely she worried for the paint on the plasterwork and the timbers in the ceiling. He was like some angel – a creature of vengeance – she remembered from Sunday scriptures but couldn't remember well enough to name.

Reg's voice, when he spoke, cut like a searchlight through the night sky: 'What? You mean you haven't spoken to her already?'

The classroom was dark and oppressive, any direct light filtered out by heavy curtains. Above dado rails, the walls were covered in children's drawings, their positioning so neat and high that they could only have been arranged by an adult hand.

There were five rows of double desks, four desks in each row and seats for forty children. Reg counted thirty-two looking up at him and one standing out the front, making thirty-three in all.

Thirty-three children, not one of them his.

Vivien Hoskins stood straight and pert. She was a small girl. Small and pretty and self-contained. Missing her front teeth, she spoke with a lisp: 'Yes, Emmy was with me before school. We played pat-a-cake. I won.' She smiled a gappy grin, pleased with the memory, pleased with herself.

Miss Fisher was kneeling in front of her, Agnes was perched on a chair by the teacher's desk and Reg leant against the wall, next to the blackboard. Miss Fisher nodded. 'And then what happened?'

'You rang the bell, Miss Fisher, we all got in line.'

'And Elizabeth Margaret? Emmy? What did she do?'

'She stayed outside,' Vivien said, distracted, still remembering how she'd won at pat-a-cake.

Agnes smiled. 'Emmy didn't get in line with you?'

The girl shook her head.

Reg sighed and Agnes shot him a look.

'Vivi, love,' Agnes said, 'what did Emmy do?'

'There was a boy. At the gate. She ran over to him.'

Agnes turned to look at Reg: still expanding, the room wouldn't be able to contain him for much longer.

'This boy,' Miss Fisher said, 'did you, do you know him?'

'No,' Vivien said.

'Now, Vivien,' the head teacher said, 'the police are going to be here shortly and you'll need to speak to them. Do you think you can do that? Will you do that for me?'

'The police?'

'You're not in trouble, Vivi,' Agnes said, 'but we need their help in finding Emmy and they'll need your help. All your help. Can you do that? Can you do that for Emmy?'

Reg stepped forward. 'There's something she's not telling us.'

Miss Fisher raised a hand to shush him. 'Is that true, Vivien? Is there something you're not telling us?'

The girl nodded and stared down at her shoes. 'I just 'membered.'

'What is it, Vivi?' Agnes said. 'What aren't you telling us?'

'The boy,' Vivien said, 'I don't know him really but Emmy shouted his name as she ran across.'

Reg took another step forward. 'And what is his name?'

The girl blinked up at the man standing over her. 'I only 'member it 'cos it sounds a bit like mine.'

'And what is it?'

'I'm Vivien, he's Vincent and he's Freddie's cousin.'

Vivien turned around and pointed at Freddie Furrell sat at the back of the class.

Freddie looked at the adults, his face expressionless, his lips closed, his mouth sealed.

5

As they stood, waiting for the tram, Harry Marsh glanced down at his watch.

'Somewhere to be?'

'As a matter of fact, yes.'

'Somewhere more interesting than here, I take it.'

Marsh looked the young woman in the face. 'That barge,' he said, 'the *Crown Victoria*, it arrived back in Gas Street late Saturday, early Sunday.'

Annie Scott nodded. 'And?'

'Get yourself down Gas Street,' he heard himself say, 'and see what you can find out about Vincent Lee. He may not be anything to do with our little Italian girl but he is still missing and I'd like to know what we can find out about him, in case his name comes up again in relation to any other little girls.'

'Just me?'

'Seaborne will see it as a family thing, so just you, *Assistant Lady Enquiry Officer Scott-Taylor*', he said, in a fair impression of the inspector.

The policewoman smiled. 'And what will DS Marsh be doing?'

Marsh looked away as if distracted. 'If you get off at the top of Bristol Street, you can cut across Holloway Head and down onto the canal there, it won't take you long.'

'Family matters aside, Seaborne said I was to stick with you and stick with you all day.'

'No need, I'll be fine. Trust me, I'll stay out of trouble. And if I don't, well, there's nothing to come back on you later, is there?'

Annie Scott nodded, moved close to Harry Marsh. '*You happen to know how many people are turning up dead these days?*' she said, her voice low and hushed, her accent broad Brummie, far broader than Marsh's own soft brogue.

Marsh smiled with deeply feigned ignorance. 'Do you? It's a good question.'

'Did you mean that?'

'Mean what?'

'It's a threat if I ever heard one.'

'Ah,' Harry Marsh said, nodding, 'yes, I can see how you might think that. Remind me to tell you about my *Little Caesar*, some-time. Toast of the Tuck Shop it was.'

Annie Scott laughed. 'Touché.' She shook her head. 'Noble wasn't much use, was he?'

'Not as much as I'd have liked but there are other options out there, it's just a question of identifying them.'

'And you have?'

He shrugged. 'Might have.'

Other options.

Had Carlo Montealto had any other options? Had his family had any choice in their fate? What choice does anyone have in the face of madness, other than *bad* or *worse*?

And now what choices did Marsh have?

On the one hand, he had to do right by the dead girl, on the other, if he didn't clear his name, chances were he wouldn't be in a position to *do right* by anyone, ever again.

No, as much as he couldn't stop thinking about that sad Digbeth attic and everything that had led up to it, he had to put it all to the back of his mind and do what needed doing now.

He hated it but the Montealtos would have to wait until he had a straight head.

Until he could see a way forward clear of any other worries which may, or rather would, cloud his vision.

Impossible as it seemed at this moment, at any moment, that is what he had to do.

6

Reg Miles ran across the playground. Back on the street, he turned right and ran some more. He passed two uniformed police officers on their way to the school. He didn't have time to explain anything to them and didn't feel the need – this, he could sort himself.

Vincent Lee wasn't a Furrell but he was a relative, Reg knew that much and he had form. Form with little girls, if the stories were true –if the stories were to be believed – and Reg had no need to doubt that they were anything but true.

After all, Emmy had been seen with the boy and now Emmy was missing.

He would find Vincent Lee and then he'd find Emmy.

Although he knew the Furrells by reputation, he didn't know them as people, didn't know where they lived. George Furrell, the patriarch, was a house painter, a drinker, a troublemaker – even a card-carrying Bolshie, by some accounts. An aunt of Agnes's knew the wife – Edith – that's how they'd heard the stories about Vincent last year.

About what he'd got up to.

Got up to with little girls.

And there were three Furrell kids. Three boys. The eldest worked as a butcher's boy, the middle one – Freddie – was at school with Emmy and there was a third, a young'un, not long out of nappies.

Vincent Lee didn't live with them but he lived close, according to Freddie, only the boy couldn't remember the number – or wasn't telling – and his mom wouldn't be in, never was on a Monday.

Never mind, Stan Smith would know where the boy lived. And then? Well, who knew? Reg didn't but he'd work something out.

He had to.

Stan Smith stood on his doorstep. 'Smith Street,' he said, 'named after me it was.' He laughed and then caught Reg's expression. 'The boy lives at 19. He in trouble again, Reg? What's he been up to now?'

Reg Miles pounded on and pounded hard until his lungs hurt and the only sounds in his ears were the rushing of blood and a voice telling him that if he didn't get a move on, all would be lost.

Elizabeth Margaret would be lost.

Gone for good.

Turning into Smith Street, he headed to Number 19, raised his fist and banged on the front door. Stepping back, he leant forward, put his hands on his knees and drew breath for almost the first time since he'd left the school.

There was a scurrying, the clack of a lock and the door opened.

'Yes?'

Reg looked at the woman in the doorway. 'Vincent Lee,' he said, more an exhalation of air than words. 'I'm looking for Vincent Lee.'

'He's not here. I don't know where he is but he's not here.' Millicent Lee started to close the door.

Reg straightened up and stuck his foot out, wedged his boot between the door and the frame. The woman glanced down at his boot. 'I don't suppose you'll be moving that anytime soon,' she said.

Reg shook his head. 'My name's Reg Miles and my girl's missing. My little girl's missing.'

'You better come in, I s'ppose.'

Sat opposite each other in the kitchen, Reg Miles looked at the old woman. He saw something familiar in her face. Some line, some cast of her cheekbone, something he recognised from somewhere else. From a different time and place. There was a picture in his head – a drawing?

An old sepia photograph?

Millicent Lee smiled. 'Had a good look at me, have you, Mr Miles?'

'I know you,' Reg said, pointing a finger. 'We've never met before but I do know you.'

'It happens,' Millicent Lee said, 'I get it a lot.'

'How do I know you then?'

'You'll work it out,' she said.

Reg breathed in. His lungs were returning to normal but the sense of foreboding he'd felt earlier was still there – worse now than ever, given that time was passing and he was no closer to finding Emmy. He wiped a palm across his brow. 'Can I get a glass of water or something?'

Millicent Lee nodded and raised her hands, fingers bent in on themselves. 'You'll have to help yourself,' she said, nodding at the sink. 'There's a glass on the drainer.'

'Thank you,' Reg said.

He ran the tap, filled the glass and sat back down. The old woman watched him drink. 'So who's missing and what's Vincent got to do with it?'

'It's my Emmy – Elizabeth Margaret – my daughter. She's not been seen all morning and last time anyone did see her, she was talking to Vincent.'

'And when was this?'

'Earlier. This morning. Before school.'

'And now you think she's missing?'

'She is.'

Millicent Lee shook her head. 'It won't be anything to do with Vincent.'

'They were seen together.'

'Just coincidence.'

'I still want to talk to him.'

Millicent Lee laughed.

Reg glowered. 'What's so funny?'

'I had the police here the other day, sitting just where you are actually and they were asking about Vincent. They wanted to have a chat with him too.'

'What about?'

'I'll tell you exactly what I told them: he does live here but he doesn't always stop here, not every night.'

'Where does he stop when he's not here?'

Millicent Lee shook her head. 'I don't know. I suspect he's got a little den somewhere, a little hideaway for when everything gets too much. I know how he feels, I used to be the same.'

'And how old is he?'

'He's fourteen. Turned fourteen last August.'

'He's fourteen and you don't care where he is?'

'He's left school, he's old enough to work, he'll be fine.'

'And what about my Emmy?'

'What about her?'

'She's just five. Is she going to be fine too?'

'If she's with Vincent, she'll be alright. He won't hurt her. I promise you that. He won't hurt her. He hasn't got it in him.'

Circles, they were going round in circles – this wasn't getting him anywhere closer to Emmy.

'But where am I going to find Vincent? That's what I need to know. Where's the boy?'

Millicent Lee felt the man's desperation – it was as hot as a burning coal – and nodded, weighing up the least she could say yet still be of help.

'Try Benson Road,' she said. 'There's a few empty houses there waiting to be demolished. I know he's played up that end in the past. You might find him there now. I can't promise anything but you might. And if not, you could always ask George.'

'You mean George Furrell?'

'That's him. He's my niece's husband. He's a difficult sod at the best of times but for some reason, he's always done good by the boy. Always shown him a decent hand.'

'And where would I find him?'

Millicent Lee shook her head. 'You might try The Grand Turk on Hockley Hill. If he's not there now waiting for it to open, he will be before long.'

'Ta.'

'And don't worry yourself so much,' the old woman said, 'if your girl is with Vincent, she'll be fine.'

'You don't know that. You can't know that,' Reg said. Standing, he finished his drink and put the glass into the sink. 'You were in the Music Hall, weren't you?'

She smiled and nodded. 'I said you'd remember.'

Reg looked at the old woman in front of him. Attempted to imagine her fluttering around the stage as she sang, hiking up her skirt and flashing her scanties to anyone who cared to look. He could see traces of the young girl she'd been in her lined face – it was what he'd recognised, after all – but somehow he found the thought of her performing to a crowd of baying and whistling men disturbing. As if she'd always been an old woman and the young girl was just a temporary disguise.

'Before my time but my dad, he used to go a lot. You were a regular at the London Museum Concert Hall in Digbeth. When my dad died, we found a load of old programmes and photographs in a box under his bed. That's where I've seen you.'

'Have you still got your dad's stuff? I'd appreciate a look-see, if you have. The good old days and all that.'

'No, not sure we have. It was all a bit old and falling apart.'

Millicent Lee sighed like a bicycle tyre with a puncture and laughed. 'Oh, I know that feeling. It's a pity though, I really would like to see something from back then, anything.'

'And I'd really like to find Emmy, Miss Lee. Let's hope at least one of us gets what we want,' Reg said, his words tight and terse, harsher than intended.

He turned and left.

7

Gas Street Basin, a washed-out dent in the middle of a washed-out day. Narrowboats, buttyboats, tugs, all parked and neatly tethered, for as far as the eye could see. The only colour, the gently undulating mass of brightly painted wooden vessels against a backdrop of buildings rendered monochrome by a flat and bleary light. It felt as if the sun had forgotten to rise and the sole source of illumination came from the even, featureless cloud that embraced the city. The buildings surrounding the basin looked like an old daguerreotype on the point of fading away to nothing, leaving behind a stained sheet of silver and little else.

A thin layer of smoke hung head high, bitter and musty, smelling of ash, coal dust, and meat fat. There was a splattering of rain, each drop an essence of cold which stung the skin on contact, burning like a wasp sting.

Annie Scott pulled her coat tight around her body – steeling herself against both the weather and her unexpected nerves – and walked along the towpath that ran under the bridge. Moving further into the dock, she looked from narrowboat to narrowboat, from name to name. As she walked, the rain turned into nothing and disappeared.

A woman holding a broom glared at her from a nearby deck. Wearing a floor-length apron over a black dress, the woman could have been a character from the 19th century, had it not been for her almost modish hair. Cut to just below ear length and side-parted, the long side – swept back over her right ear – bore evidence of a curling iron.

As soon as she saw Annie looking back at her, the woman became busy with something at her feet, brushing away with far more application and effort than was necessary.

'Excuse me?'

The woman carried on sweeping.

The policewoman took a step forward, so close to the edge now that another inch and she'd be in the water. 'Excuse me, madam, I wonder if you could help me?'

Unable to ignore the interruption any longer, the woman stopped working and leant on the broom handle.

'Probably not,' she said, looking up.

'Oh, I do hope you can,' Annie said, with her best smile. And then she laughed to emphasise her friendliness, her approachability, aware that from the woman's point of view, she was nothing more than a featureless silhouette.

The woman scowled and squinted. 'What do you want?'

'My name's Annie Scott, I'm with the Birmingham City Police and I'm looking for a narrowboat.'

'You don't look like no police to me.'

Annie Scott laughed again. 'I can assure you I am.'

The woman scowled. 'Looking for a narrowboat, you say? Well, you've come to the right place then, aincha?'

The policewoman laughed for a third time, aware the effect was becoming predictable, tired. 'Yes, I have, haven't I? No, you see, I'm looking for one in particular. One special narrowboat.'

'Thought you might be.'

'The *Crown Victoria*, it's just back from London, well, back over the weekend – ring any bells?'

The woman shook her head. 'As you can see, you being police and all, there's a fair amount of boats round here. Is that it? Can I get on now?'

A little boy appeared in the cabin door. He wore a large sweater over long shorts, his nose red and snotty. 'Momma?'

'What?'

'Thirsty, Momma,' the boy said, pointing to his mouth.

The woman rested her broom against the side of the cabin, knelt, brushed the boy's fringe from his eyes. 'You's feeling better, I take it?'

'Bit.'

'Only a bit? Then you shouldn't be up. Back to bed now and I'll fetch you something along in a minute.'

''Kay, Momma.'

The lad disappeared back below decks.

'Nice boy,' Annie Scott said.

'He'll do,' the woman said.

The policewoman turned to walk away and then paused. 'Pity you can't help,' she said, 'it's about a boy. A boy who's missing. Who may be in trouble.'

The woman looked up. 'What? What did you say?'

'The boy's called Vincent and I'm trying to find his father. His family, actually.'

'Vincent Lee's missing?' the woman said, before she could stop the words.

For a moment, Annie Scott doubted herself. It was true, the boy was missing but that wasn't why she was here, not really – it was a white lie but an expedient one. 'Well, we are trying to find him,' she said. 'So, you do know them? The Lees, that is.'

'Yeah, well, maybe.'

'And Vincent?'

The woman breathed in and nodded. 'He hasn't been round here for a while, has Vincent. Not since he had that row with his old man and got thrown out.' Realising she'd gone too far, said too much, the woman dropped her chin, avoided any further eye contact. 'I wouldn't say I know them but I do know who they are and what they are is private. Like most of us round here, they keep theyselves to theyselves.'

'I'm only trying to help,' Annie Scott said.

'I've heard that before, 'specially from your type.'

'My type?'

'Police.' The woman snorted. 'You lot treat us bargees like gyppos most of the time, like we've always done sommat wrong, when what we is is hard-working folk who just happen to move about some. Treat us proper unfair, you lot do. Always have and suspect you always will.'

Annie Scott crouched down in an attempt to put herself on the other woman's eyeline. 'I'm sorry if that happens – to bargees or gypsies, actually – it shouldn't. But I do need to speak with the Lees. It is important, what with the boy missing, I'm sure you understand.'

The woman nodded to herself, weighing up possible actions and probable consequences. 'Alright,' she said, 'reckon I can help but I didn't, if you sees what I mean? If anyone should ask, it wasn't me – I didn't help you one little bit, alright?'

Wallace Lee was a man out of proportion. Broad-shouldered but short in the leg, he looked like an oblong box which had been compressed into a cube but clumsily, unsuccessfully. He had a bowler hat pushed back on his head and wore a thick work jacket over a bulging waistcoat. A silver watch chain ran across one side of his belly, from waistcoat button to left fob pocket. Around his neck, a bow tie under a grubby white celluloid collar.

His trousers were moleskin and his highly polished boots were topped off with puttees that came up to just under his knee. His hands were strong, his fingers stained grey and black and he was filling a briar pipe, tamping the tobacco down with a forefinger.

Close up, he had an aroma of sweat and diesel.

There was a small stove on the roof of the living quarters and a kettle was beginning to steam.

'Mr Lee?'

He looked and smiled at the young woman on the dockside. His teeth – what teeth remained – were smoker's yellow beneath a walrus moustache. 'Who's asking?'

'I'm Annie Scott. Policewoman Annie Scott of the Birmingham City Police and I'm here about your son Vincent.'

The man coughed and spat into the canal. 'Vincent? What's our kid been up to now?'

'Is there somewhere we can talk?'

Wallace Lee looked around. 'Here's as good as any.'

'May I come on board?'

Lee shrugged. 'If you must.'

Annie Scott took a pace forward, rested a foot on the side of the *Crown Victoria*. The narrowboat edged itself away from the brickwork and the young woman tottered.

Wallace Lee laughed. 'Hang on,' he said, 'let me give you a help.'

He laid his pipe next to the stove and reached out. The policewoman took his hand – it felt as tough and as seasoned as a pony's saddle – and stepped down onto the boat. 'Thank you,' she said.

'My pleasure,' he said. 'You want a brew?'

'Yes, why not? That would be very welcome. Thank you.'

Tea made, they sat on small stools next to the tiller, cups in hands. 'So,' Lee said, 'what's he done now?'

'Mr Lee, I have to ask you, when did you last see your son?'

'Call me Wally,' Lee said, 'Mr Lee's me dad and he's still around somewhere, believe it or not, the old sot.'

'Alright, Wally,' Annie Scott said, 'when did you last see Vincent?'

Wally Lee sipped his tea and sucked his upper lip. 'Now that's a good question and not one to which I've got a good answer. Six months, maybe.'

'Six months? Last May?'

'Seems about right.'

'You don't seem very concerned, Mr Lee.'

'Wally.'

'You don't seem very concerned, *Wally*, if you don't mind me saying.'

'I asked what he'd done, didn't I? What has he done, you ain't said?'

'We're tying up a few loose ends on a matter and just need a chat with your son.'

Wally Lee laughed. 'A chat? Really?'

'Really.'

Lee tipped his tea dregs overboard. Annie Scott watched as they spread out and became part of the canal's oily surface.

A young couple appeared on the dockside. Laden down with groceries, they were struggling to control a small boy.

'Dad?' the woman said, a note of desperation in her voice.

Wally Lee looked across. 'Alright young Tobias, you being a nuisance?'

'No,' the child said.

'So why don't I believe you?' his grandfather said.

'Don't know,' the boy said.

'You come here,' Wally Lee said, holding out his arms and lifting the boy on board.

As he landed, Tobias looked at the policewoman. She stuck out her tongue. The boy laughed and buried his head into his grandfather's thighs. The young couple came aboard.

The woman glanced at Annie Scott. 'And who are you?'

'She's police,' Wally Lee said.

'She don't look very like police to me.'

Annie Scott smiled. 'We come in all shapes and sizes these days. And you are?'

'Glory. Gloria Tyler. I'm his daughter,' she said, gesturing at Wally Lee. 'And that's my husband Tony.'

'Afternoon, officer,' Tony Tyler said, tipping his cap at Annie Scott and sizing her up, all at the same time. 'And what can we do for you?'

'She's here about Vincent,' Wally Lee said.

Glory Tyler looked as if she'd been slapped. 'What about Vincent?'

'Tell you what, Glory,' her father said, 'Why don't you take the boy inside? You can put all this stuff away at the same time. Me and her won't be much longer.'

The young woman nodded but hesitated. Annie Scott watched her closely, sensing there was something she wanted to say.

'Yeah,' Glory Tyler said, patting her son on his head, 'he needs a lie down. Tony, give us a hand, will you?'

'Sure,' her husband said, pulling open the double doors to the rear parlour while giving Annie Scott one last glance. He smiled to himself as he disappeared below decks and the young policewoman felt she'd been assigned a value, like a prize animal being led around the ring at an auction, prior to the shambles.

Even buried deep in her overcoat, she shivered.

Wally Lee turned and looked at her. 'Like I said, I ain't seen Vincent for months, so I don't sees what I can do to help.'

'May I be frank?'

The man cackled. 'You can be anything you want to be, darlin'.'

'This is hard to say, I'm afraid, but Vincent was seen in the company of a young girl.'

'So?'

'She was five and he was enticing her.'

'Enticing her? What'd you mean by that?'

'He had a bag of sweets and he was trying to take her away from her friends.'

Wally Lee snorted. 'He wouldn't do anything like that.'

'I'm sorry, Mr Lee, but it's not the first time. There was a similar incident last year. And well, nothing untoward took place then either but we'd just like a word with the boy, explain that what he's doing is not really acceptable.'

'Bit more than a *chat* then,' Lee said. He picked up his pipe from next to the stove and lit a splint. After several puffs, he threw the splint into the canal and rolled smoke around his mouth, letting it seep out between his teeth. 'He wouldn't do anything bad, he's not like that.'

'Are you sure?'

'Sure as sure can be.' He drew on his pipe again.

For a moment, the detective felt she was being watched and glanced down into the narrowboat's parlour, convinced she'd see Tony Tyler lurking there. As she looked, a figure moved away, deeper into the cabin space.

A female figure.

Annie Scott twisted her torso. 'That boat there,' she said, pointing. 'Is that yours too?'

Lee nodded. 'That's our buttyboat.'

'Buttyboat?'

'We tow it behind us, lets us carry more stuff than this ship can on its own.'

'And what stuff's that?'

'Timber, coal, whatever load we can get, to be honest. Chocolate sometimes, believe it or not? Whatever's wanted, we'll cart it.'

'And you just tow the buttyboat behind you?'

'Tony mans it. Loosens and tightens the tow rope, when necessary. Makes sure it keeps in line so it don't swing out and don't catch in the reeds, or hit anything else.'

'Sounds like hard work, if you ask me.'

Wally Lee opened his hands to embrace the wharf. 'Life's hard work, in case you ain't noticed.'

'And all hands on deck, I expect.'

'All the time.'

The young woman smiled and nodded.

The bargee grinned. 'What? You want to give it a go?'

'No, I'll leave that to you professionals, thank you. To be honest, what I don't quite get is why Vincent isn't here? Surely, you could use his help? Use an extra pair of hands?'

Lee lit another splint, applied it to his pipe. 'He weren't up to it.'

'I heard you had a row, was that because he wasn't up to it?'

'You heard what?'

'I heard you and Vincent had a row.'

'Who said that?'

'Who said it doesn't matter, is it true?'

The man shook his head and looked perplexed, as if calculating passing space between his boat and an oncoming barge. 'He was just too sensitive, like.'

'Too sensitive? What do you mean?'

'Like I says, it's a hard life this, darlin'. Long, long hours and when it gets cold, it gets really cold. You ever tried to break ice on a canal top come Christmas morn?'

Annie Scott shook her head. 'No, I can't say I have.'

'Don't. You wouldn't like it.'

'And Vincent didn't like it?'

'No, he didn't, especially after Marge, his ma, died..'

'So you sent him to live with your aunt?'

Wally Lee laughed, choking so hard on his smoke that his eyes watered. 'No, I sent him to school first. Thought it would sort him out. Teach him a few things.'

'Which school?'

'Over in Beeches Green. It's happy to take barge kids, even finds them somewhere to stay. But he didn't like it and kept running away. And then one morning, he's back sitting where you're sitting now.'

'And after that?'

'Well, I wasn't having him here, was I?'

'It's then he went to Millicent Lee's in Smith Street?'

Wally Lee nodded. 'That's right.'

'And now? Where could he be now?'

Lee shook his head. 'No idea, darlin'.'

'And you're not worried?'

'He'll turn up. He always does, does Vincent. Always. Anything else you need? 'Cos me, I got things need be done.'

Annie Scott walked along the canal bank, towards the steps that led up to Gas Street. She heard footsteps. Turning around, she saw Glory Tyler a few yards behind her, her fast pace not far off a run.

'Wait,' Glory Tyler said, raising a hand. 'Hold up.'

Annie Scott stopped. 'Can I help you?'

'Is Vince in trouble?'

'We're just trying to find him.'

Glory Tyler shook her head in disbelief. 'If you're trying to find him, he must have done something. You lot don't go looking for no one just for their own good.'

'Glory. May I call you Glory? We just need a word with your brother, that's all there is to it.'

The woman laughed. 'Don't go fibbing on me now, what's he done?'

Annie dipped her head, ready to turn and walk up the steps. 'I've already told your father everything.'

Glory reached out and grabbed the policewoman by the elbow. 'Then tell me,' she said, 'I might be able to help, I might.'

'There was an incident with a young girl and we need to speak to your brother about it.'

The woman dropped her hand from Annie's arm and put it over her mouth. 'What? What are you saying?'

'And this incident, it's not the first time. There was something similar last year – on two occasions.'

Glory Tyler rubbed her hands. 'No,' she said. 'No, I don't believe you.'

Annie Scott looked at the young woman. There was something about the way she stood, head down, shoulders slouched, which pleaded for mercy, for consolation, for a kind word – even if that kind word was a lie.

All the policewoman had was the truth.

'Your brother was clearly identified on all occasions, by reliable witnesses,' Annie said, 'I'm sorry but he was.'

Glory Tyler looked up, tears in her eyes. 'Were they hurt, these girls?'

Annie Scott shook her head. 'No, not at all.'

'Then what's the problem?'

'Unfortunately, there's a difference between intention and outcome.'

'What?'

'Your brother was stopped as he was leading the girls away. If he hadn't been, well, we just don't know. We can't know what may have happened next. And that's why we need to have a chat with him, explain to him why what he's doing is wrong. Or could be seen to be wrong. How it can cause unnecessary distress, even if there is no actual malice or bad intention involved.'

'Vincent wouldn't hurt a fly,' Glory said. 'He's not like that.'

The young woman turned, ducked to go under the bridge, then hesitated and came back. She locked eyes with Annie Scott and for the second time that day the policewoman felt she was being weighed up again.

Judged again.

Evaluated again.

Eventually, Glory Tyler spoke: 'Can I trust you?'

'You can.'

'Good. You see, there was a row between Dad and Vince. A big one. It was the day me and Tony got married. Young Toby had just turned two and Ma had been dead a year to the day, so we decided getting hitched was the thing to do. It was part celebration, part wake, it was. And a bostin' day, Ma would have loved it. Anyway, we were all in the pub, all except Vince – he was tired and too young really, so he went back to the boat early. We stayed on. It was gone midnight when we got home. And there he was, asleep on a bunk.'

Glory Tyler hesitated.

'Yes?'

'Thing is, he was all dressed up in Ma's clothes. Must have put them on, lay down and fallen asleep, like.'

'I see.'

'Dad went off on one. Said he wasn't having no *queeny* under his roof and that Vince had to go. I said: *No, he's probably just missing Ma, I mean, ain't we all?* But Dad was insistent, Vince had to go. And a few days later, off he goes.'

'And that's when he went to the school?'

'That's it. That's exactly it.'

Annie Scott sighed and shook her head. 'It must have been difficult for you.'

'It was. Tony, he thought it was funny, like, he wanted to tell everyone. But Dad, he wasn't having that.'

Annie Scott could imagine the scene: the older man incandescent with fury and self-imagined shame bearing down on the younger man. Tony Tyler may have had the age advantage but Wally Lee had the weight, the heft, the years of looking after himself – it would have been no contest, no contest at all.

'You see,' Glory said, 'Vince wouldn't hurt those little girls, that's why I'm telling you this, he wouldn't, he just wouldn't.'

'How can you be so sure?'

''Cos he thinks he is one, that's why.'

8

Just before two o'clock, Harry Marsh walked into The Trafalgar Hotel. Charlie Tighe stood at one end of the Public Bar, hatch open, tumbler in hand.

Marsh breathed in a waft of smoke, it snagged in his windpipe and he coughed. Wheezing, he fumbled for his inhaler. Moira was right, he needed it more and more as time went by, there was no denying that. Many days were fine but on others, almost randomly and unpredictably, something would catch in his throat and trigger, at the very least, breathlessness. At its very worst, he would feel his chest collapse in on his lungs and then, unable to breathe out, fear of suffocation overwhelmed him. This attack wasn't that bad, it was just uncomfortable.

He inhaled, counted five and exhaled.

Charlie Tighe looked over. 'You want a drink, Harry?'

'No thanks,' Marsh said, waving Tighe away.

'You look like you could do with one.'

'I'm fine.'

The DS turned and leant his back against the bar, closed his eyes, breathed in again – slowly, methodically, just as Jeannie had taught him all those years ago.

'You alright, mate?' Tighe sounded concerned.

'I'm fine,' Harry Marsh said. 'I just need a minute.'

'Take as long as you want,' Tighe said, lifting his tumbler to his lips before emptying it in one gulp. He waved the glass under Marsh's nose. 'You sure?'

The policeman nodded. 'I'm sure.'

'Just me then.'

Charlie Tighe walked to the back of the bar, a slight sway to his swagger, uncapped a half-empty bottle of Kilbeggan whiskey and poured a double shot into his tumbler. By the time he walked back, Harry Marsh had his breathing under control.

'Getting worse, is it?' Tighe said, a look of genuine concern on his face.

Marsh shook his head. 'Not really. It's just I've got a bit of a chill, it's cold out there and then smoky in here. I'm fine now.'

'Really?' his friend said, 'You don't sound it.'

'No, really,' the sergeant said. 'I'm fine.'

'Good.'

The two men stood in silence as Tighe sipped his drink.

Harry Marsh looked around the room. 'Any luck then?'

'Maybe.'

'Maybe or definitely?'

'A bit of both.'

Marsh laughed. 'Let's start with the maybe, shall we?'

Tighe nodded, put down his glass and dropped his voice. 'Give it a minute, Harry.'

'Give what a minute?'

The landlord jutted his chin across the room at two men finishing off their pints. The last two customers in the pub.

'Fair enough,' the policeman said.

Over in the corner, the two men stood and walked their glasses back to the bar.

'Thanks, landlord,' one man said. The other simply nodded. They placed their tankards on the counter and left.

Harry Marsh watched them go. 'Just us now, Charlie. What you got for me?'

'I'll lock up and then we'll have a little chat.'

Closing the front doors, Tighe slid the bolts into place and rejoined Harry Marsh at the bar. Marsh grimaced, his friend's breath was ripe and sour.

'I asked like you asked me to and I got a couple of names.'

'Thank you.' Marsh gestured at the tumbler sat on the counter. 'You going to tell me what's going on then?'

'What's going on? What do you mean what's going on?'

'What's going on with you that you need a drink this early in the day.'

Charlie Tighe reached for the glass, emptied it. 'Dutch courage. Or should I say, Irish courage? You ask the kind of questions I asked on your behalf, you need a bit of something, I can tell you. The boys I had to talk to, you don't want to get on their wrong side, you really don't. I mean, asking too much of them, that can get a person into trouble.'

'What kind of trouble?'

Tighe shook his head, ignored the question, looked around the bar. 'This is hard enough graft as it is, this running a pub lark, I don't want to complicate things.'

'By being known as a copper's nark?'

'You said it, not me. And anyway, I said it was for a friend. And that's true. We are friends, aren't we, Harry?'

'We are.'

The two men lapsed into silence.

'Maybe I will have that drink,' Harry Marsh said.

'I thought you'd never ask,' Charlie Tighe said.

The publican walked behind the bar, scooping up a clean glass as he did and uncapped the whiskey. 'Double or nothing?'

'Well, I don't want nothing.'

'Double it is,' Tighe said, turning, pouring and placing the glass next to Harry Marsh's right hand. 'It'll do your chest good.'

Marsh raised the glass and put it to his nose. 'Doubt that but cheers anyway.'

Tighe refilled his own tumbler. 'Sláinte chugat.'

The two men drank.

'This is a good Irish,' Marsh said.

'You've got a good nose,' Charlie Tighe said.

'I can read,' the policeman said, inclining his glass towards the bottle on the bar.

Tighe guffawed. 'Ah yes, there is that.'

They drank.

Tighe belched and giggled and Harry Marsh realised for the first time quite how drunk his friend was. The landlord was a practised drinker and Marsh didn't like to think what time of day Charlie must have started to get into this state, so early on.

The DS emptied his tumbler and put it down on the counter.

''Nother one?'

'Better not, I am on duty after all.'

Charlie Tighe stood up straight and saluted. 'Of course you are. You are on duty after all. Not me though, I'm off till six, so you won't mind if I do.'

The publican went to put his glass down as he reached for the whiskey bottle but mistimed his move. The tumbler slid from his hand, snagged on the edge of the counter and fell to the floor, breaking into three large pieces. He looked down at his feet, in disbelief.

'Charlie,' Harry Marsh said, 'if you're in trouble—'

'I'm not, Harry. Not yet, anyway.'

'You going to tell me about it?'

'About what?'

'About what's going on?'

Charlie Tighe retrieved a dustpan and brush from under the bar and knelt, sweeping the glass shards into the pan. His arm movements were too neat and too controlled, a man doing his best to conceal his drunkenness from himself, from the world.

From an inquiring policeman.

Eventually, the publican stood, walked the length of the counter and upended the pan into a fire bucket. 'Better not forget it's there,' he said. 'Could do someone a hurt, that could.'

'It could,' Harry Marsh said.

The landlord poured himself a fresh drink and walked to a window. He pulled at a curtain and looked out. He let the netting slide back into place and slumped down onto the banquette that ran along the wall. 'OK,' he said, 'sometimes I buy stuff I shouldn't from people I shouldn't do business with but that's as far as it goes. I swear, Harry, that's as far as it goes. I wouldn't do anything else. I wouldn't. This is between friends, right?'

'Friends – as you keep reminding me.'

The publican laughed. 'I had another *friend* of yours in earlier, as it happens,' he said.

The policeman raised an eyebrow. 'A friend? Who?'

'Sergeant Greene.'

Marsh sighed. 'He's not exactly what I'd call a friend.'

'He said he was.'

'What did he want?'

'It's more what he didn't want.'

Harry Marsh sat down next to Charlie Tighe. 'What didn't he want?'

'He didn't want me to tell you anything. He'd found out we were tight as kids and he didn't want me to tell you a thing.'

'What sort of thing?'

'Anything.'

Marsh sighed. He felt as if he were running a hundred-yard race and just as the race was about to be won, the finishing line vanishes without warning, only to reappear a hundred yards behind him, back at the start. It was always the same when questioning a drunk, no matter how well you knew them.

Always the same.

And always equally frustrating.

But *tight as kids*? Maybe that was something. How did Greene know that?

'Charlie, you've got to help me here, you really have.'

'He says he's a friend but I don't think he likes you, Harry, I really don't.'

'Well, I don't like him, so it's mutual.'

Tighe laughed and slapped his hand down on his friend's thigh. 'You're a good man, Harry Marsh, and funny too. How's Jeannie? Still as lovely as ever?'

'She is and she'll still be lovely, even when we get to the end of what you've got to tell me, even if that's sometime around 1960.' Marsh reached across and pulled the tumbler away from his friend's reach. 'What did he say about me, Charlie? What did the good sergeant have to say?'

Charlie Tighe watched Harry Marsh turn the glass around in his hand and nodded. 'He said you were trouble, Harry. Proper trouble. And that I shouldn't be helping you.'

'Did he now?'

'He did he now. He said how his colleague crossed you and now he's in hospital for a good, long stay.'

'That's at least part right.'

'Which part?'

'The part about some young woodentop spending the next few nights in a hospital bed.'

The landlord nodded, his chin almost touching his chest. He peered at his old friend with a sideward glance. 'But you didn't put him there, did you?'

Harry Marsh putted air across his lips, not quite a sigh, not quite a laugh. 'Did he say anything else, this arbiter of truth? Anything else I should know?'

'Arbiter? That's a posh word, Harry. Learn that at your posh school, did you?'

'It's just a word.'

Tighe reached out for the tumbler, Marsh pulled it further away, Tighe shrugged. 'Yes, he did, come to think on it.'

'Come on then, out with it.'

'He said that if I do you any favours now, there'll only be trouble ahead. That my life could become *too hot to handle,* how my future's a real *burning issue*, if I got his drift.'

'He said that?'

'He did.'

'And you believe him?'

'He's a man capable of delivering on his promises is Sergeant Greene.' The landlord hesitated, glanced down at the floor, his tell-tale knee starting to beat out a rhythm. 'Or so I've heard.'

Marsh turned his head, stared at his friend. 'And what have you heard?'

Charlie looked up, the solemness of the seriously drunk upon him. 'Can you get shot of him, Harry, can you? Can you get him off my back?'

'Give me something to work with here, Charlie. Help me out and I'll do what I can do.'

Tighe snorted, shook his head and looked around. 'There are times, Harry, times when a little bit of what looks like good luck turns bad and before you know it you're in deeper than you wanted to be and there's no way out until you've lost everything. Ask Mos Tyber, you ask him, he'll tell you.'

'Mos Tyber?'

'Jewish bloke, owns The Narrows.'

'I heard it burnt down,' Marsh said.

'So it did but how?' Tighe sniggered. 'Some say it was the Jerries, others that Greene had a hot hand in it but who knows the truth. Anyway, I've got you that information, Harry. Like you asked for earlier, when you phoned, I've got you that info. It's the best I can do, given the people I had to ask—'

'People even you wouldn't choose to do business with?'

Tighe pulled a face. '*Even you*? Thanks for that, Harry. Let's just say I don't want to be asking them for anything else, not now, not anymore.'

Marsh looked closely at his friend, at the etched lines in his face, at the bags under his eyes, at the almost prison pallor of his skin. 'What is it, Charlie? What's happened to change your mind all of a sudden?'

The publican shook his head. 'Nothing.'

'Don't believe you.'

'I'm just tired, that's all.'

'And?'

Tighe snorted. 'Christ, you're a dogged one, ain't you?'

'It's what makes me good at my job, Charlie.'

Tighe nodded. 'S'ppose it does.' He paused, tapped his fingers on the table three times, looked up and fixed Marsh with a stare. 'Guns. I've heard that guns are part of the deal now. Rifles. Serious shooters. Serious shooters for serious people. Serious Irish people.'

Marsh looked at his friend's drunken, scared face. 'How deep you in, Charlie?'

'Me? I'm in the shallow end, Harry. You know I wouldn't have anything to do with guns, not me. You know that. Just a few smokes and a bit of whiskey.'

Marsh sighed. 'You should have told me earlier.'

'Yeah, maybe I should but you know...'

Marsh frowned: he knew but he didn't – maybe he didn't want to know.

Charlie Tighe stuck a finger and thumb into a waistcoat pocket and drew out a scrap of paper. He passed it to Marsh.

It was a lined page ripped from an order book, with a name and address scrawled in pencil: *Sean Lynch, 136 Upper Cox Street.*

9

His visit to The Grand Turk having proved pointless – Furrell hadn't been in *right now* but he might be in *later like* – he walked up Benson Road, or what was left of it. Over the last days, the last weeks, the last months, he'd seen enough death and damage to last him a lifetime – to haunt his sleeping hours for the years to come – but what he could and would never get used to, was the pain and loss suffered by the people who had somehow come through this alive.

Life was tough but he'd always believed hard work and thrift were the answers: the best way was to manage your situation, rather than allow the situation to manage you.

Agnes felt the same. That's why they were together.

One of the reasons, anyway.

They made common cause.

Only this – this wanton, random destruction – was something else. It was, Reg realised, cruelty without any ambition other than the application of cruelty itself. And all delivered by the satanic hand of his so-called fellow man.

But now, cruellest of all, Emmy was gone.

No, not gone. To say *gone* – to think *gone* – was to almost accept Emmy would never return and that Reg could not countenance.

So, not gone then, *taken*.

After leaving Millicent Lee, Reg had run back to the factory, reported a family emergency (which was nothing but the truth) and said he'd be off for the rest of the day. At that point, Reg felt dread tighten in his chest, like bindweed round a tree stump. Shivering, he knew he must find his daughter, he must bring her home safe, deliver her from the human monster who had her and he – Reg Miles – would do whatever was needed to make sure that happened.

But to find Emmy, he had to find the boy and to find the boy, he had to find George Furrell. And right now, he was getting nowhere fast.

Standing there in the bomb-broken landscape, his head light, his stomach twisted and curled, there was a sweat on his brow – at this point, this moment, the nightly inferno burnt within him, rather than around him – but he knew nothing could stop him, nothing would stop him, from finding Emmy.

Nothing.

He moved further into the ruins.

To one side, the street had been reduced to a run of facades. A flat row of brickwork, without side walls or roofs, punctuated by shattered windows, staring sightlessly into the street.

What was left of it.

On the other side, house fronts had peeled off the terrace's carcass and crashed down onto the cobbles, turning pavement and road into an elaborate obstacle course.

Reg walked to the first house on his right and picked his way inside, stepping over masonry and charred timbers, the air a mix of tar and smoke.

The front room was burnt and featureless.

He went through to the backroom.

A table lay on its side, a chair stood next to it. There was a kettle on the stove and smashed chinaware in the sink. The back door had been blown outwards into the communal yard.

Moving from house to house, Reg worked his way up the street.

Some houses were better preserved than others but none was habitable and all were beyond rescue. In time – he had no idea when – the demolition crews would come in and finish the work Hitler had started.

At the top of the street, he turned and began to walk back. The light was going now but his mission was clearer than ever.

Walking along behind a brick frontage, there was very little to see but Reg felt an increasing loss with every step, sensing every pace was taking him further away from Emmy, not nearer. It was a desolation amplified and compounded by the absence of all the people whose lives he now walked in and through. Lives that until recently would have thrived all around him.

Glancing upwards, he imagined he could see horizontal and vertical lines crossing and defining ghost spaces – rooms where people once lived and laughed and cried. The air itself seemed to beat and echo with this very recent past.

So recent as to be almost palpable.

He could almost hear their laughter.

He could almost hear Emmy laughing.

Emmy.

The sadness receded as the light faded and an irresistible wave of panic washed over him – a panic that time was running against him and that there was very little he could do to slow its progress.

Stooping down, he picked up half a brick. It was white in places, black in others – the scarring of an incendiary device. He weighed it in his hand and looked around.

There was a nearby upper window, glass somehow intact.

On impulse, he stretched his arm back and threw the brick.

It arced through space, shattering the pane with a pleasing crack and fell into the street beyond.

He laughed and for a moment, the bindweed loosened.

10

Gone four, getting dark, Marsh turned into Upper Cox Street.

The door of 136 was green and blistered, in need of a fresh coat of paint. A net curtain hung behind its frosty, dimpled glass portal. Marsh reached out to the knocker and banged three times. He sensed movement, leant back, glanced across at the front window.

Nothing, just blackout.

And then a voice from inside of the house. A woman's voice, soft, lilting. 'Who is it?'

'My name's Marsh. Detective Sergeant Marsh, Birmingham City Police.'

The front door opened and the policeman offered up his warrant card.

'What do you want?' Her face was pale and lined, a wiry strand of dark hair across her forehead. She could have been anything between twenty and forty. Her skin was sallow and the little finger on her left hand was missing, stumped off at the knuckle.

'I'm looking for Sean Lynch. I believe he lives here.'

'What's our Sean done now?'

'Is he around?'

The woman looked him up and down. 'He is. You better come in.' She pulled the door open and turned. 'He's in the back. I've made him an early tea as I'm out to work.'

'Thank you,' Harry Marsh said, stepping into her front room and heading through to the back.

Sean Lynch glanced up as a familiar figure pushed its way through the curtain hanging over the kitchen door. The young man was much younger than Harry Marsh remembered him – eighteen maybe nineteen – and looked as thin and undernourished as the broth he was spooning into his mouth. There was the smell of onions in the air. An old tin pot pootled away on a gas ring.

The kitchen was small and dingy, most of the space was taken up by the table. Beneath the smell of food, there was an odour of damp.

Harry Marsh sat himself down opposite Lynch. 'Do you mind if I sit?'

'It would appear that I don't,' the young man said, running his spoon around the bowl, chasing one last lump of carrot, ladling it into his mouth.

The DS held out his warrant card and Lynch shook his head. 'No need, I remember you well enough. There's no point in you standing there, Dee, I'll be fine.'

'If you're sure,' the woman said, from the doorway.

Lynch looked at Harry Marsh. 'I am.'

Dee turned and went back into the front room.

'She's my cousin, Deirdre is,' Lynch said, 'but she acts like she's my elder sister, like I'm something she needs to fuss over all the time. Like I'm a constant worry.'

'And are you?'

Lynch shook his head and laughed again, his bray an emphatic and forced statement of courage and fortitude. His overconfidence a thin gloss disguising nervousness. 'No, I don't think I am but then I wouldn't, would I?'

'You are,' Dee said, from the front room.

'Now don't you go listening, cuz, this here's men's talk, it is.'

Dee laughed. 'Since when were you a man? Anyhows, I'm off, so as long as you're happy, the two of you?'

Lynch stood up, walked to the doorway and pulled the curtain across. 'Still your lips and go now.' He sat back down. 'There, that's better. What can I do for you, Mr Policeman?'

'The other night...'

'At The Traf you mean?'

'Yes. What was the disagreement about?'

'Nothing.'

'Nothing?'

The front door slammed shut and both men watched the curtain in the kitchen doorway twitch in the backdraught.

'Not a thing,' Lynch said, turning back to look at Marsh. 'We were there having an early drink, then when we left your two friends set on us. Said they needed to teach us a thing or two about our place in the world. How we should stay where we belonged or else we'd feel the long arm of the law a little more often.'

'And then?'

'Then they hit us a few times and you turned up.'

'And that's it?'

Lynch nodded and stood. 'That's it,' he said, walking over to the sink and rinsing out his bowl.

'The problem is, Sean,' Harry Marsh said, 'I don't believe you.'

Lynch turned and rested his back against the worktop. 'You're free to believe what you want,' he said, a young boy playing the big man, knowing his portrayal wasn't entirely convincing. ' 'Cos that's how free will works, isn't it? You want more, you have to buy it.'

'How well do you know Sergeant Greene?'

'Sergeant Greene? Who's he now?'

'The sergeant who beat you up.'

'Ah, that one. I know his boot better than I know him, to be honest.'

'And PC Noble?'

'That's the other fella I'm guessing? No, never seen him before either.' Lynch lifted a kettle and filled it under the tap. 'Cup of tea?'

'No, thank you,' Marsh said. 'Thing is, PC Noble's been beaten up.'

'Not too bad, I hope.'

'Bad enough to be in hospital.'

'And what's he's saying this Noble? Saying I did it? Is that what this is about?'

'No,' the policeman said, 'he's saying I did it.'

Lynch giggled and placed the kettle on the stove. 'You? I don't know about a cup of tea, I should be buying you something a wee bit stronger.'

'It's not funny,' Marsh said. 'It's really not funny.'

'Not for you, maybe, Sarge. Me? I think it's hilarious. Did you? Did you put him in hospital? Tell me you did, that would make my day, that would.'

'No, I did not. But your friend, Patrick Ivers, the one who was with you the other night, all of a sudden, he's nowhere to be found – or so I've been told – and I do find that a bit suspicious. I do wonder what he might know that he doesn't want me to know.'

Sean Lynch laughed and shrugged. 'He knows a few girls about the town does Paddy, I'll tell you that for nothing. And I'll tell you this, he's probably bedded down with one of them as we speak. Or maybe two of them. He can be like that can Paddy, a bit wild.'

Harry Marsh turned, looked at the workman's bag lying next to the back door, a short length of pipe visible on top of tools. 'Tell me, Sean, what do you do?'

'I'm a plumber, I am. Well, I will be. I'm learning the ropes at the moment.' He smiled. 'Or rather, I'm learning the pipes. And we're not talking the uilleann pipes, before you ask.'

'A plumber?'

'Yes.'

'A good trade, plumbing. People will always need plumbers.'

'Let's hope so.'

Harry Marsh stood and walked over to the door. He reached down and picked up the bag. 'This will be yours then.'

Lynch turned his head, looked, nodded. 'Aye, that's mine, that is.'

Marsh dropped the bag onto the table. It clattered and clanged as it settled. He reached in. 'Now what's this?' He pulled out the length of pipe and a hammer, laid them on the table, side by side, like bones in a museum.

'My tools,' Lynch said. 'That's what that is.'

'And this?'

'A blow torch.'

'This?'

'A pipe wrench.'

The policeman hefted the wrench in his hands. 'Heavy.'

'It is so.'

Using the wrench, Harry Marsh pointed at the kettle. 'Your water's boiling.'

'Thanks,' Sean Lynch said, turning off the gas ring and lifting the kettle away from the stove. He spooned tea into an old pot and covered the leaves with boiling water. 'You're sure you won't have a cup with me, Sarge? I can't convince you now?'

'I'm sure. And these?' Marsh dropped two pieces of metal onto the table next to the tools. Both were round, highly machined, with an inner thread. 'What are these?'

Lynch walked over and looked down. 'Piping caps. For capping off pipes, you know?'

The policeman picked up the length of pipe and started to screw one of the caps onto one end. 'Not a great fit though, is it?'

'Ah well.' Lynch sat down. 'Once it's on, it needs to be braised. That's why you need a blow torch and a bit of solder. To make it secure, like.'

Harry Marsh nodded and fitted the second cap to the other end of the pipe, before laying the whole thing back onto the table. 'Well, look at that,' he said.

Lynch looked puzzled. 'Look at what?'

'Doesn't it remind you of anything?'

'Should it?'

Marsh waited and watched Lynch's face as realisation washed

over his features. The boy swallowed. 'That bit of pipe, it's nothing, it's a bit of scrap for me to practise on. It's nothing at all.'

Marsh picked up the pipe and turned it over in his hands. 'Nothing now, that's true but a clever boy like you, you could turn it into something quick. Something like, I don't know, a pipe bomb?'

'What are you saying, Sergeant?'

'The two Irishmen who made the bomb that blew up the Broadgate shopping centre in Coventry last year, you know what happened to them?'

Lynch shook his head. 'No.'

'They were hanged in Winson Green earlier this year. They claimed they didn't know what was going to happen when they made that bomb. Said the man who asked them to make it told them it was for an electricity substation, not a row of shops. Anyway, they build it, he plants it, five people die. And you know what?'

'What?'

'They hang, he's still in prison, being looked at by some psychiatrist or other. He'll never get the noose, that one. He will die in prison but he'll never hang. Wouldn't be surprised if he outlives the both of us.'

Lynch's face reddened, he seemed on the point of tears. 'I haven't done anything. I haven't made anything for anyone. I haven't done anything. Ask anyone. I wouldn't do anything like that. I wouldn't.'

'Maybe not,' Marsh said, 'but so far this year, ninety-four IRA men and women have been apprehended and convicted of either possessing or using explosives or firearms. You fancy making it ninety-five?'

'I'm not IRA. Christ, I'm not. I'm not a Reb. Not me. Look at me, for Chrissakes, do I look like a Republican?'

'I'm sure the Special Irish Branch will bear looks in mind, when they have a word and they will have a word, trust me. Once they see this, they'll want a proper word,' Harry Marsh said, pointing at the pipe and the caps on the table. 'And I'm not sure a nice boy like you wants a word, let alone a *proper* word, with Special Branch.'

Lynch shook his head, realising he was in a hole, wondering how much further he had to fall. 'You English bastards, you're all the same. All bastards.'

Marsh smiled and tapped the pipe with a finger. 'Boom.'

Lynch licked his lips, breathed in, sighed. 'What do you want?'

'I want to know who beat up Bob Noble and why.'

Lynch shivered, sipped his tea, glared at the policeman. 'I can't. I just can't.'

'You do know something then?'

Lynch nodded.

Harry Marsh started putting the tools back into the bag. 'Sean, all I want to know is why I'm being blamed for this, that's all. Everything else I don't care about, everything else I can forget.'

Lynch finished his tea, put his cup down. 'Paddy, now his brother fixes up some of the locals round here with stuff, you know? Below the counter, tax-free, cheaper than it can be bought trade – when it can be bought, that is.'

'Alcohol?'

'Whiskey, yes.'

'And cigarettes?'

'Yes.'

'And your chat with Greene and Noble?'

Lynch dropped his shoulders, defeated, nothing left to lose. 'That was a warning to stay away. They saw us in the pub, they thought we were planning to move in on their territory. That's what they said, leastways.'

'Their territory?'

Lynch looked up and smiled for the first time in minutes. 'And you a copper. Do you not know anything about anything?'

'Anything about what?'

'Your boys in blue, them up the road, they've got a sideline in the illegal booze, fags and protection, they have. You don't buy what they've got to offer, chances are you won't get anything at all. Worse, you don't pay them off, you might end up not having what you started with. I hear there was a bad fire at some bar or other on their patch recently and I'm not talking about anything the Jerries put a match to.'

Harry Marsh started. As far as he was aware, all the pubs in Moseley and Kings Heath had come through the last weeks intact, apart from one: The Narrows.

Maybe Jeannie's story about a fire at The Narrows being deliberate was true after all – perhaps her customers were better informed than his wife gave them credit. And to be fair, Charlie Tighe had suggested that there was something not right with The Narrows' incident. 'And The Trafalgar Hotel, that's theirs?'

Lynch laughed. 'Christ, well, they'd like to think it is but that landlord fella, that Charlie Tighe, he's a bit of a boyo himself, plays both sides to see what's best for him, he does. Cuts it a bit too close sometimes, I can tell you, but who can blame him? Every man for himself these days, isn't it?'

'And the other night? Were you there on business?'

'Us? No, we were not. We were having a drink, just a quiet drink, would you believe? And then those two, they pull us outside, accuse us of muscling in on their turf. How their bosses won't be happy with us at all. And if their bosses weren't happy, they'd make sure ours weren't either.'

'Their bosses?'

Lynch laughed. 'The two you saw, they're just the Tommies, they are. The young copper, Paddy's brother and a friend gave him a leathering a couple of nights later, just to show them that we can't be pushed around without pushing back.' The boy stopped in his tracks, any sense of amusement vanishing from his face. 'Not that I'm anything to do with anything, you understand?'

Harry Marsh closed up the plumber's bag and put it on the floor. 'I understand, Sean and like I say, I'm not interested in the whiskey or the fags, I'm really not. But if you know anything else, anything at all, I am interested in that.'

Lynch's face twisted in a collision of confusion, computation, fear, all of which reduced to one simple question: how best to insure his own self-preservation. The boy lifted his chin and stared at Harry Marsh. 'And if I tell you, you won't be calling Special Branch on me anytime soon now, will you?'

'I won't.'

The boy nodded, paused, spoke. 'It's not just booze and fags, there's word of shooters too. Proper stuff, like. Rifles have been mentioned. Not that you heard that from me. You didn't hear it from me, did you?'

Marsh shook his head. 'Any names, Sean? Can you put any names to any of this?'

Lynch sat back, closed his eyes and then leant forward. He shrugged. 'Jesus, why ever not?' He wiped a hand across his forehead. 'Look, as I understand it, there's two top men. One does the business, gets the gear, the other one, he makes sure that whatever they've got, it gets put about.'

'Names?'

'One's another copper, I know that but I don't know his name.' Lynch said. 'The other, I've heard a name. I don't know who he is or what he looks like but I've heard a name, I have.'

'Tell me, Sean, tell me the name.'

'Arthur Shaw mean anything to you?'

No.

But then: yes.

Sod it.

11

Reg Miles arrived home. Nell was there with Agnes. The two women looked up at him as he entered, half-expecting to see Emmy following on behind. Reg shook his head. Agnes dropped her eyes and Nell took her sister-in-law's hand, squeezed it once and then wiped a tear from her own eye.

Reg threw his jacket over the back of his armchair and sat down. 'What did the police say?'

Agnes went to speak but choked. Nell reached out and patted her on the back. 'Nothing much,' Nell said. 'Only that they'll be out looking for her. Her and that Vincent boy. They've got good descriptions they said and they'll be in touch, soon as they know anything.'

Reg nodded. 'I would hope so.'

Agnes looked at her husband through swollen red lids. 'What about you, Reggie, you have any luck?'

'Does it look like I did?'

'Reginald,' Nell said, 'there's no need to take that tone.'

And Reg was a small boy again, being chastised by his twin sister. His older sister, as she liked to remind him. Older by a whole ten minutes but those ten minutes granted her lifelong authority.

'Sorry,' he said, standing, 'I didn't mean anything by it, Aggie, you know I didn't.'

Without looking at him, Agnes took his hand, her touch a touch he knew so well: physically the leathered hand of a hard-working woman, emotionally the hand of the only woman he would ever know. Would ever want to know.

He felt her push a piece of paper into his palm. 'What's this?'

'See for yourself.'

He unrolled the paper, held it up to the light and there in green ink: *You never know who's listening, be careful what you say.* The words, a play on a popular propaganda poster, one with a swastika and a cartoon German called Furtive Fritz. 'And where's this from?'

'Got pushed through the letterbox earlier,' his wife said.

He scrunched the paper into a ball and shoved it into a trouser pocket.

'What you up to, Reginald? What's this all about?'

Turning, he looked at Nell, hands on hips, voice instantly recognisable: his mother's voice, their mother's voice always ready to chide and admonish, never to praise.

'Nothing,' he said, a small boy again, a small boy staring down at his feet.

'That's not what I've heard,' his sister said.

He looked up. 'What have you heard?'

'You've been hanging round with the wrong sorts, that's what I've heard. Doing stuff you shouldn't.'

'Who told you that?'

'Someone at chapel yesterday.'

'Who?'

'Does it matter?'

'Who?'

'A few, if truth be told but no one you'd know, you've not been to chapel for so long,' Nell stepped forward, looked up into her brother's face. 'Tell me this has got nothing to do with that.'

'What you talking about?'

'Emmy. Elizabeth Margaret. Her being missing. Tell me it's a coincidence, Reg, a sad coincidence.'

'It's a coincidence.'

'What's a coincidence?' Agnes said, her yellow hue accentuated by the downlight from the unshaded ceiling light.

'Nothing,' Reg said.

'I don't believe you,' his wife said. 'Why don't I believe you, Reggie, why?'

'Agnes,' Nell said, resting a hand on her sister-in-law's shoulder. 'Agnes, love, everything's going to be alright.'

'No, it's not. I know it's not. I know. And it's all down to him, that's what you're saying, it's all down to your brother.'

Not her husband, not the father of her child but some other woman's brother, that shook Reg – that she should call him that, shook him more than he could have anticipated. 'I'll make it right,' Reg said. 'I will.'

'You're going to make this right, are you? Make it right?' She laughed. 'Then tell me, Reginald Miles, what you done to make it wrong in the first place?'

'Nothing, I've not done anything wrong.' He looked at his sister, hoping, praying for support, feeling more isolated, more detached, more removed than he ever had in his life. 'Not a thing.'

'Them cuts and bruises on your face,' Agnes said, 'I knew they were something, I knew you'd been up to something you shouldn't, Reggie, I knew.'

'I haven't.'

Agnes dropped her head and picked at the hem of her overall.

Nell stared at Reg, unblinking. It was the stare of a sister who knows exactly when a brother's telling the truth – and when he's lying.

Without saying another word, Agnes started crying, tears of anger, frustration, despair. 'What have you done, Reggie? I know you've done something but what have you done that this should happen? What have you been up to? What you done that brought this trouble down on our little girl? Our poor little Emmy. She could be anywhere. She could be hurt, she could be scared, she could be—'

Nell tightened her grip on her sister-in-law's shoulder. 'Don't say it, Agnes, whatever you do, don't say that. And don't think it. Not for one minute are you to think that.'

Agnes reached up and grasped the other woman's hand tight. 'Oh, Nell.'

'I'll let them know you won't be in work tonight, Agnes love,' Nell said. 'They'll understand, I'm sure. And if they don't, well sod 'em.'

'Thank you, Nell,' Agnes said, blinking away tears. 'Thank you.'

'And Reginald will do what Reginald needs to do. Won't you?'

Reg walked to his chair, scooped up his jacket from the back of his seat.

'Where you off to now?' Nell said.

'It's nearly six o'clock,' he said, 'and six o'clock is opening time.'

Nell shook her head in disbelief and Agnes appeared beside her.

'If you don't bring her back with you, Reggie,' his wife said, 'if you don't manage that, then don't bother coming back yourself. You hear me? Don't bother opening this door ever again. Ever. Ever. Ever. This house is dead to you. I'm dead to you. Emmy is—Emmy is—Emmy is...' Her sentence fluttered and faltered in the air.

Reg looked at his wife and her anger, her rawness, her desperation worked into him like acid on ancient paintwork, revealing features unseen for many years. He allowed her fierceness to strip away any final detachment or restraint that remained until all that was left was his need to strike out and hurt – a primal impulse for satisfaction that only violence could supply.

Only violence could satisfy.

A brick thrown through a glass windowpane.

The big man shivered, breathed in and stretched himself to his full height, hoping that how he felt right now wasn't apparent to anyone other than himself. Pulling on his jacket, Reg left the house and walked out into the evening, not knowing what he was about to do but knowing that he would do anything, anything at all, to bring his daughter back home.

Anything so that he didn't have to see Agnes look at him with such disgust ever again.

12

Jeannie looked up from her cross-stitch: a bee floating over a red bloom. 'You're home,' she said. 'And I haven't even thought about tea yet.'

Marsh knelt at his wife's feet, folded his arms across her knees. 'Only for the moment,' he said. Reaching out and around Jeannie, he picked up a bottle from the other side of her chair and turned it over in his hands.

Kilbeggan.

'That was on the doorstep when I got home,' his wife said. 'There's a note too.' Jeannie dropped her embroidery hoop and needles onto the tabletop and passed him a piece of paper.

Marsh unfolded it: *Sorry. You know there'll always be a drink in the taps for you. CT.*

'You're home, you're sad and you're in trouble,' Jeannie said, taking off his hat, pushing his hair back and up from his forehead. 'What is it?'

'Do you remember that wedding, the first time you came up here for a visit after we got engaged? Mom and Dad were invited to the service and we stood at the back to see if you liked the church enough to get married there?'

'The one at St Mary's? The bride was the younger sister of a family friend, wasn't she?'

'And do you remember the groom's name?'

'Shaw, I think. Arthur Shaw, wasn't it?'

Marsh stood, walked across to the sideboard, took out a tumbler, poured himself a large measure of whiskey.

Arthur Shaw.

Sod it.

Sod it.

Sod it.

He emptied his glass and picked up his hat. 'I'll be late,' he said and left without saying another word.

13

Reg Miles walked up to The Grand Turk. *Maybe later*, the barmaid had said at lunchtime, *you'll almost certainly find Georgie in here later*.

Now was later.

Everything would be fine, Reg told himself.

Nothing would be fine, Reg told himself.

A barman walked over as Reg arrived at the counter. Sleeves buttoned tight at the wrist and held in place on his upper arms by gold elasticated bands, the man wore a waistcoat over his striped shirt and a silk tie, complete with a gem encrusted tiepin. He was drying a tankard with a dirty cloth. 'What can I get you?'

'Not a thing in that glass.'

The man looked at the cloth. 'You're right, it does need a bit of a rinse. Still, who'll know?' He put the glass under the counter and dropped the towel into a nearby sink. 'What was it again?'

'I'm looking for someone,' Reg said. 'Been told he drinks here.'

The barman eyed him up and down. 'That's what people do, you know? Drink here.'

Reg smiled and nodded. 'Guess they do.'

'So, my friend, what's your poison?'

'George Furrell. I'm looking for George Furrell. Is he in?'

'Depends,' the barman said.

'On what?'

'You a rozzer?'

Reg laughed. 'Do I look like a rozzer?'

The man giggled. 'Nargh but they're crafty sods these days them rozzers, always trying to catch us out on something or other, always.'

'Really?'

'Tell you what, you prove you're not a rozzer and I'll tell you if I know George Furrell.'

Reg glared at the dandy in front of him. 'How can I prove something I'm not? That's like asking me to show you something that's not here.'

The barman shrugged. 'True. Never thought of it like that.'

'I can show you what I am though.'

'Oh yeah? And what are you?'

Reg caught hold of the man's tie. Tugging hard, he dragged him forward until they were almost nose to nose. 'Angry,' Reg said, 'sodding angry and looking for someone to take it out on.'

Unperturbed, as if this threat of random violence was an everyday occurrence, the man gestured towards the next bar. 'He's in there. He's the bald bloke with the tartan muffler.'

'Thank you,' Reg said, releasing his grip and straightening his back. 'Much appreciated.'

George Furrell glanced up as Reg Miles walked across the room and gave the impression he recognised the big man. 'You're looking for me, by the looks of things,' Furrell said. 'Landlord said some big bloke had been in asking after me.'

Reg stopped in his tracks. Of all the receptions he'd anticipated, this was not one of them. All he could do was nod. 'George Furrell?'

Furrell stood. 'That's me.'

'Can we have a word?'

George Furrell looked at the cards in his hand, sighed, and threw them down onto the table. 'I'm out, boys,' he said. 'Not a good hand anyway. Now, who are you and what's this about?'

'Let's take this outside.'

Furrell laughed. 'I've had better offers in my time and from better lookers than you. Now, if you're going to wallop me, have the decency to tell me what it's about first, son. Who have I upset this time?'

'I'm not going to hit you,' Reg said. 'And I'm not your *son*. It's about Vincent Lee and my daughter.'

'Alright,' George said, standing up, 'let's go outside.'

Reg walked into the yard, turned around and watched the other man relight a cigarette. The stub was barely worth it.

'You shouldn't, you know,' Reg said. 'Not out here.'

George stared up at the sky. 'They won't see this little thing from up there, now will they? And they've not been round these parts the last few days anyway.'

Bombs, fire, water.

Water, fire, bombs.

Incessant, cyclic, never-ending.

'No, they haven't.'

'I'll carry on then.' He drew on the cigarette, all the time watching Reg. Exhaling, he took a pace forward. 'Who are you?'

'My name's Reginald Miles and I'm looking for Vincent Lee.'

'So you said.'

'My daughter, Emmy – Elizabeth Margaret – she's missing.'

'And what's the boy got to do with that?'

'Last time she was seen, she was seen talking to him. At the school gate, this morning. Then she went off with him.'

'And how old's – what did you say her name was – Emmy? How old's Emmy?'

'She's five, six September next. She's at school with your boy Freddie. Same class.'

'Is she now?'

'She is.'

Furrell took a last drag off his cigarette, threw it to the ground, stepped on it. 'I see.'

'Do you know where he is?'

'Have you tried The Old Crow?'

'The Old Crow?'

'Millicent Lee. She lives opposite us.'

'I have.'

'And he wasn't there?'

'You think I'd be here if he was?'

George Furrell smiled. 'Fair enough.'

Reg stepped off a couple of paces, circled around, came back in, stood over and above the smaller man. 'She said you and the boy were close.'

Furrell shrugged. 'He talks to me a bit. Not much but sometimes. And I lend an ear. If you call that close, then, yeah, we're close.'

'Close enough to tell you if he's got a hiding place? Somewhere he can run off to?'

George Furrell squinted as if deciding whether something was out of square or not and then nodded. 'Maybe.'

'You going to tell me where?'

Furrell peered up at Reg. 'They'll just be playing.'

'And how do you know that?'

'You got a cigarette on you? You smell like a smoker.'

Reg pulled out a packet. George Furrell took one and struck a match.

'He's a sad boy is Vince. His mom died a few years back, he's never got over that,' Furrell said. 'And then his dad threw him out. Tossed him aside like a rag doll. And he got hurt all over again. You've got to understand that about him.'

'OK,' Reg said, 'but do you know where he is or don't you?'

14

Harry Marsh raised his hand and hesitated. Annie Scott stood off to his right and a couple of uniforms loitered by the cars – Hayward and Smiley – he remembered them from the other day, from the day they'd discovered Liora Montealto's body. How long ago was that exactly? Marsh couldn't be sure, everything just blurred from one moment to the next, what with the winter coming in and the bombings – both relentless and both seemingly without pause, stitching the days together, with an invisible, unbreakable thread.

Yesterday?

The day before?

No, he couldn't be certain but there was one thing he did know, one thing he knew for sure: here he was.

Here at this door.

Here and now.

The PCs wouldn't have been his choice but they were available when needed and he didn't want to use any of the local Moseley coppers, not for this. He couldn't be certain where their loyalties would lie.

Seaborne had agreed. 'Take a car and whoever you can – even Scott-Taylor, if you want – and get over there. This needs sorting, now, tonight, pronterino.' There had been an urgency and an excitement in his superior's voice. A tone, Harry suspected, last heard when ordering a driver to chase smash-and-grab robbers through the streets of London, at high speed, in the pre-war years.

Marsh looked at Annie Scott, she nodded and the sergeant knocked.

Nothing.

He banged his fist on the wooden door.

'Who is it?'

'Harry Marsh,' Marsh said, doing his best to sound calm, measured, matter-of-fact.

'Harold Marsh,' the voice said. 'What do you want at this time of night?'

The door opened.

Alfred Henderson stood there, shirt unbuttoned, white vest tucked into uniform trousers. Trousers hiked up and over his belly by braces and held in place with a broad leather belt.

'I need you to get dressed and come with me, Sergeant Henderson,' Marsh said. 'I've got a few questions for you.'

'Come with you? What now? Tonight?'

The DS nodded. 'Tonight.'

'A few questions about what?'

'I'm sure you can guess.'

Henderson shook his head and smiled, bold and resolute in his innocence. 'Give me an idea, Detective Sergeant Marsh,' he said. 'Just one, eh?'

'Hayward, Smiley, take Sergeant Henderson inside and help him get dressed, if needs be.'

'Yes, Sergeant,' Smiley said, almost saluting. He looked at Henderson and pointed into the house. 'Shall we?'

Henderson scowled at Smiley. 'Shall we what? Dance?'

Taking a sideways glance at Harry Marsh, Alfred Henderson shrugged and disappeared back into his unlit front room. Hayward and Smiley followed him.

Harry Marsh breathed out and looked down at his feet. He looked like a schoolboy disappointed with an exam result.

Annie Scott stepped in close. 'You like him, don't you?'

'Why'd you say that?'

'You hesitated. You didn't knock right away and you looked at me for reassurance. You like him.'

Him.

Alfred Henderson.

Charlie Tighe.

He liked them both and they'd both changed, or so it seemed. But then how can you say someone's changed when it turns out you didn't really know them at all?

And it turns out he never did, never had – and what sort of copper did that make him?

Pretty sodding useless.

But then what defines *useless* when the world's going to hell?

He had a decision to make, responsibilities to bear, actions to take for which he felt entirely unequipped and yes, in truth, he felt *useless*.

Henderson.

Charlie Tighe.

The Montealtos.

Especially the Montealtos.

A father who believes he has no other option than to kill his beloved daughter in order to protect her – there were no laws on the statute book conceived to deal with a situation like that, no court on earth able to pass judgement.

No man or woman able to face the baseless horror of the action.

The more Marsh thought about it, the more it seemed to him that the Montealto case was just an extreme example of the old madness returned, the madness he had seen face to face on a battlefield in France and the madness he swore he would do his best to prevent reoccurring.

But he'd failed.

And as it turned out, was failing daily by not recognising elements of that madness when it infected people he thought he knew.

Christ, what kind of a world were they living in right now?

Sod it right to hell.

And back again.

'Everyone changes,' he said, the taste of bile in the back of his throat. 'No one's ever quite what you think they are in the first place and then everyone changes anyway.'

15

They were smart houses – once. Mid-Victorian villas designed and built for the up-and-coming middle-classes. Attic rooms for the servants, cellars for ice and coal. Reception room, a dining room, a withdrawing room and gas-heated bedrooms. But now they were deserted and boarded up. Condemned before the war for being in a part of town no longer desirable – at least, not by the more recently affluent.

George Furrell pushed open the rear garden gate and Reg Miles followed him down the path.

At the kitchen door, Furrell raised a finger to his lips and then pointed at the ground: there was broken glass all over the floor. Stepping over and around the glass, he edged forward and into the house.

The kitchen had been stripped. Where there should have been sinks, there was bare plaster. Pipes had been ripped from walls and the large fireplace was missing its iron work.

George Furrell crossed the room and eased open a corner door. Joining him, Reg found he was looking down a flight of stairs into a cellar passageway, its far wall lit by a throw of flickering light.

At the foot of the stairs, the two men turned left, towards the source of that light.

The coal cellar was a parody of a family room. In the centre, a table covered with a singed, red-checked cloth and surrounded by four mismatched chairs. There was an equally mismatched tea set laid out, ready for non-existent guests.

An old oil lamp hung from a beam, casting its blue hue over the entire space.

A moth-eaten chaise longue was pushed up against the far wall, a pile of sheets at one end, two pillows at the other, a leg missing and the corner propped up with a brick.

The room had been done out in what could be salvaged from wrecked houses or what had been thrown away, no longer fit for purpose.

A young boy sat in the middle of the chaise longue, wrapped in an eiderdown, thumbing through a colouring book, a box of No 52 Crayola crayons next to him. He was shovelling sweets into his mouth from a white paper bag.

Vincent Lee.

But no sign of Emmy Miles.

No sign of Emmy – Reg felt the fire inside flame higher.

The boy looked up as Reg bounded over to him and grabbed him by the collar, pulled him onto his tiptoes. The eiderdown and colouring book fell to the floor.

'Where is she? What have you done to her?'

The boy stared up at Reg. He was a good-looking lad, with dark hair and big eyes and the expression on his face reminded the man of nothing less than an animal caught in a trap, paralysed by fear, unable or unwilling to move. Maybe this was the sadness that George Furrell had described. Or maybe it was something else. It struck Reg more as a complete absence of anything – for a moment, it seemed the boy was a shell and nothing more.

Reg didn't care. He shook him. 'Where is she?'

Furrell appeared at Reg's shoulder and the boy looked across at the other man.

'This won't help. Won't help anything at all. Best put him down.'

Reg grunted and took his hands away.

Vincent settled back onto his feet.

Furrell bent down, picked up the colouring book, looked at the cover: *New York World Fair 1939*.

'That's mine, that is,' the boy said, reaching out.

'This man,' George Furrell said, pointing at Reg. 'This man is looking for his daughter. Elizabeth Margaret Miles. Emmy Miles. Have you seen her?'

The boy stared at Furrell and then looked over at Reg before looking back to his uncle.

'We know he's seen her,' Reg said. 'He saw her this morning.'

'Is that right, Vince, son? Have you seen this kid? His kid?'

Vincent stared straight ahead, motionless, wordless, blank.

'He knows where she is,' Reg said, reaching out to grab Vincent again. 'I know he knows.'

Furrell swatted Reg's arm away. 'That won't help. Now, Vince, this girl Emmy, you did see her, didn't you?'

Vincent nodded.

'Is she alright?'

Vincent nodded again.

'Where is she, Vince, son? Can you take us to her?'

Vincent nodded for a third and final time.

16

Waxy and unforgiving, the light in the windowless interview room made the three people around the table look as if they'd just been released from the Little Bromwich Fever Hospital.

Or worse, were on the point of admission.

Harry Marsh, Annie Scott and Alfred Henderson sat in silence, the only sound the occasional rattle and rumble of heating pipes, as they coughed, heaved and sighed deep within the building.

Henderson was down to his shirt sleeves again, both of which were rolled up to his elbows. Tie askew, his jacket hung off the back of his chair, he smelt of brown ale and cigarette smoke – the cigarette he'd requested and Marsh had allowed, before entering the station.

'Arthur Shaw,' Harry Marsh said, 'you're familiar with him?'

Henderson nodded. 'Should be. Artie, he's my brother-in-law. But you know that, Harold, your mom and dad were at the wedding. You too, if I remember right, though you weren't invited.'

'You remember right.'

'What's Artie done now then?'

Annie Scott leant forward. 'We have reason to believe he's involved in black marketeering. Mostly but not exclusively, whiskey and cigarettes. Would you happen to know anything about that?'

Henderson sniggered. He looked at the young woman as if she was the most clueless person he'd ever met. 'Who isn't involved in a bit of dodgy dealing these days, bab?' he said.

'Most seriously, there's been mention of—'

'Not now,' Marsh said, with a shake of his head. 'We'll come to that in a bit.'

'As you wish,' the young policewoman said.

Henderson looked Annie Scott up and down. 'Where'd you find this one, Harold? She's proper posh, like. A bit too good for you, I'd have thought, despite your hoity-toity schooling.'

'Think what you like,' Marsh said, 'but please answer the question: are you in any way involved with Arthur Shaw?'

Henderson dropped his head to one side and smiled. 'He's married to my sister, so yes, you could say we're involved.'

Harry Marsh stood, stretched out his back, leant forward and rested his hands on the table. 'And his trade in alcohol and cigarettes?'

Henderson sighed, a grown-up losing patience with a slow child. 'Like I say, everyone's a bit bent these days, even people who don't mean to be. The number of laws this government have brought in of late, you don't know what's legal one day to the next. Truly, you don't.' He sat back, a self-satisfied grin on his face. 'And I'm a policeman, it's my job to know, so if I don't, God help the ordinary joe on the street.'

'Yes,' Marsh said, 'I do get that. But this isn't crime by accident, this is methodical, well-thought out, exploitative criminality, at its worst.'

'Highfalutin' words, those – you get them from her by any chance?' Henderson said, smiling at Annie.

'The thing is,' Marsh said, 'if it was just alcohol and tobacco, well, it would just be alcohol and tobacco, which is bad enough. But, it seems, there's a level of protection being offered too. A bit of proper gangsterism. And that rather lifts it to another level, don't you agree? Tell me, Sergeant Henderson, what do you know about The Narrows?'

Henderson laughed. 'The Narrows? Got bombed out, didn't it?' He crossed his arms in front of him. 'That's what I heard, anyway.'

'That's what everyone heard,' Annie Scott said. 'But we have new information indicating that what everyone heard may not be correct.'

'Oh look,' Henderson said, turning to stare at the young woman, 'cat's given that one back her tongue.'

'This is not,' Harry Marsh said, 'a joke.'

Henderson pointed at his own face. 'Am I laughing, Harold? Look at my face, is this me laughing? It is not. I'll tell you what is funny though.'

'What's that?'

'The Narrows. That's what's funny.'

'It is?'

Henderson cackled. 'If I was you, I'd be talking to the owner of The Narrows. Ask him what he knows about the fire.'

'And who's the owner?' Marsh said, walking around and behind Henderson. 'Who should I be asking?'

Henderson looked over his shoulder and grinned. 'Some Polack tatter man from the other side of town. Bought the club last year as a bit of investment and then only goes and loses the whole shebang in a card game. And from what I've heard, he's a bad loser. And a yid, to boot, some greedy old Jewboy who don't like giving up what is no longer his.' He laughed again. 'Still, if word gets around that what happened to him you made happen and you can make it happen to others, why not take some credit?'

Yid.

Jewboy.

Juden.

Liora.

The words burnt like magnesium in water – bright, piercing, blinding – and Marsh felt that old feeling again, that sensation he always got when humanity's mask slipped, revealing the capricious, cruel primitive beneath.

Without thinking, Harry Marsh lunged at Henderson and slammed the man's head down onto the desk. Moving in closer, Marsh made a fist, ready to pull Henderson upright and punch him in the face.

Winding his arm back, his elbow hit something.

There was a yelp of pain.

He turned to see Annie Scott standing close behind him, one hand raised to her face, the other pulling a handkerchief from a pocket.

'Annie—'

'Don't,' she said, wheeling away, wiping around her right eye with the handkerchief, 'don't do anything else to him you'll come to regret and don't worry about me, I'm fine.'

Henderson sat back up and grinned, blood running out of one nostril. He spat on the floor. 'You do surprise me, Harold, I'd never have thought you had it in you. Never. What you going to say? I walked into a door or something?'

Harry Marsh shook his head, felt a tightness in his chest, took a pace away. He closed his eyes and slowed his breathing.

Not now, Christ, not now.

Opening his eyes, he glanced across at Annie.

His elbow had connected with the right side of her face but there were no cuts, no blood that he could see, although there would be a black eye, that much was certain.

Henderson rubbed a hand across his mouth and looked at Annie Scott. 'You're going to get a right reputation for beating up coppers, you are, Harold, if you're not careful.'

'Shut up,' Marsh said, as he sat back down. Reaching into a pocket, he pulled out his PNB, thumbed through a few pages. 'Being, as you say, *a proper copper*, I spoke to a young Irish lad earlier. He had a few things to say. Interesting things.'

Henderson spat on the floor again. 'I wouldn't go believing what any of them bogtrotters tell you. You can't trust a single one of them. Not one of them.'

'He's one of the two that got beaten up outside The Trafalgar Hotel the other night. Him and his mate Patrick Ivers.'

'I'll believe you.'

'Beaten up by Greene and Noble.'

'Ah,' Henderson said. 'And how is poor old Bob? I hear you went to see him at the hospital this morning. And then sent in some nice lady doctor to make sure he was doing alright.'

'I did.'

'Guilty conscience, eh, Harold? You take him grapes or flowers or something else nice?'

Marsh looked down and reread a page in his police notebook, slowly, deliberately. 'We had a nice chat me and Bob and I think he appreciated it, I certainly did,' he said, without looking back up.

'What'd you talk about?'

'What do you think?'

'I couldn't say, seeing as I wasn't there.'

'Surprised your ears weren't burning because you were there in spirit. Thing is, I was there in person,' Marsh said, closing his PNB and placing it on the table in front of him, hoping his bluff would work, knowing that Noble had refused to name anyone and that they were only here now because of Sean Lynch. 'All of which gives me something of an advantage, seeing as I know what was said and you don't.'

A pulse started to beat in Henderson's left temple, as regular as a metronome. He glanced down at the tabletop, at the notebook. 'Does it now?'

'It does now.'

'Good for you,' Henderson said, a quiver of uncertainty in his voice, like the first drop of sweat on a summer day, unwanted but unavoidable. 'Good for you.'

Harry Marsh stood, moved around the table, sat on the corner nearest the sergeant, positioning himself so he could see both Henderson and Annie Scott. 'Do you want to know something, Alfred?'

'Depends on what you've got to say. Or maybe you're just going to hit me again. In which case, I don't want to know.'

'Let me tell you what I think's going on here,' Marsh said. 'You taking notes, Policewoman Scott?'

'Yes, Sergeant,' Annie Scott said, holding up a notebook and a pen.

'Good,' the DS said. 'Good. So. What I think is this: a man hears about a stash of illicit alcohol and tobacco that's just come into the country, almost certainly smuggled in from the Irish Republic. Now, this man, he works at a factory producing goods that the importers of said alcohol and tobacco would like to get their hands on. Which is both convenient and useful, as it means no cash layout upfront, just a simple exchange of goods.'

'It would be convenient that,' Henderson said. 'And useful. Some might say a proper business opportunity.'

'It would. Anyway, first up, this man he gets himself a partner, a well-connected type, a man well known in his neighbourhood. This man, he really knows his patch. All the local pubs and hostelries. How am I doing so far?'

Henderson shrugged. 'You should be on the wireless, you tell good bedtime stories, you.'

Marsh nodded. 'Maybe I'll try it one day, when I get sick of nicking criminal types,' he said. 'Anyway, these men, they approach all these local businesses and like all good salesmen, they offer them an incentive to buy their goods, rather than anybody else's. A bonus offer. Good salesmanship that, I'm sure you'll agree.'

'I might if I knew what you were going on about.'

Harry Marsh laughed. 'It's very simple: buy our stuff and stay in business, don't buy our stuff and well, we can't guarantee you'll still be in business next week.'

Henderson peered up at Marsh, pulled a face of mock horror. 'That sounds like a threat that does.'

'Doesn't it? What do you think, Annie?'

'I think it's called protection, in criminal circles,' Annie Scott said. 'Or demand with menaces, in legal ones.'

Harry Marsh smiled. 'Only there's no protection money involved here, just a request that specific goods are purchased from a specified supplier for a set price and this price carries a guarantee that certain premises remain intact and in business. I'm getting a bit ahead of myself but how am I doing so far?'

Henderson shook his head. 'Couldn't tell you.'

'Now, as in all successful businesses,' Marsh said, 'these men, they find they're onto a good thing, a winner. So, they decide to recruit some help, which they do. Anyway, this help, it goes around, knocks on a few more doors, makes the pitch and starts to get even better results. Not surprising, given the very unique offer. And the fact that the help, well, they're in uniform.'

'I can see how that would work,' Henderson said, with a nod.

'And it works very well. So well that they think about expanding and there's a sortie or two up the road, just to test the waters,' Harry Marsh said. 'Only thing is, up the road is taken, so no luck there, as they get told in no uncertain terms. And then one night, the help come across two lads from up the road drinking in a place they consider their own. Seeing it as a threat when it's genuinely nothing but two young men having a drink, they take them outside and give them a beating. And two unlucky Irish fellas get a kicking they don't deserve, not only for being Irish but for being Irish in the wrong place, at the wrong time. Is that about right, Alfred?'

Henderson shook his head. 'Like I say, I wouldn't believe a word that Sean Lynch tells you, he's what them bogtrotters call a gob-shite – he'll say whatever it takes to stop him getting it in the neck. Or, hung by the neck.'

17

Leading George Furrell by the hand, Vincent Lee dragged him up onto the pavement. Reg followed on behind, each step adding to his impatience, the twist in his guts, his need for outlet. He was shocked at how he felt but not surprised.

'There,' Vincent said, pointing at what looked like any and every other house in the row. 'That one. That's the one you want.'

Furrell knelt down in front of the boy. 'You sure now, son?'

The boy nodded. 'I followed them. After they got me to talk to Emmy at the school, after they said her mom wasn't well and that she needed to go with them, after the man give me the colouring book and the crayons and the lady, she give me the gobstoppers, after all that, I followed them and that's where they went. That's where they took her.'

George Furrell put a hand on the boy's shoulder, stared him in the eyes. 'You go home now, Vincent, and by home I mean Aunt Millie's, not that cellar we found you in – you understand?'

The boy nodded again. 'Yes,' he said, before turning and scarpering off.

Furrell straightened up as Reg joined him. 'You care about that boy,' Reg said.

'Some kids, they're strong,' the other man said, 'you know they are from the minute you meet them. From the minute they're born. They just need toughening up, seasoning, something that makes them ready for whatever this tatter wagon of a world throws at them or tries to steal off them. Do that and they'll be alright. Be better than alright.'

Reg grunted. He'd have never put it that way but it was a fair assessment.

'Others,' George Furrell said, 'they need looking after. Vincent, he's like that.' He bent his neck and stared up at the big man. 'What'd you want to do now?'

'Don't know about you but I'm going in.'

'Best to have a look round first, don't you think?'

Reg glared down at Furrell but then twitched his jaw up and down in agreement.

One behind the other, the two men walked down the nearest side passage. Exiting into the terrace-wide yard, they turned left and pushed themselves against the wall, next to a blacked-out window and a back door.

Reg got his head as close to the glass as he could.

'Hear anything?' George Furrell said, mouthing the words.

'Nothing.'

'What do you want to do?'

'You go back to the street, knock on the front door, distract whoever's inside. I'm going in this way.'

'You sure?'

Again, the jaw.

Furrell disappeared into the gloom.

A minute later, Reg heard a beating on a wooden door and then a woman's voice from inside the house: 'What? Who is it?'

'ARP,' a male voice said, 'you've got a light showing.'

'I never.'

'You have. I need a word, missus.'

The sound of footsteps inside the house and then the front door opening, followed by the same female voice as before: 'Hello? Hello?'

Reg pushed on the back door and eased it open, pulled back the blackout curtain that covered the entrance on the inside.

He saw a kitchen with a fireplace, a sink, a cheap cooker, a table and four chairs.

A young girl sat at the table, her back to him.

Elizabeth Margaret.

Emmy.

And the nausea he'd felt all day changed. The relief wrenched his gut, made him want to double over and throw up on his shoes, while tears pricked in the ducts of both eyes.

But not now – he wasn't going to give into these feeling now – because right now he had things to do. Matters to put right.

As he watched, the girl carefully wetted the nib of a brown-handled dip pen in a small bottle of ink and wrote on a sheet of paper. He could tell from the way she was bent over the table that she was concentrating hard and he knew that her tongue was undoubtably held between clenched teeth.

He crept up behind her. Reaching out, he placed his hand across his daughter's mouth. She squirmed around and looked up at him – even with her mouth covered, he knew she was grinning. 'Shush,' he said, 'shush. Shush.'

Emmy nodded.

He looked down at the table.

Numbers, all written in green ink.

She'd been doing her numbers on the back of what looked like an official document. Reg turned the paper over. It was a BSA scrap release form signed by Byfield but signed several times, the shape and form of the lettering significantly different on each occasion – someone had been practising their signature.

Or rather, practising someone else's signature.

Each signature a rehearsal in green ink.

Reg heard a woman sigh and the front door close.

At the same time, a man's voice called down the stairs: 'What's that all about then?'

'Don't know,' the woman said, 'claimed to be ARP but when I opened the door, there was no one there. Had a look up the street but couldn't see anyone.'

The woman appeared in the kitchen doorway at exactly the same time as the man came down the stairs.

Reg knew them both.

The woman was Lucy Potter, Byfield's secretary.

The man, Arthur Shaw.

18

Harry Marsh walked across the interview room and sat down. 'We'll come back to the gobshite in a bit,' he said. 'Anyway, a couple of days after the Irish boys get a seeing to, PC Robert Noble gets done over in return and then what happens?'

Henderson smiled. 'I'd ask but I'm sure you're going to tell me.'

'What happens is that he points a finger at me. Accuses me of having some personal feud against him – exactly what, he's not certain, he doesn't say but yes, I'm definitely the one who put him in the hospital. But why me? Why accuse me?'

Henderson pouted and shrugged. 'No idea. What did he say?'

'Because it's another opportunity just like The Narrows,' Marsh said. 'And these boys, this firm, they love an opportunity. Especially an opportunity snatched in the face of adversity.'

Henderson smirked. 'Don't we all?'

'Can we quote you on that?' Annie Scott said.

Henderson cranked his neck around. 'I'd forgotten all about you, bab. How's the shorthand going over there? I can speak nice and slow if you like. Or if you need me to repeat anything, just ask.'

'I will,' Annie Scott said, 'don't you worry.'

Henderson swung back and squinted at Harry. 'You were saying, Harold.'

'Bob Noble's in hospital,' Marsh said, 'nothing to be done about that but why not use what's happened, why not take advantage of it? Exploit it.'

'I don't get you.'

'There's a detective sergeant from the city police, he's been asking questions, sticking his nose in where it's not wanted and to make matters worse, he's local and not only that, he's friendly with the landlord at The Trafalgar Hotel. In fact, it was probably the landlord who told him who Greene and Noble were in the first place, so it's anyone's guess what else this landlord might have said. And given that, this detective sergeant, he might uncover something he shouldn't. I'd want to get shot of him, wouldn't you?'

'S'ppose I might.'

'And what better way than, I don't know, suspension on the suspicion he's bent and out of control? Beating up a fellow officer, it's not good for a reputation. Could be career ending. No, it would be career ending.'

Henderson nodded. 'Yeah, it would. But what's this got to do with me?'

'Fair point,' Marsh said. 'As I mentioned earlier, after I visited Bob Noble, I went into Balsall Heath and had a nice chat with a very obliging Irish fella. The *gobshite*, you called him.'

Henderson coughed and then spat on the floor. He glanced over at Annie Scott. 'Sorry about that.' He turned to look at Marsh. 'You're right, that Sean Lynch is a gobshite. Like I said, he'll tell you anything to save his own skin.'

Annie Scott glanced at her notes, looked up at Henderson. 'Such as telling us his name?'

'What?'

The young woman smiled. 'Sergeant Marsh named Patrick Ivers but never mentioned any other name, not once. He didn't know it when he first came into your station and inquired after Greene and Noble. At that time, he didn't have a clue who the boys were. And tonight? Well...' Annie Scott pointed at her notes, 'It would seem you were the first to mention Sean Lynch by name.'

Henderson glared up at her. 'You sure about that?'

'Oh I'm positive. You see after graduating, I took a Pitman's course, so my shorthand is not only fine it's absolutely first-rate.'

Marsh laughed. 'Anything to say, Alfred? Anything you'd like to add? Any other names?'

Henderson leapt to his feet, the metronome beating in both temples now. His skin was florid, even under the spiritless lighting and his breath raw with alcohol and stale smoke. 'Harold Marsh, you always were a pompous little snit, even as a kid. Got yourself into that posh school on the one day, by the next day everyone knows about it. A snob and a snit back then and look at you now, a snob and a snit still. Just a bigger snob and a bigger snit.'

Pleased with his outburst, Henderson fell back onto his seat, crossed his arms and shook his head – this game wasn't over until he said so.

Marsh looked on, speechless, lost, hurt even, not quite knowing why and not knowing where to go next.

19

'Artie,' the woman said, staring at Reg Miles, 'Arthur, do something.'

'Reggie,' Shaw said, pulling his braces up and over his undershirt. 'Nice to see you.'

'Can't say the same,' Reg said, forcing his desire to hurt this man down deep. 'Come on, Emmy, we're going home.'

The little girl stood and took her father's hand.

Shaw was by the table now. 'Is that it? Is that all?'

'Would appear so.'

'What, no fuss, no threats, no demands? You don't want an explanation, nothing?'

'You can tell the police everything, when they arrive.'

'The police?' Lucy Potter said. 'Artie, stop him, make him stop.'

Arthur Shaw smiled and the circling shark returned. 'It's not that easy, Reggie, it's not. Your Emmy here, she's vulnerable in such dangerous times –today's proved that. That poor girl they found dead under a door over the way, she was young too. Not much older than your Emmy, from what I hear. You think about her, that poor dead girl. Next time, before you speak to Byfield, you think about her – and Emmy.'

Beyond words, Reg stared at Shaw.

'What you going to say to the police anyway, Reggie? I know what we'll say. We'll say we found little Emmy here out on the street. She was lost, wandering around on her own, scared of the dark, poor kid. Really terrified. The dark's scary, isn't it, buttercup?'

Emmy nodded and turned, pushed her head into her father's coat.

'You ask me,' Shaw said, 'that's proper cruel, letting a kid out on her own in a time like this, proper child abuse. The authorities, they won't like it, they won't. Might even take her away, for her own safety, and all. So what say we say nothing? We shake on it and we go about our business. Business as normal, like we discussed. You might even find that benefits you, Reggie. You and your little family. A little bit of extra tin in your pocket and the knowledge that little Emmy here's just that bit safer. You might enjoy that, you know?'

Reg stared at the table. At Emmy's paper. 'That's how you do it, eh?'

'Do what, Reggie?'

'The scrap permissions, all signed by Byfield, in green ink. Her green ink. Her hand.' He tilted his head towards Lucy Potter. She let out a groan and creased forward and inward, like a party balloon found behind a sofa a week after the celebrations. 'Artie,' she said, 'get rid of him. Get him out my house. Get him out now.'

Arthur Shaw leered at Reg and stuck out his hand. 'We got a deal?'

Reg looked at the outstretched hand, at the pink palm, the plump fingers, the manicured nails – how had he ever mistaken Shaw for a working man? 'Emmy, go and stand by the door.'

''Kay,' the girl said.

As she moved away, Reg reached out his own right hand and Arthur Shaw smiled. The smile vanished as Reg grabbed Shaw's right wrist with both hands and rotated it around until the wrist was raised, forced back and locked, the little finger and thumb spread to breaking point. Reg stepped in and the forward motion pushed Shaw down, bending him at the waist until his head was as close to the ground as Reg's had been the previous Saturday.

Reg pushed further and now Shaw's cheek was flush against the linoleum.

Swinging a leg across the man's back, Reg shoved his knee into Shaw's lumbar region and wrapped an arm around his throat.

'Lucy, do something,' Shaw said, his voice choked, hoarse.

Lucy Potter ran across the room, fumbled open a drawer, pulled out a pair of scissors, moved towards Emmy. 'You let him go,' she said. 'Let him go now.'

'That's not nice,' a voice said, 'threatening a little girl. Especially not twice in one day.'

Lucy Potter looked up to see George Furrell emerging from behind the back door's blackout curtain. He slapped her hard across the face. Her head twisted around, her grip loosened, the scissors fell to the floor. Furrell kicked them away.

Lucy Potter slumped to the ground, pushed her back against the wall, dropped her head to her knees and wailed: 'Don't hurt me, please don't hurt me.'

20

'What do you see when you look at Sergeant Marsh, the boy he was or the man he's become?'

Henderson glanced across at Annie Scott. 'What?'

'What do you see? It's a simple question.'

'I don't know how to answer that.'

'You already have – you see the boy. And what do you think he sees when he looks at you?'

Henderson frowned. 'Where's this going?'

'He sees a man he trusts,' Annie Scott said. 'A man he's known since childhood. A good man, in his childish eyes, a man he hopes is still in there, somewhere. The good bobby, the local bobby, the bobby everyone can rely on. You.'

'I was a good bobby.'

'Maybe you were once but you know what I see now?'

'I'm sure you're going to tell me,' Henderson said. 'You won't be able to stop yourself, will you?'

'I don't have memories of you,' the policewoman said, 'no nostalgia for long-lost salad days, I see you for exactly what you are now, not for how you were thirty years ago.'

'And what's that then?'

'A bully, a coward, a thief and a traitor.'

'Traitor? I'm no traitor.'

Annie Scott smiled. 'Black marketeering is bad enough, Sergeant Henderson, but selling arms to Irish Republicans? There's a case to be made for treason, in my opinion.'

'Guns? Irish Republicans?'

She shuffled her chair closer to the table. 'And what did you think they wanted the arms for?' she said. 'A country weekend?'

Marsh nodded at Annie Scott – now was the time.

'It might help your case,' she said, 'if we could speak to your associate, or should I say, your brother-in-law, Arthur Shaw.'

'He's at home I would have thought.'

Annie Scott shook her head. 'Only he's not. We sent a couple of officers around to his house earlier and he's not there.'

'Ahhhh,' Henderson said, the sound drawn out like a gas leak. 'He's not at home, is he?' Henderson shook his head. 'Then I don't know where he is.'

'You don't seem to know much,' the young woman said.

Henderson laughed. 'What I do know is that he's got a bit on the side, somewhere in town. That I do know.'

Annie Scott scowled. 'And you don't mind that he's got *a bit on the side*?'

'None of my business,' Henderson said.

'But he's married to your sister?'

Henderson smirked unconvincingly and a streak of sweat ran down the left side of his neck. 'Don't know much about men, do you, bab?'

The policewoman smiled, looked at her notes, looked over at Marsh. He smiled back. The interrogation was turning and turning in her favour. The fact of her sex was making Henderson uncomfortable – his latest barbs proved that – he'd never been questioned before, let alone by a woman.

'And what I do know,' she said, 'something I know very well is that treason during wartime, Sergeant, carries a serious sentence. A sentence some would only be too happy to pass.'

'Who would?'

Annie Scott moved forward. 'My grandfather would, almost certainly.'

Henderson looked at her in confusion.

'Annie's grandfather, he's a judge,' Harry Marsh said. 'Sir Anthony Scott-Taylor, you may have heard of him.'

Henderson squirmed and dropped his head. 'The Hanging Judge?'

Annie Scott smiled. 'I prefer Gramps.'

'Christ,' Henderson said. 'Christ on a bike.'

'Let's just hope he's doing something else on the day of your trial,' Annie Scott said.

Henderson shook his head, a drowning man reaching for a lifebelt that was beyond his grasp. 'I didn't know they were Rebs, I didn't. That was all part of Arthur's dealings. He sorted all that out. If anyone knew that, he did. I didn't, I swear it. I didn't.'

And now Henderson was the small boy cornered at the foot of the apple tree, his hands and pockets full of scrumped fruit.

'What I still don't get,' Marsh said, 'what I still don't get is why? Why this? Why now?'

'Why not?' Henderson said. 'When you get to my age and you're about to be kicked into the long grass with a pittance for your time, you look back and you wonder where you went wrong. You look at all the criminal types swimming in comfort and you wonder what's wrong with this world that you have nothing and they have everything. And that's when you realise that you're the wrong 'un, you're the one the world's taken for a mug and what have you got in return? Nothing. All I'm doing here is bending the world's troubles to suit me and mine and I don't see anything wrong with that. No, given my time over, I wouldn't change anything, not a thing. Except maybe the Rebel bit. Would never have had anything to do with them sorts, not had I known.'

Harry Marsh shook his head. 'I suspect a good percentage of what time you've got left is going to be spent doing time, so your future upkeep's the least of your worries.'

'About that,' Annie Scott said, 'if you can see your way to providing us with an address for this *bit on the side*, Sergeant Henderson, I can always try and have a word with Gramps on your behalf.'

Marsh laughed out loud – he couldn't stop himself, the sheer sense of fierce pleasure in her voice was just too much.

21

'You took your time,' Reg Miles said.

'I've been out there listening,' George Furrell said. 'What you going to do?'

'Not sure. Any idea how easy it is to snap a neck?'

George shook his head. 'No.'

'Nor me. Want to find out?'

'Not particularly. And you don't either, trust me. Think of your girl. Think about her.'

'I am thinking of her. Emmy, go stand outside. George Furrell, you go with her.'

'No,' Furrell said, 'I'm not doing that. Emmy, stay where you are.'

'Elizabeth Margaret, go outside.'

George bent forward, lowered his voice. 'Reg, whatever you're feeling now, it's going to be different later. When they arrest you, when they try you, when you get measured for the drop, it's going to be all different. You don't want that. Not for you, not for this sweet little girl of yours, you don't want any of that.'

Reg tightened his chokehold around Shaw's neck, pulled upward. 'Don't tell me what I want.'

'Reg, he's not worth it. Whatever he's done, he's not worth it.'

'Who's going to know?'

George turned and looked at Lucy Potter, her soft moan fading as she rocked herself into a near-catatonic state. He jerked a thumb in her direction. 'What you going to do about her then? You do anything stupid now, she'll know about it and she don't seem the sort to keep her mouth shut.'

'I'll tell her to say nothing.'

Furrell laughed. 'What, with threats? Even if that works, which it won't, you'll be no better than him. He needs locking up, not killing.'

'No one's getting locked up, not tonight, not ever, right?'

Reg and George Furrell turned.

The man known as Baz stood in the back door, hat pushed back, coat open, Webley Mk IV in his hand.

In the corner of the kitchen, curled up against the kitchen dresser, knees to chin, Lucy Potter started to laugh.

And laugh.

And laugh.

And laugh.

22

The cars sped on through the dark.

Dark.

The whole city was dark.

Buildings once so recognisable by their line, spire, curve were now nothing more than rubble stacked on rubble: grey, asymmetrical piles against a black sky.

And in the dark, street lamps unlit, visored traffic lights flickered and changed, throwing red, amber and green slits of light down, onto and across broken cobbles and ruptured tarmacadam.

The leading car bounced on the road's ruckled surface and for an instant, its masked headlights lit up a pavement.

Illuminated pedestrians pushed themselves back against shopfronts, panicked by the sudden light. Hoping they weren't about to become another statistic in the recent surge of road traffic accident fatalities, they stood frozen like criminals caught in a flash-lit photograph – fleeing but static, guilty but unable to move. In flagrante.

The police cars lurched around a corner and the street vanished back into the night.

Marsh swayed across the rear bench seat and found himself pressed up and against Annie Scott. She smelt of perfume, soap and smoke but mostly smoke. 'Sorry,' he said, as he righted himself.

'Don't worry,' she said, 'I've experienced far cruder advances in the back seat of many a car, I can assure you.'

And in the dark he couldn't tell whether she was joking or not. From her clipped but ironic tone, he suspected not.

The car was stuffy. He wound down the passenger window, let air blow in and across them. 'Thank you, by the way,' he said, after a moment.

'For what?'

'For the way you handled Henderson. For how you took the whole thing over, actually. I appreciate it.'

'It wasn't anything you wouldn't have done,' she said.

'Maybe so,' Marsh said, 'but I didn't.'

Annie Scott nodded – Marsh couldn't see her nod but they were still so close he could feel the movement.

'You could have,' she said, 'if he hadn't wrongfooted you. He's not a nice man that Sergeant Henderson, whatever you might think – or rather, might have thought. Often, it can take a stranger to see a friend for what they really are. But then you know that. What was it you said to Miss Lee? *It's sometimes the people we think we know the best who surprise us the most.*'

'Exactly that,' Marsh said, nodding, knowing that she was right, knowing that he'd allowed himself to be goaded, baited, distracted. And glad that she couldn't now see how embarrassed he was to have been so easily thrown by something even a somewhat green cadet could have avoided.

The car lurched again and this time they bounced upwards, Marsh's hat catching the roof.

'Watch it,' Marsh said.

'Sorry, Sarge,' Smiley said, from the driver's seat.

'Any idea what to expect?'

Marsh looked over at Annie Scott, the whites of her eyes just about visible in the gloom. 'What?'

'Any idea what we should expect?' she said.

'I don't know,' Marsh said. 'I really don't know.'

'Just a bit of advice, if you don't mind,' Henderson had said earlier, standing at the interview room door, wrists cuffed, ready to be led away. 'He's not a man you want to mess with is Arthur Shaw. He's always prepared is that man and he has a habit of getting his way no matter what gets in his way, if you see what I mean?'

Marsh did.

Or at least hoped he did.

The cars sped on.

23

Barry 'Baz' Kiteley took a step into the room, looked over at Arthur Shaw, waved the pistol at Reg Miles.

Reg let Shaw go and stood back, moving across and in front of Emmy, standing side by side with George Furrell.

Baz looked confused. 'Boss?'

Shaw pushed himself up off the floor, rubbed his throat. 'What kept you? And where's Keith?'

'He's in town, boss, doing a bit of business.'

'I told him to be here, same time as you.'

'Sorry, boss.'

Shaw shook his head. 'Not your problem, Baz. I'll have a word with him later.'

'Thanks, boss.'

'He won't be thanking me, not when he's heard what I've got to say. And Baz—'

'Boss?'

'Do me a favour, point that thing at them, not at me.'

'Yes, boss.'

Shaw spun on his heel and looked around the kitchen, weighing and then evaluating every item in it. His tongue flicked out and licked his lips. 'Now isn't this a fine mess?'

Reg and George looked at him but didn't say a word.

'A bit of a pickle. A dilemma, you might say. How would you describe it, Reggie? What would be your choice of words for how we find ourselves?'

Reg stared down at Shaw, at the grinning, malevolent face daring him to say something he didn't like. 'I don't have any.'

Arthur Shaw shrugged and bent down. He smiled and held out a hand towards Elizabeth Margaret. 'You alright back there, buttercup? You want to come out and say hello to your Uncle Artie?'

The girl twisted away, pushed her face into the gap between the blackout and the door.

'Oh, don't be like that, Emmy,' Shaw said, 'you'll hurt my feelings, yes, you will.'

'You touch her, I'll hurt more than your feelings, Arthur Shaw,' Reg said, 'I'll sodding kill you.'

'Will you now?' Shaw stood, wound back his right arm and punched out and up. The blow hit Reg just below his chest and above his stomach. His diaphragm spasmed and he found himself bent forward, gasping for breath, about to black out.

'Daddy!'

Furrell looked down at her. 'Don't you worry, love, don't you worry, he'll be alright.'

'Wish I had your confidence,' Shaw said, following through with a punch to the back of Reg's head, collapsing him to the floor, 'but I don't.'

Lucy Potter was on her feet, working her way around the walls, heading to the stairs. Her face was pale, her eyes empty and unfocussed, as if she'd switched her attention from something close to something in the distance and now both objects were blurred.

Shaw watched her crablike progress. 'And where do you think you're going?'

'Upstairs,' she said, her words as blank as her face. 'Don't want to be here, not no longer. I want my bed, Artie, my bed. That's what I want.'

'Fair enough,' Arthur Shaw said, 'you go to bed, I'll come and see to you once this is all over.'

The young woman nodded, manoeuvred herself up the steps, disappeared from sight.

Shaw walked over to Baz, stood next to him, stared back at the two men and the girl.

Reg was still bent over, his hands on his knees, his breathing less ragged now. His cap was on the floor and his Brylcreemed hair had lost its set – he glared at Shaw from beneath a fringe.

The little girl was peering out from behind her father and the other man – the man Shaw didn't know – had a hand on her shoulder.

'And who are you?' Shaw said. 'Should I get to know you? Are you worth my time?'

Furrell shook his head. 'From the looks of it, you're not worth mine.'

Arthur Shaw laughed. 'Funny, eh? You're a funny man, are you? Let's see how funny you are, shall we?' He stepped forward, picked a knife up from the kitchen table and swung it at George.

George flinched.

Shaw moved closer, prodded the other man's belly with the tip of the knife, leered. 'Knife between the ribs, a quick twist easy as opening a lock and you're bleeding out all over this nice lino, a proper goner.' Shaw brought the knife up and rested it on George's cheek, just below his left eye. He scratched at the skin. 'Tell me, who feels like being funny now, eh? Sorry, I didn't catch your name. What's your name, funny man?'

Off to Shaw's left, Reg sighed and gasped.

Shaw glanced at him and the big man exploded up and outwards, caroming into Shaw's extended right arm and punching at his throat.

The knife arced through the air and clattered into the sink, the punch failed to connect.

Shaw spun around to face Reg. 'You think this is a good idea, Reggie? You really think this is a good idea?'

'Haven't got a better one.'

Kiteley moved forward, arm outstretched, pistol wobbling, looking at Shaw for reassurance, for permission.

'Just do it,' Shaw said. 'For God's sake, just do it.'

Out front, in the street, brakes grated, a car pulled to a stop, then another. Car doors opened, feet hit stone, car doors slammed.

'Boss?'

'It's just a couple of cars, Baz, maybe it's Keith.'

'He don't drive,' Kiteley said.

There was a thundering on the front door and then a voice: 'Police, open up.'

'Get the girl and let's get going,' Shaw said, pointing at Emmy.

'You, stop where you are.'

Kiteley turned to face the back door. A man in a hat and overcoat stood there, a uniformed constable just behind him, holding back the blackout.

Marsh took a pace forward and swung his arm up and down, too fast to follow.

Kiteley's wrist exploded in a web of pain as the radius snapped near to where it connected with the bones of the hand on the thumb side. His fingers flexed and loosened – they had no choice, his hand was hanging off his arm as useless as a puppet whose strings had just been cut – and the gun dropped to the floor. He screamed in pain. Marsh's arm swung again and this time he connected with the back of Kiteley's head. The man fell forward and as he passed out he heard the distant sound of the front door being kicked open.

Marsh pocketed his cosh and moved towards the gun.

Constable Hayward appeared from the front room, Annie Scott next to him. 'Need a hand?'

'If you don't mind, Constable.'

As they spoke, Arthur Shaw lunged forward, pushing the kitchen table up towards Marsh, pinning the policeman against the sink, winding him.

Bending over, Shaw tried to scoop up the gun.

Marsh pushed the table back and Shaw stumbled, almost fell. Getting to his feet, Shaw decided the gun was out of reach and rushed to the back door. Smiley moved to stop him but Arthur Shaw's momentum bundled the policeman to the floor and Shaw ducked out and into the night. Without a moment's hesitation, Reg leapt over a fallen kitchen chair and chased after him.

Annie Scott stood in front of Marsh. 'Harry?'

Marsh was leaning on the table, inhaler in hand, sucking hard. He waved her away. 'I'm fine, you go, I'll catch up. You,' he said to Hayward, pointing at the gun and then at Kiteley, 'you can secure that thing and then cuff him. Might hurt him a bit when you do, mind, what with his poorly wrist, poor lamb.'

Outside, heart pounding, boots clattering on stone, Reg Miles ran. 'Shaw, Arthur Shaw,' Reg said, his voice loud, almost biblical, 'you're going nowhere.'

A light came on in an upstairs room and broke blackout, casting a long yellow spike across the courtyard.

Running, Shaw glanced up, saw a face in a window staring down at him and slipped on an uneven cobble. Down on all fours, he scrabbled forward, like a water boatman on a pond.

Reg pounced and looped his arm around Shaw's neck, pushed his knee into the smaller man's back, yanked.

Harder, harder, harder.

One pull.

One more pull.

And maybe a twist.

'I don't know who you are and how you figure in any of this,' Annie Scott said, closing in on Reg, 'but let that man go and let him go now, please.'

PC Smiley, truncheon out, circled the two men on the floor, tightening the radius with each rotation.

Annie Scott looked on, uncertain, feeling her words had vanished into the air, unheard.

Harry Marsh trotted across the courtyard towards them, George and Elizabeth Margaret not far behind.

Reg held tight to Shaw.

One pull.

One more pull.

And maybe a twist.

That's the way to do it.

That's the way to do it.

That's the way to do it.

Mr Punch.

Why Mr Punch, why now?

That walk along Blackpool promenade.

The hot day, the cold ice cream, the street photographer, the puppet show, Agnes pregnant with Elizabeth Margaret.

And then he remembered the promise he made to himself, to his family, the promise he made that day and had meant to honour forever more: *no evil shall befall you, nor shall any plague come near your dwelling.*

Well, Shaw was both: he was both evil and a plague and he should get what he deserved.

Would get what he deserved.

'Sir,' Annie Scott said, 'please desist now or face the consequences. Please, sir.'

'She's right, Reginald Miles, she's right,' George Furrell said, standing close behind the police officers, his arm around Emmy, trying to turn her away. 'Never thought I'd hear myself say this, Reginald, but sometimes you've just got to turn the other cheek. Now the boys in blue are here, let them deal with him.'

'He's mine,' Reg said, 'mine to do with what I want. And after what he did to my Emmy, I want this.'

Annie Scott nodded to herself: the little girl was this big man's daughter. What had the other man called him? Reginald Miles, that was it.

'Tell me, Mr Miles,' Annie Scott said, 'how old are you? Thirty-five, thirty-six?'

'Thirty-three.'

'So, if you're lucky enough to get through this war, what have you got? Another thirty years at the very least, I would say. Are you going to be able live with what you do tonight for all that time? Are you? That is, if you don't hang.'

'Maybe.'

'And Emmy, what about her? What about your daughter?'

'What about her?'

'She'll know all about this too. Do you want her to have to live with what you do tonight? Live with the loneliness and separation which will come from not having the chance to know her father?'

'No.'

The policewoman shook her head. 'Then don't do this. I can see you're not a bad person, Mr Miles, and you don't want to be the one we lock up. You want that to be him, I would have thought.'

Reg peered around in confusion, perhaps seeking absolution or at least an absolute answer. He saw the two plain-clothed police officers, the constable and George Furrell standing around and over him but mostly he saw Elizabeth Margaret.

He saw his little girl looking back at him – almost looking into him – and it was as if she was seeing Reginald Miles, the man who was her father, for the very first time.

But what did she see?

What was there for her to see?

He'd never known that himself but maybe now, now was a self-defining moment.

A moment that determines everything that must and will happen afterwards.

A moment that can go two ways and only two ways: a virtuous life lived without obvious reward, or an amoral life lived in the knowledge that potential punishment lurks in every nook, curve and shadow yet to be encountered.

Reg looked back at his daughter – guileless, innocent, no longer scared but calm and expectant – and he saw her future was yet to be written and it was not a future for him to burden down, not with these memories.

More than that, her day had been bad enough, she didn't have to witness his pain, too.

Reg nodded at Annie Scott, moved by the deep and personal honesty in her words and loosed his arm.

Shaw squirmed away and started to push himself up, attempting to grin through the pain in his neck, shoulder, wrist.

Without saying a word, Reg swung his right leg back and kicked Shaw in the head, once, hard.

The man crashed back to the stones, bounced and then settled – lights out, unconscious.

'Guess he owes you that much,' George Furrell said, his hand over Emmy's eyes.

Reg Miles nodded in agreement. 'He wants to turn the other cheek, I'll kick that one too.'

TUESDAY 26 NOVEMBER 1940

1

For the longest time, he sat in the rattan chair in the corner of the girl's bedroom and watched them.

Watched over them.

Reg Miles was far beyond tired but knew that even if he lay down, he would still be awake hours later. He could try reading – there was a half-finished Edgar Wallace next to his side of the bed but given the last few days, the book's appeal was thin, contrived, superficial.

The police had listened to what Reg had to say and then taken Arthur Shaw, Barry Kiteley and Lucy Potter into custody. No fuss was made about the state of Shaw's face although Reg could have sworn the detective sergeant smiled at him when noting down the black and closed eye, the bruised cheek, the split lip.

'Fell, didn't he, while being chased?'

'Fell he did,' Reg said.

'Then fell it is,' the policeman said, writing it down in his notebook.

And for a moment, Reg had felt guilty but that feeling was as transitory as the smile.

After insisting that Emmy wasn't in need of medical treatment, he'd been allowed to bring her home but was under strict instruction that he must report to Steelhouse Lane in the morning. Full statements would be required and his presence was not a request, that much was made clear.

The plain-clothes policeman had identified himself as Detective Sergeant Harold Marsh, Birmingham City Police.

Policewoman Annie Scott, the plain-clothes female officer, would visit Elizabeth Margaret at home in the morning and ask her a few questions, in her mother's presence.

But that was all hours away.

For now, Reg sat and watched his wife and daughter sleep.

Emmy turned and sighed, pushed her head deeper into the pillow. Agnes – still fully clothed and lying on top of the bed – twisted to accommodate her daughter's new position but never opened her eyes.

He'd get a message to the factory later, explain his and Agnes's absence. At some point he'd have to speak to Byfield, tell him what he'd found out. Despite what the man had already said about Reg's record, he knew there'd be awkward questions: specific questions about the thefts, implied questions about his competency, even perhaps, his complicity.

And maybe he had missed things.

Maybe he should have spotted something was amiss much earlier.

But how? Given the daily need to improvise after the nightly upheavals and from a selfish point of view, the hours he worked – both as an Assistant Works Manager and auxiliary fireman – how could he be expected to keep a tight rein on every aspect of their output?

How could anyone?

He'd done his best in very difficult circumstances.

Circumstances that changed from day to day.

Without doubt, the police would speak to Byfield, too – they may have already done so – but should he go in before the police or after?

Was there a matter of form to this?

What was the right thing to do?

What was expected of him?

The thoughts ran around and around his head like a mechanical hare at a greyhound track – insistent, unrelenting, uncatchable.

He yawned.

Tired, yes, sleepy, no.

No doubt things would be clearer in the morning.

He hoped.

Just after seven, he stood. Tea, he'd make tea. Agnes and Emmy were asleep and not going anywhere, he was sure of that now.

As sure of anything as he could be.

Looking back from the doorway, he saw his daughter had one eye open and was watching him, her other eye hidden in a pillow fold. She smiled and raised a hand. Holding her palm towards him, her fingers folded up and down, up and down, up and down, before she dropped her arm back to the bed. She smiled again and closed her eyes.

Agnes stirred but didn't wake, her right arm tightening its grip around Emmy, as if by instinct. Content his wife and daughter were safe, for the moment at least, Reg went downstairs.

Cup in hand, he wandered out of the kitchen veranda and into the backroom. He crossed to the corner closet and slid open the plastic louvred door. He reached inside and right at the back, found what he was looking for: an old canvas satchel, its shoulder strap worn, stained and semi-detached, its two front buckles still done up, as he'd done them up years before.

He sat into his armchair, sipped his tea, put the cup down next to him and opened the bag.

An old newspaper announcing the death of the Queen, a collection of football reports clipped from the local press and then there she was.

Just as he remembered her.

Skirt hiked, leg raised, hat perched on the back of curly hair and smiling directly at him.

Miss Millicent Lee.

There were a couple of programmes for The Canterbury, too. One dated 1890. He put both this and the photograph aside. He'd visit Millicent Lee later and give them to her as a gift. Returning something of her youth to the old woman, it was a gesture of gratitude, a small act of kindness.

At least, he hoped it would be a kindness and not a cruel reminder of all that was gone, never to return – that wasn't his intention, not his intention at all. He was just trying to do what he always tried to do: to be a decent and honest man, even in the worst of all possible times.

2

Dr Moira Penny stared at Harry Marsh in disbelief.

'Tell me, Moira, how certain are you that she was suffocated deliberately and not just suffocated by accident?'

'As certain as I can be.'

'And she was deliberately drugged?'

'Definitely.'

'But the dosage wasn't fatal?'

'No, it wasn't. Even given her size and age, she hadn't been administered a fatal dose. There was just enough in her body to guarantee that she would fall into a deep sleep.'

'And how long after she took the drug would she have fallen asleep?'

Moira Penny shook her head. 'Impossible to say.'

'But it wouldn't have been instantaneous?'

'No, it wouldn't. Harry, what's going on here? What are you up to? Or, more importantly, what are you asking me to do? Because you're obviously asking me to do something – or *not* do something, more to the point.'

Moira Penny turned from Harry Marsh to Annie Scott, a look of angry enquiry on her face – an enquiry demanding explanation.

The policewoman looked down and stared at her feet, unable or unwilling to meet the doctor's eye.

'What I'm saying,' Harry Marsh said, 'what I'm asking, is how certain are you that she was killed deliberately and didn't just die by accident?'

'Fairly certain.'

'But not entirely?'

'Nothing's ever entirely certain until it is.'

'And this isn't entirely certain, is it?'

The doctor sighed. 'Harry,' she said, 'you know what I think and you've seen the lab's preliminary report, which says nothing to contradict me. Dear Lord, what do you want me to do? Get Bernard Spilsbury himself in for a second opinion? Just what do you want me to say here? I really don't understand.'

'Say what you think is right, that's what you always do.'

Moira Penny got up from her desk, became a black shape against her office window. 'The girl had a drug – Veronal almost certainly – in her bloodstream. It was enough to render her unconscious but not enough to kill her. She had fibres in her nostrils, upper respiratory tract and lungs, suggesting that cause of death was suffocation. A conclusion supported by the burst blood vessels in her eyes. The fibres we found seem to match the cushion that was under her head. She had not inhaled any dust or brick particles relating to where she was found, which suggests that she was killed – or died – elsewhere and then moved. Her livor mortis – blood pooling—'

'I know what livor mortis is, Moira,' Marsh said.

The doctor ignored him. 'Her livor mortis indicates that she died on her back or was put on her back very soon after she died but the patterning doesn't match the rough ground we found her on, suggesting—'

The DS nodded. 'That she was moved there at least two hours after she died.'

'That she was moved there at least two hours after she died, yes,' Moira Penny said, 'that's right.'

'Two hours?'

The doctor glanced across at Annie Scott. 'Livor mortis is set in by around two hours and is best observed at around twelve hours.'

'Thank you, Dr Penny,' Annie said. 'I didn't know that.'

'Good to know that you're not infallible, Policewoman Scott, even if your boss thinks he is.'

'Suppose,' Harry Marsh said, 'suppose the girl had taken the sleeping drug by accident and had wandered away from home in a stupor. Lost in the dark, when the bombing started, she hid under the first thing she could find and pulled the cushion over her face to deaden the sound of bombs going off. Then she fell unconscious and suffocated.'

'The cushion was under her head when she was found, Harry, we both saw her. And to repeat, she hadn't inhaled any particles from her surroundings.'

Marsh ploughed on, ignoring the expression on his friend's face. 'Who's to say,' he said, 'that her actual position wasn't caused by the door being lifted? Or the kids who found her, they could have rolled her over and back again, just to see if she was alive – you know what kids are like.'

'And what about the missing particulates, Harry?'

'If she breathed in for the last time with a cushion over her face, couldn't that stop any dust inhalation?'

'Possibly. And the livor mortis? The patterning?'

'An unhappy anomaly, perhaps? They do happen.'

'Do they? Do they indeed?' Moira Penny moved around the desk and stared down at Harry Marsh. 'You want this to have been an accident, don't you, Harry? I have no idea why. You've seen the poor wee child but you want this to have been an accident. Your investigation's got nowhere and now you want to move on because you're frustrated and you've got more important things to do, maybe. Is that it, Harry? More important things are calling, are they? But answer me this, what if she's just the first of many? What happens when the next dead girl turns up? Another Vera Page, another Phyllis Hirst, another little girl, name unknown, case unsolved. What if there's a maniac out there, Harry? Have you thought of that, have you?'

Marsh dropped his chin to his chest and then looked back up. 'Moira, do you think her death is the work of a maniac?'

'No, I don't but I can't be sure. Unlike you, I believe in science, not my gut.'

'And does your science say or imply maniac?'

'No.'

'Good, because neither does my gut, so at least we agree on something,' the DS said.

'Moira,' Annie Scott said, 'you should know, we've identified the girl.'

'You have? Who is she?'

'Liora Montealto. She's Italian and she was living with—'

'She was living with her uncle down in Digbeth,' Marsh said.

'I suppose he has an alibi?'

'He didn't kill her, Moira, I'm sure of that.'

'So she is Italian. That would explain her appearance, for sure,' the doctor said.

'And Jewish,' Marsh said.

'And she's an illegal,' Annie Scott said, 'or was an illegal.'

Moira Penny sighed. 'It must be hard to be a Jew right now, Italian, illegal or not.'

The policeman looked at his friend. 'When's it ever been easy, Moira? Being something some people despise must be really difficult, even at the best of times.'

The doctor stared at DS Harry Marsh. He stared back, his expression non-committal, neutral. Walking back behind her desk, Moira Penny sat down. 'I'm guessing you'll want her body released then? Now that you know who she is, and all.'

'Yes, please.'

'And before that can happen, I need to submit a report, with my conclusions?'

'Yes.'

'My non-conclusive conclusions?'

'Yes.'

Moira Penny shook her head – her face conveyed concession, regret, distaste. 'It'll be with Seaborne by the end of today, I'll make sure of it, I'll fetch it over myself. And then we can all forget about this poor girl and move on. Which is what you've already done, Harry, obviously.'

'Thank you, Moira.'

'Now get out, Detective Sergeant Marsh, before I change my mind and don't you come back for a long wee while.'

The police officers walked out of the hospital. Harry Marsh knew Annie Scott was staring at him. Knew the expression on her face was both curious and accusatory. Knew all of this without even looking. Knew what was going through her mind, too.

Eventually, when she spoke, Annie Scott said only one word: 'Why?'

Harry Marsh smiled, his expression rueful but neither ashamed nor embarrassed, not for a moment.

Her question unanswered, the policewoman turned on her heel and started to walk away. 'Someone needs to know the truth,' she said.

'Like who?'

'Seaborne, for a start, I would say.'

'Really? Especially with everything else he's got on his plate today.'

Annie Scott stopped. 'Isn't the truth what we do? If we don't tell the truth, who will? If we're not honest, who is?'

Marsh nodded. 'That is a fair point.'

Annie Scott spun around. There were tears on her cheeks. 'We need to tell Seaborne.'

'Tell him what?'

'What we know. Everything about how Liora Montealto died.'

Marsh moved closer to the constable until their breath billowed and buffeted around them, so close that to the casual observer they could have been mistaken for lovers.

The DS raised a hand and put it on the young woman's shoulder. She pushed it away. 'And what have we found out,' he said, 'apart from the fact a man loved his daughter so much he would do anything for her? Did everything he could do for her. Thought that, in the end, he was doing the best.'

'He killed her.'

'And then he tried to kill himself.'

'That's both mortal and venial sin right there,' the policewoman said, the beat of anger almost visible in her words. 'His actions go against all law, reason, truth, and conscience.'

'Mortal and venial? Once a Catholic, always a Catholic, eh?'

'You may mock but even if you don't believe in actual sin, I'm counting two crimes here. Two *actual* crimes here on earth. Here in the realm of man. What about you?'

Marsh shook his head. 'I'm not mocking but I am seeing a man who will carry his grief to the grave. Who will punish himself every day he's got left – every waking moment of every single day. And I don't see how anything we can do to him will get anywhere close to what he's doing to himself.'

'You can't believe that? Surely not?'

'I'm not sure what I believe, to be honest. Not anymore.'

'But you can live with this... your solution?'

'Live with what? The guilt that I let a man get away with murder? Or the guilt that this one man felt he had no choice but to commit that murder in the first place? I honestly don't know but then

I don't think anyone with a degree of humanity would.' He took a deep breath and exhaled with a hint of a wheeze. 'I'm going to try though. How about you?'

'I'm not sure I can, I'm really not sure.'

Marsh turned and took in their surroundings. 'Tell me, what do you see when you look around?'

Annie Scott smiled, a watery, thin smile. 'Birmingham?'

The policeman laughed. 'True. But beyond that? Out there, in the world of men and women – what do you see?'

'Right now? A madhouse, actually.'

'*The Dog-star rages! nay't is past a doubt, All Bedlam, or Parnassus, is let out*.'

'Alexander Pope, yes?'

'*Epistle to Dr Arbuthnot*,' Marsh said. 'What we do, all we can do at times like this, is to try and bring a bit of sense to all this insanity. In the end, who's to tell the difference between what's right and what makes life acceptable for the most people?'

'Such as the Montealtos?'

'I wouldn't presume to know what's right or acceptable for the Montealtos.' The DS reached into a coat pocket, pulled out his inhaler, puffed, held, relaxed. 'And I'm not sure I ever will.'

The policewoman stared at Marsh, watched him slide the device back into a pocket. 'Hang over from the last show,' he said. 'Doctors warned me it might get worse as I got older, just never thought forty-one was older.'

'How much worse?'

'We'll have to wait and see, won't we? Talking of doctors, did I detect a note of awkwardness between you and Moira, by the way.'

Annie Scott shook her head. 'No. Why?'

'You didn't fall out the other night, did you?'

'I don't think so.'

'Good,' Marsh said, 'she may hate me right now but that's because she's a decent woman is Moira. A decent, righteous woman as well as a good doctor and a good friend.'

'If she's such a good friend, why don't you tell her the truth?'

'Because she *is* a decent, righteous woman and given what she does on a daily basis, you really think she needs anything else to worry about?'

'I don't know,' Annie Scott said, 'but knowing might help her, actually.'

Marsh nodded. 'I'll think about it. When she's talking to me again.'

They walked over the road, approached the steps to the station.

'What happens now?'

'With what?'

Annie Scott hesitated, for once in her life doubt outweighed confidence. Or maybe she'd reached a fork in the road and lost her sense of direction. 'Liora's body,' she said, eventually.

Marsh nodded. 'Moira will file her report and with any luck the girl's body will be released to her uncle as soon as is reasonable.'

'And her father?'

'What father?'

The policewoman shook her head. 'I won't ever agree with you, not for one moment, you must know that, not ever. You do know that, don't you?'

'I believe I do.'

'Nor forgive you.'

'That I can live with but I'm hoping you won't report me either.'

Annie Scott laughed, a sound as bitter as a northerly wind.

Marsh frowned. 'I am right about the Montealtos and right about you.'

'What about me?'

'That deep down you know that there's no point in prosecuting the Montealtos. That it would be a waste of our time, a waste of the court's time and all for what? To send a man to jail or maybe even the gallows when he's already in a prison of his own making.'

Annie Scott bit her lip, shook her head and then nodded once. 'Yes, as you say, *what father*?'

Marsh shrugged at the young woman, at the stern face, at the emanant sense of disapproval. 'For what it's worth,' he said, 'I am sorry.'

'Sorry? For why?'

'For putting you in this position.'

'And for your deception – are you sorry about that?'

Marsh nodded. 'It's for the best, I honestly believe it is. And maybe, given time, you will too.'

'I doubt it, Detective Sergeant Marsh, I really doubt it but if anybody asks, I will neither confirm nor deny anything about the Montealtos and refer all inquiries to you. And on that, you have my word. This is between you and your principles, or you and your god, or you and whatever it is you might think you believe in.'

'Thank you,' Harry Marsh said, 'that's very good of you. Out of interest, the boy, Vincent Furrell, what's the story there? I know he's nothing to do with the Montealtos but is he somebody we need to keep an eye on?'

'No, I don't think he is. There's nothing to tell really. He's just a sad and lonely young boy who's a bit lost in the world. He's not a danger to anyone. More in danger, if you ask me.'

Marsh sighed and nodded, turned and started to walk away, towards the centre of town.

'Where are you going?'

'Seaborne's up to his neck picking through the Moseley business right now and he doesn't want me anywhere near it, not for the moment. Means I've nothing until eleven when that Miles bloke is due in and apparently I need a new coat – have you seen the state of this one? Jeannie's not happy. She's given me all our clothing vouchers and told me in no uncertain terms to go to Lewis's or Grey's. Why don't you come along? Jeannie would appreciate it. She thinks I've got terrible taste when left to my own devices – apart from marrying her, of course. I'll treat you to a coffee at the Kardomah.'

'Thank you but I won't. I need to get myself sorted and then I'm due at the Miles's house myself in an hour.'

'Yes,' Marsh said, 'of course. See you later then.'

'You will.'

Annie Scott watched Harry Marsh stroll up Steelhouse Lane, cross Hill Street, disappear into the crowd. She was tempted to follow him, to keep him company, to give herself some company but instead she turned and mounted the station's steps.

'Morning, Sergeant' she said, passing the desk officer.

'Morning to you,' he said, looking up and smiling, noticing her black eye beneath the face powder. 'Seems like we got away with it again last night, just about.'

'Yes,' she said, 'it would seem we did – just about.'

ACKNOWLEDGEMENTS

Big thanks and big love to Jenny Lecoat and Gary Lawson who, at the beginning of lockdown, insisted I start writing what would become *Fire Damage.*

Garrie Fletcher and Peter Haynes from Floodgate couldn't have been more supportive of this book – I can never thank them enough for making *Fire Damage* Floodgate's first published novel.

I must also thank John Beaton and Colin Murray, who read an early draft of *Fire Damage* and were extremely encouraging, as well as Frank Gresham of the Moseley Society History Group and Bernard May from the West Midlands Police Museum, both of whom supplied key information during my research. I should also mention Ian Jelf, his knowledge of Birmingham's trams, buses and trains across time is immeasurable.

Huge thanks too to Elizbeth Lee for her always incisive editorial skills, Su Turner for her eagle-eyed proofreading and Peter Burgess for making the whole thing look so damned fine.

And to Jeremy Pattle, whose music complements, underscores and amplifies much of my recent film work.

Finally, thanks to everyone who's ever taken Floodgate seriously by buying a copy of *Digbeth Stories* and/or *Night Time Economy,* or stocking both on their bookshop's shelves. And a special thank you to Clive and Maria at Voce Books, whose kind support has been the making of Floodgate.

And now to influential books.

Fire Damage could not have been written without Professor Carl Chinn's *Brum Undaunted*, an unparalelled account of the Birmingham Blitz; *Bella Brum* by Doreen Hopwood and Margaret Dilloway, a history of Birmingham's once-thriving Italian Quarter; *The Father of Forensics,* a biography of Bernard Spilsbury by Colin Evans; *An Underworld at War* by Donald Thomas; Lorenza Mazzetti's heartbreaking *The Sky is Falling*; and Eric Ambler's timeless thriller, *The Mask of Dimitrios* – there's an Ambler Easter Egg in *Fire Damage* and the first person to find it will get an actual Easter egg. Or the most seasonally appropriate chocolate gift at that time.